Seasons of the Sword #2

明眸

BRIGHT EYES

A Kunoichi Tale

David Kudler

S

Stillpoint/Atalanta

Also by David Kudler

RISUKO (Seasons of the Sword #1)

BRIGHT EYES (Seasons of the Sword #2)

Coming Soon!

KANO (Seasons of the Sword #3)

Kunoichi Companion Tales (Seasons of the Sword Prequels)
DEADLY BLOSSOMS:
White Robes
Silk & Service
Waiting for Kuniko
Wild Mushrooms
Ghost
Schools for Gifted Youngsters Headmistresses' Monthly Dinner

Shining Boy*
Blade*
Little Brother*

* Coming soon

Winter Tales (with Maura Vaughn):
The Seven Gods of Luck
Shlomo Travels to Warsaw
How Raven Brought Back the Light

Find out more on **SeasonsoftheSword.com**

Follow on:
twitter.com/RisukoKunoichi • risuko-chan.tumblr.com
facebook.com/risuko.books • instagram.com/RisukoKunoichi
risuko.livejournal.com • tiktok.com/@kanomurasaki

BRIGHT EYES

Bright Eyes: A Kunoichi Tale
Stillpoint Digital Press
Mill Valley, California, USA

Copyright © 2022 by David Kudler
All right reserved.

Cover design by James T. Egan of Bookfly Design

Book design by David Kudler and Stillpoint Digital Press

ISBN: 978-1-938808-64-7 (hardcover)
ISBN: 979-8-446495-93-1 (convention hardcover)
ISBN: 978-1-938808-63-0 (pbk.)
ISBN: 978-1-938808-62-3 (e-book)

1. Japan—History—Period of civil wars, 1480–1603—Fiction. 2. Ninja—Fiction. 3. Conspiracies—Fiction. 4. Determination (Personality trait)—Fiction. 5. Young adult fiction.   I. Title.

First edition, May 2022
Version 1.0.0 (rev 25)

SeasonsoftheSword.com

To Brenda and Donal Brown

Risuko's true godparents

———

などて君むなしき空に消えにけん

淡雪だにもふればふる世に

———

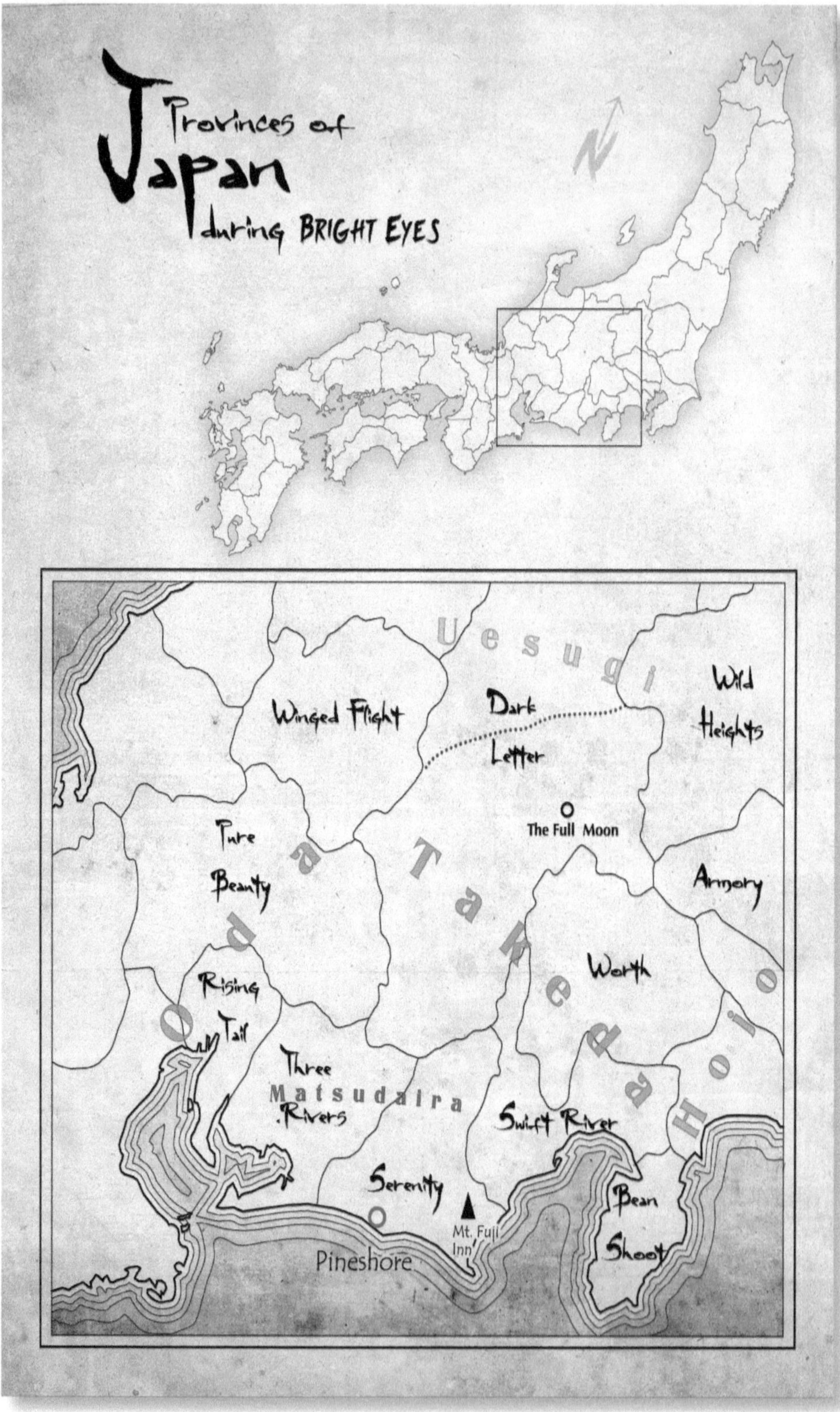

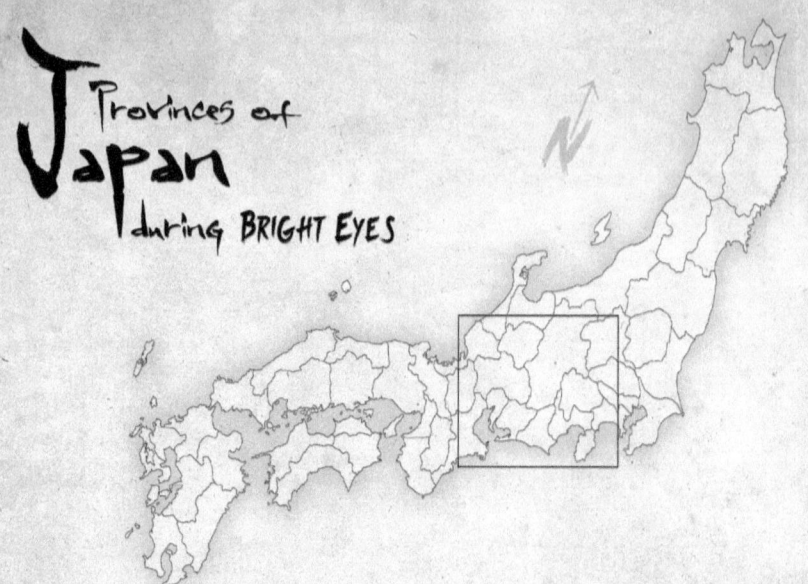

Provinces of Japan during BRIGHT EYES

Uesugi

Winged Flight

Dark Letter

Wild Heights

The Full Moon

Pure Beauty

Oda

Takeda

Armory

Rising Tail

Worth

Hojo

Three Matsudaira Rivers

Swift River

Serenity

Bean Shoot

Mt. Fuji Inn

Pineshore

Contents

Characters

Note: *In Japan, as through most of East Asia, tradition places the family name before the given name. For example, in* Kano Murasaki, *Risuko's proper name,* Kano *is her family's name and* Murasaki *her given name— what English speakers would call her first name.*

Historical figures are marked with an asterisk (*).

Residents of the Full Moon:

Risuko—Proper name: Kano Murasaki. Called "Squirrel" and "Bright Eyes." Junior initiate

Mochizuki Chiyome*—Mistress of the Full Moon

Mieko—Lady Chiyome's maid. *Kunoichi* teacher; *miko* dance master

Kuniko—Lady Chiyome's maid. *Kunoichi* (deceased)

Tarugu Toumi—Called "Falcon." Junior initiate

Hanichi Emi—Called "Smiley." Junior initiate

Aimaru—Called "Moon-cake" and "Moon-face." Servant

Little Brothers—Servants

Takeda Masugu—Takeda cavalry lieutenant

Mai—Called "Foxy." Senior initiate.

Shino—Senior initiate

Kee Sun—Cook (Korean)

Residents of the Full Moon (continued):

Sachi—called "Flower." *Kunoichi* espionage teacher; *miko* music master

Hoshi—called "Horsey." *Kunoichi* sword teacher; *miko* calligraphy master

Mitsuke—*Kunoichi* strength and archery teacher; *miko* etiquette master

Rin—*Kunoichi* garrote teacher

Suzume—*Kunoichi*

Aoki—*Kunoichi*

Fuyudori—called "Ghostie." Former senior initiate (deceased)

Takeda Forces

Takeda Shingen*—Lord of the Takeda clan of Worth (*Kai*) Province. Called "The Mountain" and "The Tiger of Kai." Allied with the Oda and the Matsudaira

Baba Nobufusa*—Takeda captain

Hara Masatane*—Takeda captain

Torimasa Noritada—Takeda Lieutenant

Itagaki Harashubo—Takeda Lieutenant

Sato—Takeda guard

Kotoku—Takeda guard

Tadashi—Takeda guard

Torai—Takeda cook; called "Shorty"

Matsudaira Forces

Matsudaira Motoyasu*—Lord of the Matsudaira clan of Three Rivers (*Mikawa*) Province

Tokugawa Tokimatsu—Matsudaira captain

Matsudaira Ietada*—Matsudaira captain

Hattori Hanzō*—Matsudaira captain

Sakai Tadashige——Matsudaira lieutenant

Matsudaira forces (continued):

Kobayashi—Matsudaira guard

Yukishiro—Matsudaira guard

Kumo—Matsudaira cook; called "Fatso"

Others:

Okā-san—Risuko's mother; proper name: Kano Chojo

Usako—Risuko's sister; proper name: Kano Daini

Otō-san—Risuko's father, former samurai, turned scribe; proper name: Kano Kazuo (believed deceased)

Junkeishō—Buddhist monk

Father Francisco—Jesuit priest traveling with Matsudaira (Portuguese)

João Afonso Alves de Sousa de Mandrágora—Novice traveling with Matsudaira; called "Jolalo" (Portuguese)

Major Historical Figures (mentioned but not appearing):

Oda Nobunaga*—Most powerful lord (*daimyo*) of Japan, controlling the capital in Kyōto and the military government headed by the warlord (*shōgun*). Head of the Oda clan of Rising Tail (*Owari*) Province. Allied with the Takeda and the Matsudaira.

Imagawa Ujizane*—Head of the Imagawa clan, former lord of Serenity (*Tōtōmi*) Province

Uesugi Kenshin*—Lord of the Uesugi clan of Crossover (*Echigo*) Province

Hōjō Ujimasa*—Lord of the Hōjō clan of Armory (*Musashi*) Province

Ashikaga Yoshiaka*—Hereditary warlord (*shōgun*) of Japan. For all intents and purposes Oda Nobunaga's puppet since Oda-*sama* took contol of the capital.

The Full Moon

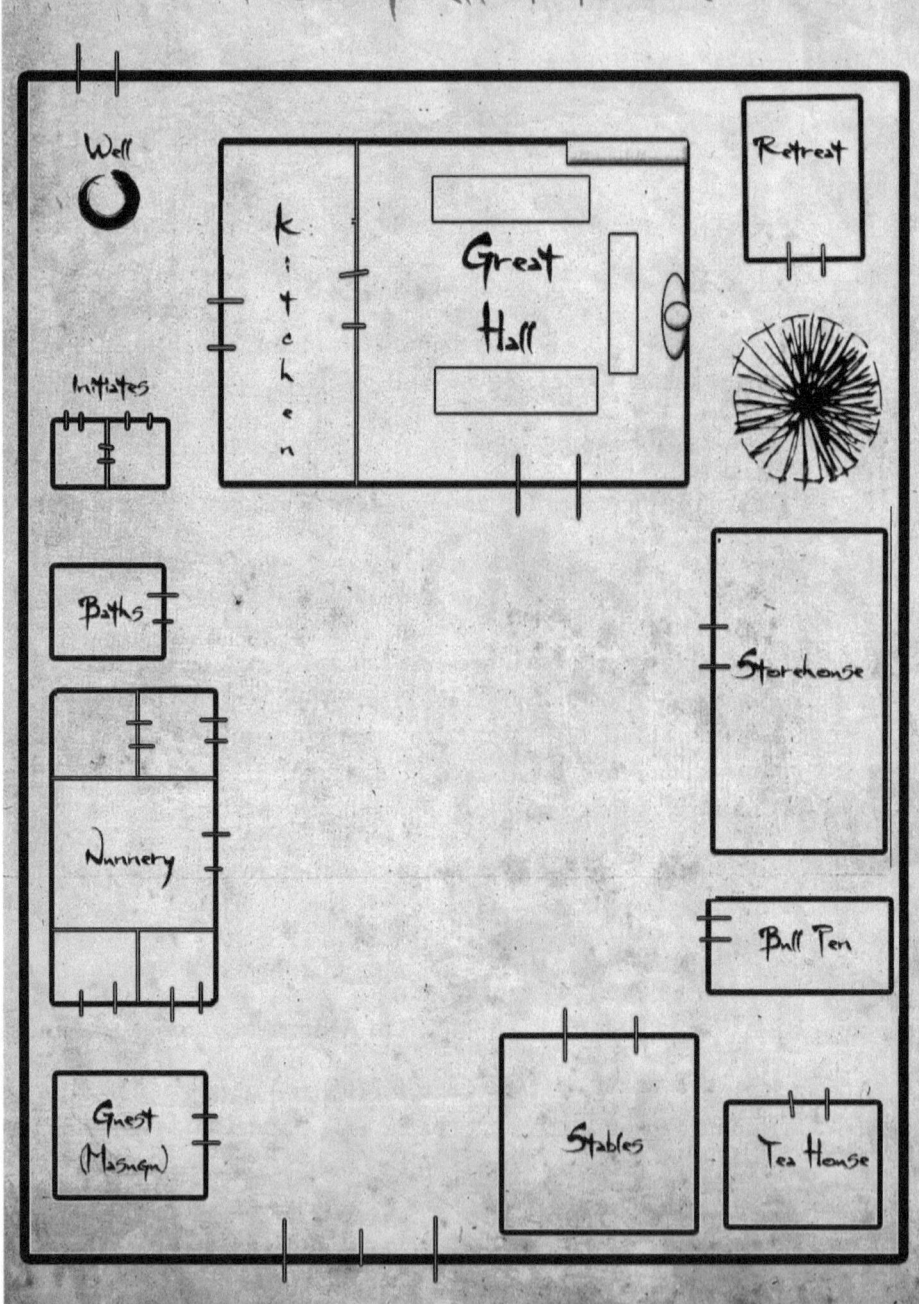

Prologue—Special

My name is Kano Murasaki, but everyone calls me Risuko. Squirrel.

Everyone but Kee Sun, the Korean cook. He calls me Bright Eyes.

He says it's because he can't remember Japanese nicknames. But how is *Bright Eyes* easier to remember than *Risuko?*

When Lady Chiyome brought me, Emi, and Toumi to her estate, the Full Moon, she told us that she had it in her power to give us something that we didn't know we wanted.

None of us know what that is.

What we do know is that we are being trained at the Full Moon to become *kunoichi.*

Spies.

Bodyguards.

Assassins.

Also, Kee Sun has taught us to cook, and we've learned to dance and play music and assist in rituals as shrine maidens, *miko*, under the tutelage of the older women.

The *kunoichi.*

A very special kind of woman, says Lady Chiyome.

I don't know if I am special. I just like to climb trees.

1—The Rising Wave

*Dark Letter Province, Land of the Rising Sun, Month of the Hydrangeas
in the Second Year of Genki*
(Shinano Province, Japan, spring, 1571 A.D.)

I meant to take the knife that Mieko held out to me, the handle toward my hand.

I meant to. But I couldn't.

"Risuko," whispered Mieko, her eyes locked on mine. I could feel the stares of the rest of the Full Moon's girls and women, chilling as white snow even on this blue-skied spring morning.

My own eyes flicked toward the pig, which struggled against its bonds, squealing.

We were outside the Full Moon kitchen, next to the well. The pig struggled, but its legs were tied to the four heavy pegs that Emi, Toumi, and I had hammered into the packed, gravel-strewn earth.

What stopped me, what kept me from being able to take the long, narrow blade from Mieko-*san's* hand, wasn't that the pig was in distress. Its squeals knotted my stomach, but I had slaughtered animals for the Full Moon's kitchen before—chickens, rabbits, even a goat.

But this animal had been dressed in a samurai's battered armor, with a helmet over its head. And all I could think . . .

Through the long, snowbound winter, Mieko and the other *kunoichi* had used this armor to teach us its weak points—to show us where even the most heavily armed warrior was vulnerable. As we stabbed under the armpits or between the front and back plates with daggers, it hadn't seemed real; the armor had been on a kind of straw dummy, like the ones we used to put up next to the rice paddies to keep the birds away.

But screaming and straining, the pig was very real. It looked like a person, almost. It looked like a samurai. Like . . .

I looked down and shook my head. "I can't," I mouthed.

Mieko started to say something but then shook her head and held the knife handle out to Emi, who frowned but took it.

I ran.

———

I was still running—past our dormitory, past the white length of the Great Hall—when I ran into Lieutenant Masugu. Or rather, I ran into his huge black horse, Inazuma.

"Going for a climb, Murasaki?" The lieutenant was leading Inazuma by the reins.

I blinked up at him and shook my head.

"I haven't seen you climb since . . . In a while." His eyes were small, concerned half-moons under his helmet.

I blinked again. "Are you leaving, Masugu-*san?*" Inazuma carried a pack of supplies, and Masugu was dressed in a full set of armor—not his usual shining black armor with the four diamonds of the Takeda emblazoned on his chest but rather a battered brown set with the white disk *mon* of Mochizuki— the Full Moon.

He was dressed, in fact, very much as the pig had been.

I couldn't hear the squealing anymore.

The lieutenant nodded. "It's time to go."

"You're not going to wait for Lady Chiyome to return?"

Now he shook his head. "She knew I needed to leave once the passes to the west were clear. She won't be surprised."

I wrapped my arms around myself. "I . . . We will miss you." *Mieko*-san *will miss you the most,* I thought, but thought it best not to say.

"Well, it shouldn't take me more than a month to get to the capital, deliver my . . . the letter you returned to me, and get back here. No time at all."

I shrugged. *The letter.* A battle map showing a combined Takeda-Matsudaira attack on Lord Oda's troops in the capital, signed with the Matsudaira crest of the the three wild ginger leaves. The letter that white-haired Fuyudori had tried to kill us all to retrieve, the night. . .

Masugu smiled and patted my arm. His horse whickered impatiently. "Besides, Inazuma wants to run."

I nodded.

"Say, don't you have a lesson? Shouldn't you be with the others?"

My gorge rose, but I stared up at him. "Did you know that if I were to slip a very sharp blade up beneath the back of your helmet, I could push the tip just under your skull and sever your spinal cord?"

Masugu's face froze.

"Mieko-*sensei* was teaching us to do that. On a pig dressed in armor."

"That . . . would be very effective."

"I couldn't do it."

"No," he sighed. "There is a purpose for your being here, Murasaki-*san*. I do not know the reason that Chiyome-*sama* brought you to the Full Moon. I do not know the reason that the gods brought you, Emi, and Toumi here— but there is one." He squeezed my shoulder. "Learn what Mieko and the rest have to teach you."

I pleaded dejectedly, "I don't want to be a killer."

"No," he sighed again. Then he patted the swords that stuck out of the pack on Inazuma's back. "Neither do I. And yet I am a Takeda warrior. It is my duty. We live in dangerous times. If I were not to fight to protect our provinces and our people, how many more would die?" His sad smile reminded me of the one that Mieko gave me so often. "You are a samurai maiden, Kano Murasaki—the daughter of a warrior. You too have a duty."

Now he had me crying. "I'm n-no samurai. Lord Oda stripped my f-family of its honor." I thought of my father, walking toward the Imagawa castle. Walking toward his death. *Do no harm.*

"And yet your duty remains. If I know anything about your father—or his daughter—I do not believe that any power on this earth would take that away." He squeezed my shoulder again and swept the tears from my cheeks with a gauntleted finger. "In the meantime, Murasaki, why don't you forget about knives and samurai and duty for a bit. Climb." He nodded toward the tree.

I nodded back and gave him a smile, though it was the last thing I wanted to do. "Thank you, Masugu-*san*. Come back soon."

"As soon as I can, Murasaki-*san.*" He began to turn, but then stopped and turned back. "May I . . . Would you take care of something for me while I am gone?"

Wiping my nose on my sleeve, I blinked at him. "Of course, Masugu-*san*."

He reached up and took the shortest of his swords from the pack. He held it out to me.

I stared at the sword in its silver-trimmed black scabbard. "I . . . I cannot . . . Masugu-*san*, it is too fine!"

He gave me a small shrug. "That's why. It's a beautiful blade with the Takeda emblem on it." He tapped the four-diamond *mon* embedded in the hilt. "I'm supposed to be a poor soldier, someone no one would notice. This kind of gives me away, don't you think?"

"I suppose." Still, my hands were at my sides.

"Take it, Murasaki. You need to get comfortable holding a sword—a real sword. And I can't leave this with just anyone."

Scowling at the ground, I held out my hands.

When he placed the *wakizashi* in them, however, I gasped in surprise. "It's heavy!"

"It's not made of bamboo." I could hear the laughter in his voice; when I glanced up, I could see that he was indeed grinning. "Get used to it. Learn to use it with the same comfort that you do the practice sword. Just be careful: this blade has removed its share of limbs—and lives."

I had to fight the urge to drop the blade. "Th-thank you, Masugu-*san.*"

"You are very welcome, Murasaki-*san.* I know that you will treat this sword well until I return. If you need help caring for it—keeping it clean and sharp—the Little Brothers or Kee Sun can teach you. Or Mieko." His smile faded like a springtime snow. "Goodbye, Murasaki."

"Goodbye, Lieutenant."

He ruffled my hair, something I don't think he'd ever done before. "Now go climbing."

As the lieutenant led Inazuma toward the front gate, I tucked the scabbard into the back of my red-and-white belt. Then I scrambled up into the lower branches of the enormous hemlock that grew on the eastern side of the Great Hall.

It wasn't until I threw my leg over the biggest of the branches, waving at Masugu as he mounted and rode out onto the ridge beyond the gate, that Fuyudori's ghost came to visit.

Not her actual ghost. Angry though the white-haired girl's spirit must have been, we had performed all of the proper rites for her. Her body had been burned and the ashes buried in the icy ground behind the compound. We had left out a bowl of rice and a cup of *sake* at our meals. (They had been small ones, though—no one felt she deserved more.) No one had spoken her name. It had been longer than the forty-nine days it would have taken for her spirit to reach the next world.

But sitting there on the branch, feeling the wind stirring my hair, I found it hard not to remember cowering on that same limb, watching her climbing after me, furious. Murderous.

I took a deep breath and did my best not to think of her.

I had not had a sword then. Could I . . .

Already, Masugu-*san* was only half visible, disappearing over the edge of the ridge down the road that led to the valley and the road west, toward the imperial city.

I waved again, though I knew he would not see.

It was nice to be up in the tree again. Nice to feel the wind. Across the valley, beneath the deep blue sky, the mountain peaks were still covered in snow, but lower down all was green—a deep, rich green broken by flashes of silver where streams poured the melting snow down into the fields below.

The ridge top too was green. Fresh shoots pushed up through dead grey grass. White wildflowers frosted the meadow.

"You staying up there all day, Mouse-*chan*, or are you getting your mousy tail into the kitchen to help make dinner?" Toumi glowered up at me from the corner of the Great Hall.

"Can you see anything interesting?" asked Emi. She too frowned—but then, she always frowned.

"I was waving goodbye to the lieutenant."

"Oh. He's gone?" Emi's frown deepened into a pout.

Toumi made a retching sound. "Come on. We had to bleed the stupid pig. You get to butcher it."

When I felt the blood leave my face, Emi said, "Killing it was very easy. And put the animal out of its misery."

"I know," I whispered.

"Then why didn't you just kill the stupid thing, *baka!*" growled Toumi.

"I couldn't help . . . " I didn't want to, but I shuddered.

"What?" Both girls walked below my branch.

I closed my eyes. "I couldn't help thinking . . . of whose spirit might inhabit the pig."

"You—what?" Toumi gaped up at me.

"I couldn't help but think . . . that it might be . . . I don't know. Fuyudori." I gazed at the opposite side of the valley. "My father."

"Oh," said Emi.

Toumi gave a harsh laugh. "Unbelievable! Do you go around worrying about crushing your father when you step on ants?"

Again I blanched. "I . . . I will now!"

"*Baka!*" Laughing again, Toumi shook her head. "Come on down here, Mouse. You've got your dad to cut up."

"Toumi!" whispered Emi.

I took another breath, trying to steady myself, and looked back out over the landscape.

Over the edge of the ridge, where Masugu-*san* had disappeared, there seemed to be a hazy wave rising. A wave of vertical lines tipped in steel. Spears. Dozens bearing blue flags showing the Matsudaira *mon*: three wild ginger leaves.

"Uh . . . Toumi? Emi?" They both looked up at me. Now, instead of feeling bloodless, I could hear the blood pounding through me. "I think we're being invaded."

2 — Guests

Kee Sun banged on his gong. The rest of Mochizuki's inhabitants poured out into the courtyard.

"Glaives!" called Mieko. Somehow, she had armed herself with her long black bow. A quiver of arrows hung at her back.

Mai and Shino, the senior initiates, ran out of the storeroom holding armloads of the long-bladed spears and began to distribute them. Shino's flat face was set in a grimace while Mai grinned like a crow that's spied carrion.

The Matsudaira soldiers had continued to flood up over the edge of the ridge top. They marched eight abreast—mostly pikemen, but every other line had four or five samurai.

"Emi, Toumi, get bows, get up on the roof of the stables. Don't shoot without my order, do you understand?"

"Yes, Mieko-*san*!"

Kunoichi had stationed themselves on the rooftops, behind the bamboo spikes that decorated the walls of the Full Moon.

"Risuko!" Mieko stared up. "You've already got a sword?"

I realized with a start that Masugu-*san*'s blade still lay at my back. Without meaning to, meaning only to hand it to her, I drew it. "Um. Yes?"

Her eyes narrowed for a moment, but then she nodded. "How many? Soldiers?"

Trying to keep my shaking hands from dropping the blade, I looked back out at the invaders. "Still coming," I called through dry lips. "Nine ranks of eight so far, mostly pikes, and some horsemen flanking them." Remembering what Masugu had told me about his lancers and the other mounted troops in the Takeda army, I said, "Heavy cavalry, I think."

"Archers? Muskets?"

I shook my head.

"Good," she said, though she didn't look at all pleased. "Get farther up and call out if you see anything change." Then she sprinted to the Guest House, scaled the walls, and was at the corner of the wall with her bow drawn before I could climb to my feet.

The *wakizashi* in my hand was impossibly bright. The edge looked every bit as sharp as one of Kee Sun's knives. Carefully—remembering what Masugu had said about severed limbs—I slid the sword into the scabbard at the back of my belt and clambered three or four branches higher until I was above the wall and could see all around the compound.

Below me, the Full Moon's women were armed and at their stations. We had practiced this every third day since Lady Chiyome had left on her latest *miko*-hunting expedition.

Hoshi, the calligraphy and *katana* teacher, was distributing helmets to the Full Moon's defenders. Like me, she had a sword at her back; unlike mine, hers was a full-length *katana*. Her job was to guard the front gate in case the enemy breached it. Kee Sun would be by the smaller back gate, armed with his lethally sharp cleavers.

Why do I have to learn to use a sword? I whined to myself. A bow would have been much more useful up there in the tree. Not that I would have been any more willing to use it.

The last rank had now cleared the ridge—eleven rows making eighty-eight foot soldiers and a dozen mounted troops.

Against eighteen women, five girls, and a cook.

Behind the last soldiers came two high blue banners bearing the Matsudaira crest. Between them were a pair of shiny black palanquins, one carried by four armored soldiers and the other by two large men in blue.

Someone must have called out an order, because the entire company came to a halt fifty paces beyond the wall. It was like watching a flock of birds all deciding to light on a tree all at once.

The smaller palanquin moved forward through the troops. I heard Mieko call out something; high as I was, I couldn't make out what she said.

I had just noticed the plain white disk *mon* on the side of the palanquin when Toumi loosed her bow.

"*Stop!*" I screamed, but it was too late. The arrow arched toward the Matsudaira troops, planting itself in the top of Lady Chiyome's box.

A figure I hadn't noticed trailing the palanquin dropped to the ground, but the Little Brothers simply stopped.

Without realizing it, I had drawn my blade. Why, I couldn't begin to tell you, but the gleaming steel reflected the green of the hemlock boughs in a way that made my breath catch.

Chiyome-*sama's* grey head poked out of the palanquin. Her I could hear distinctly, even at that distance. "What in the names of all of the hells are you shooting at?" She looked up at the arrow still quivering in her palanquin's roof. "Nice shot. Now let us in. I want a bath."

By the time I reached the ground, Kee Sun, Hoshi, and one of the other women had opened the gate. Mieko had kept the remaining *kunoichi* at their stations but had sent the initiates—Shino, Mai, Emi, and Toumi—down to greet our mistress. When we'd lined up in front of the door to the Great Hall, Mai snorted and pushed Toumi. *"Nice shot."*

Gripping her bow, Toumi grunted.

"Actually," Emi mused, "it *was* a nice shot. I don't think I could have hit a moving target at that distance."

"Slipped," said Toumi through gritted teeth. Emi's compliment seemed to make her more uncomfortable than Mai's teasing.

"Finally out of that prison!" Lady Chiyome grumbled, stretching, as she stepped onto the gravel of the courtyard. She looked around at us and gave a sour snort. "You look like a bunch of little boys playing soldiers. You can sheathe the blade, Risuko. What have you been doing, slaughtering chickens?"

Blushing, I returned the short sword to its scabbard.

While the Little Brothers walked the palanquin toward the stables, the lady called, "Stand down, Mieko. We wouldn't want to hurt any of Lord Matsudaira's servants. I know they're just men, but he's rather fond of them. And they're our guests. Once all of your toys are put away, gather everyone in the Great Hall."

Mieko snapped off a crisp bow, and soon all of the women were making their way back down to the ground.

"You two," Chiyome-*sama* barked at Shino and Mai. "Make sure the baths are ready."

The two girls sprinted toward the bathhouse, which I knew was clean—Toumi, Emi, and I had cleaned it the night before—and whose water I assumed was hot, since we had lit the fires that morning.

Lady Chiyome chuckled, clapping her hands together. "Kee Sun, you lucky rascal!"

The cook huffed to a stop next to me. He'd shoved his three longest knives into his sash. He actually looked as close to happy as he ever looked. "Yeh're back."

"Of course I'm back, silly man."

"One o' these days, yeh're gonna get a body so riled up, yeh'll have to kill him, and they'll have to arrest yeh."

"Don't make me have the Little Brothers give you a caning," she said, but she was smirking. "In any case, I've brought you a hundred soldiers to practice your craft on. They'll be with us for at least a week."

The cook whistled. "Well, we just slaughtered us a pig, and we got some . . . But we'll need . . . C'mon, girlies—"

"Before you scurry off," the old woman said, "take Aimaru with you. He's missed the company of the ladies." As Aimaru stepped out from behind the palanquin, she gave us a backhanded wave and strode off toward the baths.

"Aimaru!" said Emi, closer to smiling than I'd seen her in weeks. She looked as if she were about to embrace our tall friend but stopped herself, her almost-smile shifting to a ferocious frown. "You've grown."

Aimaru ducked his head. "Couldn't help it." Like Emi's, his ears were turning pink.

"You two are disgusting," said Toumi, rolling her eyes.

"How was the trip, Aimaru?" I asked, trying to cut short the teasing. "Did you make it to Pineshore?"

He was about to tell how things were near my home, but Kee Sun growled, "Afore yeh girlies get to gossipin', we've got work to do. So, Moon-cake, yeh ever worked in a kitchen?"

Aimaru blinked, started to shake his head, but then shrugged, smiling.

The cook chuckled something in Korean, then smirked at him. "Fine. Try not to get chopped up. Go with these two"—he gestured at Emi and Toumi—"and bring some rice from the storeroom. Bright Eyes, yeh're comin' with me to butcher that pig." He strode back toward the kitchen, and I had no choice but to scurry after him.

Somewhat to my relief, the hog had been stripped of its armor. It hung by its hind legs from a hook that stuck out from the walls of the Full Moon. Its throat had been cut into a grotesque grin, and it had bled out into a huge, steaming vat.

"We'll make *soondae* with the guts and blood." Kee Sun patted the vat. He had a particular fondness for the Korean boiled blood sausages. It was one of the few dishes that he made that I couldn't stand. Not that I ever complained. "But first, let's see how that fancy carver of yehrs'll quarter this carcass."

"Carver?"

"Is that blade at yehr back just for decoration, Bright Eyes?"

My hand flew to the handle of the short sword before my mind had even registered what he'd said. "Shouldn't . . . This oughtn't to be used for cutting up a hog, should it?"

"Oh, I reckon it's carved less noble beasts than that afore now. The lieutenant's, is it?"

I nodded.

"Well, girlie, get'er out for me now."

I drew the blade, conscious of the edge as it cleared the scabbard.

It lay in my grip more heavily than the bamboo practice swords, it is true. But once I held it in both hands before me—in the stance of the Two Fields—it felt like nothing more than an extension of my arms. "Whew."

"Ayup." He squinted at the blade. "All right then, girlie, yeh'll take yehr best, strongest horizontal cut, just like the Little Brothers and Horsey-girlie and all have been showing yeh. I want to see how many cuts it takes yeh to cut all of the way through."

I scowled at him. Butchering a pig wasn't as hard a job as butchering a cow, say, but even then, we'd never started by trying to cut the thing in half. We'd always cut off the bits from the outside in; he'd taught us that that was more efficient. "Are you—?"

"Now, Bright Eyes. We got a hundred soldiers to feed. And yeh'll only feed one or two."

I knew he was joking but couldn't help gawking at him.

Kee Sun snorted and stepped back. "Now, give it a whack."

Stepping forward toward the carcass, I measured the distance.

I had been doing this exercise for months. Had seen my father do it for years.

Clamping my teeth together to keep my tongue from sticking out, I took a closed stance—knees bent, one foot behind the other. I took a breath, let the blade swing back until the guard hit my bicep, stepped forward, and swung.

Watching my father, I had always thought the strength of the cut came from the arms. Hoshi (who Kee Sun called *Horsey* for her long face) and the Little Brothers had taught me that this wasn't so. The force came from the legs and hips.

As they had taught me, I snapped my hips around and extended my rear arm, so that the blade made a distinctive *whew* sound—*swing* through *the target, not* at *the target . . .*

Where that movement had always brought a satisfying *smack* of bamboo against the straw men I'd practiced with, however, now I heard a sound I knew from the kitchen: the wet *ssss* of steel slicing through flesh.

The blade passed cleanly through the hog's midsection, severing the ribs and head from the hips and legs in one clean cut. The head dropped into the vat of blood.

After a moment, entrails slithered out and joined it.

I stared at the animal—at its two halves. I stared at the *wakizashi.*

"Ayup," said Kee Sun. "Thought so."

I stared at Kee Sun.

"See that mark there?" He pointed at where tiny characters had been etched into the steel, just above the guard.

In miniscule *hiragana* script, someone had carved into the blade *Cut through three bodies with a horizontal cut.*

I stared at the mark. Gore slowly obscured it.

"That, Bright Eyes, is a mighty fine carver."

I nodded.

———

Quickly, the cook showed me how to clean off the blade—first with straw and then with a cloth soaked in pungent oil of clove. The edge didn't seem to have been nicked even slightly.

It hadn't been easy, not exactly. The blade was heavier than I was used to, and I had used all of my muscles—from my feet up through my shoulders— just as I had been taught.

But that sword had cut a body cleanly in half. I had cut a body cleanly in half.

Even after I had sheathed the weapon at my back, I couldn't help but be terrified of the power that lay against my skin, contained by no more than a rice grain's thickness of lacquered wood.

Excited too, a bit. But mostly terrified.

———

The other girls and Aimaru appeared carrying a bag of rice. Well, Aimaru was carrying it. Emi and Toumi were walking along in front and behind, like a lord's honor guard.

They all gaped at the pig's body.

Emi stood wide eyed but thoughtful.

Toumi spat, incredulous. "Where'd you get *that?*" she muttered as we moved the pieces of the carcass into the kitchen. Kee Sun was cutting off the extremities and letting us work with those.

"What?" I worked to remove the loins from a leg, trying hard not to remove my fingers at the same time.

"That sword. That's not one of the ones from the armory."

Before I could answer, Emi said, "It's Masugu-*san*'s." Her perpetual frown was neutral. I couldn't tell what she was thinking.

"He asked me to take care of it while he's on his mission."

Emi nodded but her face remained a mask.

Toumi's eyes narrowed.

"Enough yacking," Kee Sun growled. "Let's get this animal butchered!"

———

Once the pig that I had been too weak to kill had been rendered into all of its edible parts—meat, organs, guts, blood—and just as we were about to start cooking, Hoshi stuck her head into the kitchen from Great Hall.

"Don't you all look lovely," she said with a smirk.

We were all covered in blood. We looked like . . .

Well, we looked like a bunch of children covered in blood. And more.

When we all scowled, Hoshi laughed. "Get cleaned up. You're all needed in the hall. Lady Chiyome wants to speak with everyone. Even you, Aimaru." When the cook started to speak, she said, "Not you, Kee Sun. You get to keep cooking, lucky man."

He actually did look pleased. He was stuffing intestines with *kimchee*, noodles, and blood. *Soondae.* The sausage looked disgusting and smelled worse, but he seemed as happy as a pig in a mudhole.

A pig.

Aimaru jogged off to the Bull Pen, where the men slept. We girls stumbled out the back door of the kitchen—Toumi wiping her gory hands on the jacket of Emi, who was still lost in thought. Toumi never liked anyone to be left out when it came to misery.

Emi barely seemed to notice, which didn't improve Toumi's mood.

We grabbed clean clothes from the storage bin in our dormitory and went to the baths.

It was a blessing to wash off the mess. Even nicer because we didn't usually get to use the baths until the end of the night.

But before we could get comfortable, Sachi-*sensei* came in and hurried us out.

Sachi was one of my favorite teachers at the Full Moon. When she wasn't out on a mission (most often accompanied by her friend Hoshi), she was our music teacher, and she was almost always full of good humor and dirty jokes.

No jokes or humor now: she barely waited for us to get dressed before she marched us back to the Great Hall.

There we were met by nearly all of the current inhabitants of the Full Moon: the eighteen *kunoichi*, five initiates, Aimaru, the enormous Little Brothers, and Lady Chiyome. Only Kee Sun was missing.

Kee Sun and Lieutenant Masugu.

"Nice of you to join us," said Chiyome-*sama* with a sour smirk.

Sachi herded us to the front, where we knelt.

After a moment of silence, Lady Chiyome said, "As you may have noticed, we have some visitors."

A flurry of laughter passed through the hall.

Once it had settled again, our mistress continued, "Lord Matsudaira and his followers will be our guests for the next week. While I cannot tell you their purpose yet, it shall become clear soon enough."

She let another silence settle before continuing. "There are several things that we need to remember—particularly our initiates." She glared at us. "We have become, here in the mountains, used to forgetting that what we do is not . . . general knowledge. What we do, what we study, who we are—these are secrets known to few outside of these walls. And Lord Matsudaira and his followers are *not* among that number."

I looked around. The older women were all nodding somberly.

"We must behave like nothing more than we are supposed to be: a school for shrine maidens. So walking around with swords strapped to our backs"— she arched an eyebrow at me—"will not be tolerated."

Now a grumble rippled through the hall.

"It will not be tolerated," she continued, chin high and both eyebrows raised, "while the gates are open. Once we are amongst ourselves, you may return to your peculiar pursuits as much as you'd like. Just don't kill each other, please."

Laughter again.

"In the meantime, pretend to be the weak, brainless creatures they believe you to be. If you need a refresher course, I'm sure Sachi-*sensei* there would be happy to oblige."

This time a guffaw, led by Sachi herself.

"I will expect *all* of you to entertain our guests. Make them feel welcome. Should any of them become overly friendly—well, the Matsudaira commanders understand that, decorous though you may all be, the maidens of the Full Moon are not playthings. If any of them become rude, please let me or Mieko or— Yes, let us know, and we'll be sure to cool their ardor."

Again, the older women nodded, and we all joined in.

"Chiyome-*sama?*" The quiet voice came from Mitsuke, the young *kunoichi* who taught us etiquette and who worked with Emi and Toumi on archery. "If we're not supposed to be . . . who we are, what do the Matsudaira think about us being up on the walls?"

"They thought you were cute." Lady Chiyome gave what was for her a broad grin. "Even though one of our runts managed to fire a longbow a hundred paces into the roof of my palanquin."

Hoshi and Sachi, who were both back in a good mood, gave Toumi a mocking cheer.

Toumi blushed at the floor and ground her teeth.

Chiyome-*sama* gave a low chuckle and continued. "They have no idea how few of them would have survived if I hadn't been there."

At her lady's side, Mieko gave a small, gratified smile.

"Now go," barked Lady Chiyome. "It's time to get this place ready to host a lord of the realm. We open the gates at sunset."

3—Wild Ginger

As I reentered the kitchen, Kee Sun held out his hands.

It took me a moment to realize that he wanted the sword. With a sigh, I removed the scabbard from my sash and laid it and the blade it held in his palms. I had possessed the blade only a few hours, had truly wielded it just once. But I suddenly felt naked without it.

"Don't yeh worry, Bright Eyes." Reverently, he placed the blade in the topmost space of his rack of knives. It stood above the cleavers and skinners and fine filleting blades like an emperor above his court. "Everyone knows better than to play with any of these here blades."

"Yes, Kee Sun-*san*." It wasn't as if anyone but us came into the kitchen. But . . . "But Masugu-*san* made me promise to take care of his sword."

"Well, yeh can clean it. And yeh can practice with it. But otherwise, it stays here. Yeh follow?"

I nodded.

He turned to the others. "And none of yeh will touch that sword." Aimaru nodded, his usual broad smile in place, so Kee Sun glared at the girls. "Understood?"

"Yes, Kee Sun-*san*," said Emi and Toumi. Toumi said it with a scowl, but she said it.

"After all," he said with a wink, "what are a sweet group o' girlies like yeh going to do with a sword?"

"Nothing good," muttered Toumi, but Kee Sun laughed. "Fair enough. Now let's get cookin', shall we?"

We worked hard, preparing five times the food that we usually had to. And where Kee Sun always made sure we were careful in our preparations, now he demanded nothing less than perfection. Aimaru, who had never worked in a kitchen, mostly tried to fetch what he could and otherwise stay out of the way.

In the meantime, whenever I left the kitchen—to get extra bamboo steaming trays or dried mushrooms from the storage room—the Full Moon bustled like an anthill that's been kicked open.

The *kunoichi*—killers and spies and bodyguards—cleaned the hall, adding tables, sweeping the floors, and laying out bowls and chopsticks. The Little Brothers raked the courtyard with military precision. Sachi had Mai and Shino bring in wildflowers from outside and showed them how to arrange the fragrant white and blue blossoms in bowls on the tables in the dining room.

In the kitchen, under Kee Sun's direction, Emi, Toumi, and I proceeded to transform a pig, some rice, mounds of spinach and soy beans, three bulbs of garlic, and some leeks into a feast for a lord. He kept wandering in and out of the pantry, muttering under his breath, hands white from the chalk he used to mark the slate on which he kept track of our supplies.

As the sun began to set, Lady Chiyome called us all out into the courtyard.

Mieko and the other *kunoichi* had changed. They were dressed not in the wide red *miko* trousers and white blouses that I had grown used to but in fine silk kimonos. Mieko's was midnight blue with a pattern of chrysanthemums and wisteria trailing down the sleeves. Sachi's was white and green, decorated with peacock feathers. Mitsuke, the most forgettable-looking woman I've ever known, was dressed in a spectacular robe covered with a pattern of autumn maple leaves.

Their faces were painted white, their hair shiny and up off their necks.

They looked . . .

They were beautiful.

Toumi gave a choking sound.

"Well," called Lady Chiyome, walking in front of us, "don't you all look lovely. Not you, Aimaru. You don't look lovely at all."

Now it was Emi choking.

"Little Brothers," called Chiyome-*sama*, "open the gate."

They pulled back the huge bar and slid the doors open.

———

I had grown up in the shadow of the Imagawa castle. I had seen plenty of Lord Imagawa and his followers, enough so that I didn't think I'd be particularly impressed by the Matsudaira leader.

To be honest, I didn't know what to expect after that morning's invasion. But what I didn't expect was for Lord Matsudaira to enter the Full Moon in a simple dark blue kimono—no armor, no sword. Not even a knife at his belt.

He was a tall man, as tall as the Little Brothers, which meant that he was even taller than Masugu-*san*. His face was broad and open, but his eyes . . .

His eyes were piercing. Even across the entire courtyard I felt as if he were staring at me—staring into my soul, like a hawk at a rabbit. At a squirrel. It made me want to run to the tree I'd just been in and climb to the top.

Three men walked just behind him, no more armed than their lord—armed only with the Matsudaira emblem of the three wild ginger leaves on their robes. Two were older, with grey hair. One was young and carried himself lightly, as if he were about to tell a joke.

Lady Chiyome walked forward to meet them. "Lord Matsudaira, welcome to the Full Moon. You honor my humble school with your presence."

Now Matsudaira-*sama* smiled, though his eyes remained serious. "Mochizuki Chiyome, it is you who honor me." He glanced up at all of us. "It is rare for soldiers such as we to get so gracious and so lovely a welcome."

They bowed to each other, Chiyome-*sama* bowing slightly lower than Lord Matsudaira.

"Of course," Emi whispered, "she was with him this morning."

Mai shushed her.

"Lady Chiyome," continued Matsudaira-*sama,* "may I introduce my captains—my brother Matsudaira Ietada and my old friend Hattori Hanzō." He gestured to the two older gentlemen, who bowed respectfully. "And my nephew Tokugawa Tokimatsu." The younger man bowed as well, just as deeply if a bit more rakishly.

Chiyome-*sama* smirked at the young man, whom she'd obviously already met—I had to assume that the introductions were for our benefit. Bowing to the three men to almost precisely the same depth as they had, she then turned and indicated Mieko. "My lords, may I introduce my . . . lieutenant, if you will. Mieko is the principal teacher at the Full Moon, instructing the young women here in how best to serve the gods."

Mieko bowed low to the captains, and after a gesture from Sachi, we all joined her.

When we straightened, Mieko (who had that morning been showing us how to kill an armed man with a knife) remained in a demure pose, her head lowered and turned to the side. "It would be our honor and pleasure, sirs, to pause from these studies so as to serve you." She gestured toward the front doors of the Great Hall, which Hoshi and Mitsuke opened, revealing the brightly lit, brightly decorated room within.

Grinning, Lord Matsudaira and his two elder captains swept past them and into the hall. The younger one, Tokimatsu-*san*, stared briefly at Mieko as if trying to remember something before he laughed and followed the others.

Chiyome and Mieko followed them, as did we.

As Emi, Toumi, and I sprinted back to the kitchen, the rest of the soldiers streamed into the hall, laughing and jostling as they found their way to the tables. Aimaru started to follow us, but the Little Brothers led him over to the tables. He gave an apologetic shrug and sat as we disappeared back into Kee Sun's domain.

In the kitchen, our cook faced off with an enormously fat man with a long white beard. "And yeh think yeh can just come into my kitchen, do yeh, yeh vat o' lard?"

"And you think you can serve your Korean slop to my lord, you pickled cabbage?"

Each of them held a gleaming cleaver in his fist.

"Um, Kee Sun-*san* . . . " I wanted to ask if everything were all right, when it clearly wasn't. My fingers itched for the sword, just behind the interloper. "Can I . . . Do you . . ."

Both men looked at me, looked back at each other. They started laughing then and threw their arms around each other.

"Girlies," chuckled Kee Sun, "this here is Lord Matsudaira's cook, Kumo. Me, I call him *Fatso.*"

"Like you're so skinny," snorted the big man.

"Well, it's like yeh always said," Kee Sun began, and they finished together: "Never trust a skinny cook!"

They both laughed for a few moments more before Kee Sun slapped his knife down on the cutting table. "Fatso's going to help in the kitchen while our guests are here."

"*Help!* I'm going to be showing these poor, lovely girls the proper way to prepare food after you've led them all astray with your peculiar Korean cooking habits!"

Kee Sun laughed again, and Kumo joined him, and they both began sending us out with platters of boiled soy beans and bowls of spicy *kimchee.*

Lady Chiyome was at present the only woman seated. She was deep in conversation with Matsudaira-*sama.*

"*Girl!*" shouted one of the soldiers, "get us *sake!*"

That meal blurred by even more than most.

While we served, the older women kept the guests entertained. Sachi played the flute while Mieko danced. Hoshi sang, which I had never heard her do, while Sachi accompanied her—a song about a bird seeking its mate after a long winter. Mai and Shino even played, and while their plucked *koto* and *samisen* music may not have been quite as achingly beautiful as Sachi's flute, it was certainly better than Emi, Toumi, or I could have produced.

Two things stick out in my memory.

First, the young Matsudaira captain, Tokimatsu, kept staring at Mieko, while a samurai beside him with a scar on his cheek seemed to be muttering jokes into his ear.

Second, I noticed two odd creatures seated at the very bottom of the tables, closest to the kitchen: a tall, slender man and a boy. Their skin had a peculiar hue, a bit like bronze that's just started to turn green, and they were both dressed strangely. The man wore black robes like none I'd ever seen, with a solid white band at the neck. The boy wore a heavily embroidered jacket, but his pants came only to mid-thigh, and he had some sort of tight material covering his legs the rest of the way down. Their eyes seemed almost lidless, with an odd, roundish shape. And they spoke a language together that sounded as if it were made completely of vowels.

I asked Aimaru about them—he sat just to their left, beside a Matsudaira surgeon who seemed to have had too much *sake*—and he told me that they were from far to the west. That the man was a priest and the boy his novice.

I nodded, but I didn't understand. The man didn't look like any kind of priest I had ever seen.

Even their oddity was odd. I had heard of folks from the lands of the setting sun—that they were "ghosts," all white, with white hair and pale eyes. These people didn't look like ghosts. But they didn't look like anyone I had ever seen.

I noticed that the boy's eyes were following me, so I hurried back to the kitchen.

Once we had finished serving the meal, the folks at the head table—Lady Chiyome, Lord Matsudaira, and his captains—began giving speeches. At that point, Kee Sun allowed the three of us to come in and eat.

I felt so tired and hungry that even the memory of the pig squealing, bound in armor on the ground outside the kitchen, didn't stop me from eating and enjoying the pork.

I didn't eat the *soondae,* though. The blood sausage still made my stomach churn.

Kee Sun and Kumo were both laughing and swapping stories about meals cooked on military campaigns—horse meat, fox meat, herbs that turned out to be foul tasting, mushrooms that turned out to be deadly. They kept drinking *sake*, and they let us have some too—watered down, of course.

It didn't make me want to laugh. It made me want to go to sleep.

But we couldn't—not until the dining room and the baths were clean.

And I kept staring up at Masugu's sword, lying atop the rack by the cutting table. Its black scabbard seemed to absorb all of the light in the brightly lit kitchen.

In the dining room, a sudden burst of sound came from the guests as they began to rise from the tables.

The kitchen doors flew open, revealing all the women of the Full Moon—plus Aimaru—their arms laden with bowls and platters and cups and jugs, which they deposited, laughing, in the washing tub.

Well, I say all of the women—I mean all except Lady Chiyome, of course. And Shino and Mai, whom Kee Sun had exiled from the kitchen on pain of having their limbs removed.

"Thought we'd save you the trouble," said Sachi, "since you carried these all out!"

And then all of the women left, escorting the guests to the gate.

"What a lovely bunch of young ladies," chortled Kumo as Aimaru slid the last bowls into the overfull tub.

"Ayup, that was mighty nice of 'em." Kee Sun grunted and pointed at the enormous mound of dirty porcelain that filled the tub near to overflowing. "Mind, yeh girlies—and yeh too, Moon-cake—still need to finish cleanin' those for tomorrow mornin'."

We groaned but began cleaning up.

4—Shadow of the Moon

Once the dishes had been washed and the baths cleaned out and readied for the next morning, the cooks and our friend bid us good night, and we all stumbled into our dormitory.

Toumi grumbled and muttered her way into her bed and began snoring soon after.

Emi whispered, "So why do you think the Matsudaira are here?"

"I don't know." I had been asking myself the same question. "Do you suppose they could have been trying to stop Masugu-*san*?"

"It would make sense out of why he suddenly rode off."

I shook my head in the dark. "He was waiting for the passes to open."

"Hmm."

"And Lady Chiyome was traveling with them."

Silence.

At first I thought Emi was thinking, but then I heard the whistling breath that characterized her sudden descent into sleep.

I lay there, thinking through the day, my body exhausted but my head unable to let go. I found my mind circling around the arrival of Lord Matsudaira and his troops, around Lady Chiyome's warning to keep our secrets, around Masugu-*san*'s departure.

The sword.

The feel of it in my hands, as if my arms were at last complete.

Lady Chiyome and Kee Sun had said that I couldn't carry it or practice with it where anyone might see. But when would I be able to?

After a long debate with myself, I slipped out of my bedroll, stepped carefully around the lump that was Emi, and sneaked out into the clear, chill night.

The moon had not yet lifted above the compound wall, but the stars were bright. The Great Hall rose, still and star frosted, before me.

I walked over to the kitchen door and slid it open as carefully and as quietly as I could.

The door wasn't made for silence; it squeaked and groaned as I slid it open, and my breath caught, sure that Kee Sun or Lady Chiyome or Lord Matsudaira or someone would spring on me from the shadows and demand to know what I thought I was doing.

No one sprang.

On tiptoe, I made my way over to Kee Sun's shrine of knives. There at the top lay the short sword, its scabbard blacker than the shadows that surrounded it. I had to push up as far on my toes as I could, but I stretched to reach it and bring it down.

Sheathed, held to my chest, it somehow felt lighter than it had when I had wielded it that afternoon. Not even thinking about it, I drew the blade.

In the dark kitchen, the steel seemed to flare with silver light—like a frozen lightning bolt there in my hand. I placed the scabbard in my sash and took a ready stance, gripping the hilt in both hands, raised at my right shoulder, the blade pointed straight upward. The Eight Phases.

The sword knocked a bamboo beam from which herbs hung. I had to catch a bag of dried ginger root. Using the tip of the blade, I lifted the bag back to the beam.

If I wanted to see what the blade really felt like, I would need to go outside.

Keeping my grip tight, not wanting to let the lightning loose, I peered out the door. Nothing moved.

I stepped out into the space between the kitchen and the well where I had failed to kill the pig. Near the place by the wall where I had sliced the dead pig's body in half.

Taking a deep breath, I pulled myself into the pose of the Two Fields: blade before me, hands at my belly button, feet spread and knees bent, balanced.

I stepped back and to the right, raising my hands above my head and angling the blade down toward my left foot—the Bamboo Bud.

A downward slash—the Key of Heaven.

The blade *was* heavier than I was used to. But it was also so exquisitely balanced that changing its angle or position felt as natural as breathing. And the feeling of that blade slicing through the air filled me with glee, a desire to howl and scream with the fierce pleasure of it.

Obviously, I could do no such thing so late at night. But I wanted to.

Facing east, I went through the entire dance, the Sixty-four Changes. Then I turned to the south and repeated it, then repeated the whole sequence again to the west and finally to the north.

By the time I completed the fourth pass through, my whole body felt warm in spite of the cold. Nothing existed in my world except for the flash of the starlit blade and the roar of my blood through my veins.

It wasn't just that the sword made me feel powerful, though it did. I also felt as if the whole of the Sixty-four Changes, which I had been practicing every morning and afternoon since before Fuyudori's death, had ceased to be simply a series of movements that my body made, hands empty or not.

Now it felt as though the sword and I were going through the dance together. Or that the dance was going through us.

And the sword had none of my uncertainty, none of my moral scruples. It knew what it was. It knew its purpose. It sought nothing more than to fulfill that purpose. It was a sword just as I was a warrior.

I turned to the east, ready to begin again, but nearly dropped the blade in surprise at finding Mieko standing just inside the open kitchen door.

She smiled and tilted her head. "A beautiful blade, isn't it?"

Stunned, my body caught between the exultation of moments before and shock, I stammered, "Y-yes, Mieko-*sensei.*" Shock. Humiliation at being caught doing something that felt so . . . private. Fear that I was somehow breaking the rules.

"May I?" She held out one fine-fingered hand.

I couldn't have refused her even if I'd wanted to. Which I suppose I did. Even so, I held the handle out to her, letting that frozen lightning bolt rest on my two sweaty hands.

"*Dōmo arigatō,*" she murmured, and stepped past me into the open space near the well, letting the weight of the blade roll from one hand to the other, testing its balance, feeling its weight.

With no warning, she spun, stepping forward and then delivering a sweeping horizontal cut so fast, so beautiful, that I would have gasped even if she had stopped the blade more than a mere finger's width from my neck.

And so I did gasp, and the impulse to dive out of the blade's path only caught up after there was no need. I exerted what little discipline I had just to keep from moving or screaming.

Mieko smiled again, a wilder smile than I was used to from the ever-graceful *kunoichi.* "Again, thank you." With a bow, she presented the blade back to me, lying across her two open palms. "It truly is a beautiful blade. Masugu honored you in giving it to you."

I took the *wakizashi* and, not trusting my now-shaky grip, hugged it to my chest with the tip down. "I . . . He just asked me to take care of it while he was away on his mission."

Now her smile softened. "I'm sure he did. Do you know the history of this blade?" When I shook my head, she continued, "It was forged nearly a hundred years ago for Masugu's grandfather, who served as a captain to the then-Lord Takeda." She touched one finger to the four-diamond emblem on the hilt. "When Masugu's mother was a young girl, her mother was . . . taken advantage of by one of the other captains. Her attacker was sentenced to death, but Masugu's grandmother was so mortified by the stain on her honor that she begged her husband to release her from the shame. Which he did, with that blade."

"Oh." I stared down at the remorseless steel.

"The story that is widely known says that the grandfather then took his own life with this same *wakizashi* in order to erase his family's dishonor completely. But when Masugu told it to me . . . " Her eyes narrowed in sad memory. "His mother told him that she believed that her father had killed himself out of sorrow—sorrow at his wife's death, sorrow at her dishonor, sorrow at having had to take his beloved's life."

"Oh." I thought for the first time in weeks of my own mother—of her wails after my father walked to his death in the Imagawa castle. I thought for the first time in years of my earliest memory: my mother sitting in the middle of the floor of our tiny new home in Serenity Province, Usako held to her breast, weeping in this memory too. Weeping, I now realized, because she had lost everything—home, family honor, prospects for me and my sister—because of my father's refusal to kill a group of Imagawa children for Lord Oda—Imagawa children plus one hostage, Masugu.

"Risuko," Mieko said, and reached out a hand, touching my cheek, which I realized was wet. She looked into my eyes. Whatever she saw there, she nodded. "So. This sword holds a great deal of significance to Masugu. He would not have let just anyone take care of it for him."

Not able to meet her gaze any more, I frowned down at the sword's handle and nodded back.

"You wield it well—remarkably well for someone so young. Your movements flow beautifully. But then, you have always taken to the Sixty-four Changes."

Again I nodded. Even before I had known its purpose, my body had remembered it as *Otō-san*'s daily practice with his sword.

"What you need to work on, now that you have a real sword to practice with, is precision. I know that I frightened you just now when I swung the blade at your throat, but I know this sword, and I knew precisely where I needed to stop. Let me show you."

And she proceeded to give me a lesson in swordsmanship unlike any that I had received from Hoshi, from the Little Brothers, or from Masugu. Part of it was her almost supernatural grace. Part of it was that where, for the men, the wielding of the sword was all about generating power—using their legs and arms to create devastating force behind the blade—for Mieko-*san*, it was all about placement—as she said, precision. She worked with me until the half-moon had crept over the wall of the Full Moon, causing the sword to flare as I swung it, trying to keep my cuts and my parries as elegant, as efficient, and as lethal as hers.

Finally she bowed to me again. "Well done. We should go to sleep; morning will no doubt bring more adventures."

I bowed low in return. "Thank you so much, Mieko-*sensei.*" She gave me a small smile, but as she turned, I said, more loudly than the whispers we'd been using, "Will you teach me again?"

Now the smile widened, becoming once again her most frightening grin. "Oh, Murasaki-*san,* you can count on it."

5—Jotaro-san

For months, the only dream I ever had was of Fuyudori falling backward from the top of the huge hemlock into the snow-filled night. Her open eyes, her open mouth, the white of her hair whipping through the white snow—these haunted me in sleep more than her spirit could have done in my waking hours.

That night, however, after I snuggled into my bedroll, still sweaty from working with Mieko out in the brisk night, I dreamed about my mother.

She was sweeping the floor of our house—the *tatami* mats were all up, stacked outside the front door, and she was sweeping away the dust.

She wasn't sweeping with the stiff broom she usually used, however. She was sweeping with *Otō-san*'s *katana*. And she was crying.

Sweeping and weeping.

I was yanked out of the dream by a shove and a sharp voice saying my name over and over again and repeating, "Get up."

My eyes unglued themselves unwillingly.

Mai was prodding my shoulder with her foot, her face set in a grin that lacked any warmth.

"What?" I asked.

She snarled, "You need to help fill and light the baths. Now. If you don't, Toumi's going to make sure you're the only one helping in the kitchen today." She narrowed her eyes. "And I'm going to practice on you with Mieko's blades."

Groaning, I pulled myself from my bed and threw on clothes.

Once I stumbled from our dormitory to the bathhouse, Emi murmured, "You went out last night."

"Couldn't sleep."

She said nothing for a moment and then said, "I guess that's why you didn't wake up with the rest of us."

"I guess."

I joined in carrying buckets of water from the well to fill the two tubs, cool and hot.

Emi started muttering that if we had just a few more people, we could just stand in line and pass the buckets back and forth, rather than each of us running between the tubs and the well.

She even tried to talk about it to Shino, who was carrying water to the store-room, where she and Mai were helping do the laundry. Shino simply growled and turned her back.

———

Aimaru was waiting for us in the kitchen, looking more awake and cheerful than anyone should have had a right to look. Toumi told him so, and for once neither Emi nor I tried to stop her. Even so, we were all happy that he was helping.

Once we had prepared everything, Kee Sun sent him out to eat.

"After all," said Kumo-*san* with a smile, "who wants to be served at table by a man when there are such lovely young ladies about?"

Aimaru rolled his eyes but happily left the serving to us.

The morning meal wasn't as busy as the evening meal had been, but it lasted much longer. Matsudaira soldiers and inhabitants of the Full Moon trickled steadily into the Great Hall.

This time, the *kunoichi* weren't helping serve; we would bring the platters of scrambled rice and egg and of reheated *soondae* out to the serving tables, but Mai and Shino were the only ones distributing the food to the people eating. Shino's expression was resigned; Mai had an almost manic grin on her face that made it look as if she were about to take a bite out of someone.

When I mentioned this to Kee Sun, he scratched his beard for a moment. "Well, I think Falcon-girlie and Smiley can keep the platters coming and going. Why don't yeh help those two clowns out in the dining hall."

Kumo winked at me and chuckled, "It will make the soldiers happy to see another pretty face."

I bowed, as much to hide my blush as out of politeness.

As I helped Toumi bring out more sausages, she muttered, "Pretty face."

"I'm sure he thinks you're pretty too."

Toumi snorted. "Like I care."

"Well," I said, frowning at her. "Why would you?"

"Exactly."

There were times when agreeing with Toumi was even more confusing than disagreeing with her. It wasn't just that she was such a prickly, contrary person. It was that, more often than not, I actually had no idea what she was saying, let alone what she was thinking.

I put down the tray of sausage that I was carrying—Mai picked it up immediately and took it toward where Lord Matsudaira chatted with his youngest captain.

Toumi was already stomping her way back to the kitchen.

It looked as if a number of the guests' teacups were empty, so I picked up a full pot from the center table—still hot, thankfully—and walked toward where Aimaru was speaking with the bronze-skinned boy. "Would you like some tea?"

"Thanks, Murasaki-*san*," said Aimaru and added in a whisper, "Sorry."

The other boy just held up his cup without looking at me.

The old priest next to him said something in that birdsong language of theirs, and suddenly the boy's eyes were on me. "Thank you very much, it is," he said, and though his accent was good, it sounded more as if he were apologizing.

Aimaru smiled broadly. "This is Murasaki."

I bowed, not knowing what else to do.

"Good morning, it is, Murasaki-*san*." He gave his head a shallow nod. "I am João Afonso Alves de Sousa de Mandrágora, at your service."

At my . . . "Good morning, um, Jo . . . "

"Jolalo-*san*," said Aimaru, his smile just as bright.

"Um, tea?"

"Thank you, it is." Jolalo held out his cup again, and I filled it.

As I filled Aimaru's, he added, "Jolalo-*san* has been telling me about his country far to the west."

"Portugal," the other boy said. "A great country, it is. A very long journey, it is. It is taking us almost a year to sail here."

Not knowing what to say to that, I bowed again. "Welcome to the Full Moon, Jolalo-*san*."

He scowled. "Thank you, it is."

I poured tea for one of the Little Brothers and for the strange priest, who bowed his head slightly as the boy had done.

When I went to pick up a fresh pot, Shino stood by the serving table, an expression on her face as if she had smelled spoiled meat.

I followed her eyes; she was glaring at Mai, who was smiling at the Matsudaira captain Tokimatsu and at a samurai who was laughing next to him, the one with the fine scar below his right eye.

"Disgusting," muttered Shino. "She's flirting with them."

It was true. Mai tittered and blushed at something the samurai was saying, looking like anything but the vicious girl I'd come to know over the previous months.

"Well," I said, "Chiyome-*sama* did say we should follow Sachi-*sensei*'s example." I nodded to where the music teacher had a knot of Matsudaira soldiers listening wide eyed to a story.

"Fine," grumbled Shino, "but she can't leave us to do all the serving." She strode off toward Mai with a full platter of eggs and rice, and I wasn't sure she wasn't going to bang Mai over the head with it.

Chiyome-*sama* gestured for me to come bring tea to her and Lord Matsudaira. As I approached, Shino used her hip to bump Mai out of the way—she was stronger at hand-to-hand combat than Mai. Mai, however, was stronger with weapons and looked about to smash the teapot in her hand against Shino's face when Mieko spoke, somehow having appeared just behind Captain Tokimatsu. "Girls," she said, managing to keep her voice both soft and knife edged, "do you need some help?"

Mai and Shino, who knew just how sharp Mieko could be, bowed to her and muttered, "No, *sensei*." They slinked apart, leaving Tokimatsu and the samurai looking amused—but also leaving their plates empty.

"Risuko," said Lady Chiyome with a chuckle, "go fill the captain's cup first. He looks as if he needs it more than I do."

———

Aimaru once again came and helped out in the kitchen once he'd eaten. After breakfast, all four of us headed out to the Tea House with Hoshi-*sensei*. We spent the morning writing out in our best, flowing calligraphy a section of the Sermon of the Flower Wreath: The flowers of enlightenment lie like a net of gems, each reflecting the others' brilliance like clouds of thought.

As we walked away from the Tea House, Mitsuke approached us with her face as blank as ever, Aimaru trailing behind her. "All of you, follow me. The young man here will help Kee Sun today. The rest of you will be going outside."

Shrugging, Aimaru shuffled off toward the Great Hall.

"Now, the rest of you are going to be helping with food as well." When Mai started to object, Mitsuke continued, "Not with the cooking—with the gathering. Emi and Toumi, get your bows; you are going hunting in the woods. Mai and Shino, you are going to hoe the garden."

"The garden!" moaned Shino.

"With your glaives," said Mitsuke, voice flat as ever. "If, while no one is watching, you should happen to practice the thrust-parry sequence Rin-*san* was showing you the other day, I am certain that no one will object." Then she turned to me. "You, Risuko, are going to be hunting birds' eggs."

I nodded. "Climbing trees?"

"No, I think even our hemlock here doesn't challenge your skills enough. You will be searching for eggs up there." She pointed over the Retreat, over the wall at the back of the Full Moon, to the sheer, rocky cliff that loomed over the compound.

I gulped. I had climbed the Imagawa castle, which was even taller, but which had easy hand- and footholds—easy for me, at least. This looked . . . not easy. For anyone.

Mitsuke raise one eyebrow.

I sighed. "Yes, Mitsuke-*sensei.*"

6—The Mountain at the Full Moon

love to climb.

I suppose that's a silly thing for me to say at this point. Of course I love to climb. Still—it's true. It's always been true. That earliest memory—of my mother weeping with my sister in her arms—I see it from above. Even though we had just moved into the tiny house, even though I was just four years old, I had already found my way up into the rickety rafters. I always felt more at home up in the air than on the ground. Safer.

There was a reason that my mother came to call me Squirrel.

Yet as I stared at that sheer rock face from within the confines of the Full Moon, I just stood there, looking up.

Toumi snorted as she and Emi shouldered past me, bows and quivers over their shoulders. "Scared, Mouse-*chan?*"

I shook my head. But we both knew it wasn't true.

Emi smiled as they walked out the gate. I think she meant it as reassurance. It felt as if she were consoling me: *It's been a pleasure knowing you, Murasaki.*

"Come along, Risuko-*chan,*" said Mitsuke. "Lady Chiyome tells us you climbed up the side of the Great Hall to her window on a snowy night. If you can do that, this should be no problem."

We walked through the rear gate, and the cliff loomed over us.

"Has anyone else ever climbed it?"

The teacher with the forgettable face shrugged. "You'll have to ask Mieko-*san.* She's been here longer than I have."

Again I nodded, though my mouth was dry. "Let me . . . find the best way up."

She held her hands out, palms up, as if to say, *Don't let me stop you.*

Mouth parched, heart in my throat, I crossed the small kitchen garden that lay behind the rear wall of the compound. Then I clambered over the brush-choked pile of rubble at the cliff's base, staring up at the rock.

Closer up, the face no longer looked sheer. It was steep, it is true, but not straight up and down, and there were cracks and fissures where I could see my toes and fingers finding purchase.

Just to the right of the center of the precipice was a slight crease. An indentation no more than a hand's breadth or two deep that ran at least two-thirds of the way up the cliff to an angled shelf. It had been invisible from a distance, but close up, I knew.

There, I thought.

Feeling breath and strength return, I approached the wall and began to climb.

Let me tell you one other thing—and this is a secret: when I climb, I am not thinking of the fall or of the distance above. I am thinking about the wood or rock or plaster immediately in front of me. I am thinking about possible hand- and footholds.

I know that, as long as I can find them, I can keep climbing.

And this little fissure in the cliff's face made finding those easy. It was full of cracks and irregularities that I could wedge a foot or hand into. The depression in the rock and the slight angle of the slope meant that my fingers and toes didn't carry all of my weight. I won't say that it was a climb that anyone could have done. I won't say that it was easy. But quickly I was free of the ground and back up in my element.

I felt as if the rocks existed to help me climb, as if the mountain itself were aiding my ascent.

Here's another secret: I often feel that way. Not always. But there are times—my favorite climbs—when it doesn't feel as if I'm climbing. Instead, the cliff or tree or wall seems to be lifting me, higher and higher.

I have never been one to feel the presence of gods and monsters. Yet in those moments I know with all certainty that I am in the presence of something much, much larger than myself. I feel both humbled and alive.

You may think me silly or peculiar; my sister always did.

When I reached the shelf, I was almost disappointed. My muscles were warm, but it was a good feeling; I had not yet begun to tire. Still, I knew it would be good to pull myself up onto the ledge and find my best starting point for the rest of the climb.

I clambered up onto the relatively flat surface and sat. For the first time, it occurred to me to look down.

Below me, I could see Mitsuke, Mai, and Shino, their faces upturned, their mouths open. By the walls of the Full Moon stood a handful of Matsudaira samurai. I could also make out the black silhouettes of the old Portuguese priest and the boy, Jolalo-*san*. They too seemed to be staring up at me.

Grinning, I waved to them all.

Of course, at just that moment it began to rain.

Weather comes quickly up there in the mountains, especially in the warm months. Blue sky can give way to storm in the blink of an eye. A blizzard can change to rain just as quickly.

Fat drops began to splash off of the dusty rock and to cool my pleasantly warm neck. The sun disappeared and the sky darkened as clouds poured over the mountain above me.

Below, everyone scattered.

I looked around for what shelter I could find. I didn't expect much.

The shelf wasn't level. Water was already beginning to trickle down. I stood before it soaked my trousers. Toward the upper end of the ledge, where it narrowed away to nothing, I saw a dark crevice.

Thinking I might be able to shove myself at least partially out of the rain, I shuffled up toward the shadow.

The rain turned to hail, springtime as it was. Icy pellets pelted my head.

The crevice looked wide enough that I would be able to huddle out of the weather. I turned sideways and pushed . . .

And suddenly found myself through and completely out of the hail.

Relieved, I watched the pea-sized hailstones bouncing off the stone shelf.

Shaking myself, I looked behind me. It was completely dark. I reached out with my hands; there was open space. Rock walls widened out on either side, but I couldn't feel a back wall.

I'd never been in a cave. As I've said, I have always been most comfortable above the ground, not beneath it.

Yet I could not help but feel a tickle of curiosity urging me deeper.

I took a step into the dark and then two more. The air was cool and still and smelled of . . . something. Birds. Something.

A sound at odds with the high drumbeat of the hail behind me rumbled out from the black depths. It sounded like distant rain, though the floor that I could see was completely dry. An echo, maybe.

I turned back to the opening. It was a vertical slash of bright light. Hail still bounced off the ledge and into the cave, scattering at my feet.

I squinted into the depths of the cave, trying to peer into the gloom.

One of Mieko-*sensei*'s lessons came back to me. When moving from the light into the dark, she had told us one afternoon as we practiced stabbing the dummy blindfolded, keep one eye closed—both if you can safely manage it. That way, you will not be left blind in the darkness.

I knelt and closed both eyes, letting light seep away. I counted ten breaths and then ten more. I listened to the *tic-tic-tic* of the hail behind me.

I opened my eyes.

Though the cave was still dim, I could see that it expanded out from the narrow entrance—as wide at the widest spot as our dormitory down below, though not as high.

In the dim recesses of the cave, against a night-black abyss, crouched a creature of nightmares. Atop a massive body that was pressed low to the cave floor, a lumpen head threatened, with enormous fangs and tusks thrusting out of a cruel, black-splashed mouth. Its eyes were lost in shadow, but I had no doubt that they were focussed on me, the invader.

The hair rose on the backs of my arms, on my neck. My breath caught, and I had to fight the urge to run screaming out of the cave. Never turn your back on an ogre. My father had said it as a joke, but I know that he'd meant it nonetheless.

Barely daring to breathe, I inched my way backward.

The thing's eyes remained locked on me, but it made no sign of following.

My foot bumped up against the wall. Light spilled onto my hands from behind me. Without blinking, I edged my way back out of the cave and onto the wet, welcome ledge outside.

Still there was no sound of the monster pursuing me.

I edged my way back down to the far end of the shelf and turned to find my bearings again. The rain had lessened; across the valley it was sunny. And down below, on the road up to the ridge where the Full Moon and the Matsudaira camp perched, a swarm of soldiers were making their way up the hill.

Not blue flags this time. Red, with a four-diamond emblem that I knew well.

Takeda.

I scrambled over the edge and down the mountainside as quickly as I could without flying.

As I reached the bottom of the cliff, the field was still empty, and so I ran on shaky legs toward the rear gate. I burst through it to find only Jolalo, who was staring at me as if it were I and not that apparition in the cave that was the *oni*.

"You . . . climbed," he said.

"Yes." I looked around, trying to find someone to tell. The kitchen . . .

"You climbed like a . . . like a . . . "

"Like a squirrel," I said. I bowed, pressing my wet, raw palms to my wet, cold thighs. "Excuse me, Jolalo-*san*." I ran past him and burst into the kitchen, where Aimaru was helping Kee Sun and Kumo-*san* shell peas, tiny in his enormous hands. "Takeda," I gasped. "Takeda soldiers, coming up the hill!"

Kee Sun grunted and Kumo-*san* snorted. "Hope they brought some food," the huge cook said.

Aimaru's eyes stayed on me. "Did something happen, Murasaki-*san?*"

Before I could think how to answer, Kee Sun said, "Later. Well, Bright Eyes? What're yeh waiting for? Ring the gong and get all of the girlies ready to welcome our patron as our guest."

We stood once more in a line in front of the Great Hall. Half of us were wet, but Chiyome-*sama* didn't seem to care. Her focus was on the figure striding through the gate toward her.

"Chiyome, it is always a pleasure."

Lord Takeda was smaller than I had expected. His face was a perfect oval, kindly, though his eyes were cold. He was almost completely bald—a dark stubble showed that he shaved like the Little Brothers—but over his mouth he wore a thick mustache.

"My lord honors this humble household with his presence," said Chiyome-*sama,* bowing low. I was astonished to hear her speak in a tone that was respectful. Almost. With a sly grin, she began to sweep her hand toward us initiates. "If I may—"

At just that moment, the only person in the compound who could have interrupted the meeting swept in through the open gate. Lord Matsudaira called out, "Well met, my lord governor of Worth!" Three samurai stood between him and Lord Takeda, their hands near but carefully not on their swords.

"Well met, my lord governor of the Three Rivers," Takeda-*sama* replied. "I hope that your travels through my domain have been pleasant." A quartet of his guards stood at the open gate, ready to draw.

At the time, it was only the fear that a battle was about to break out in the Full Moon that allowed me to forget about the monster in the cave.

When Matsudaira-*sama* and his soldiers didn't move, Lord Takeda turned to Lady Chiyome and said, "Chiyome, it is a pleasure as always to be under your protection. As I was saying, we will of course be happy to forgo our swords within the Full Moon's walls."

"You honor me, my lord."

Lord Matsudaira smiled, his eyes focussed on Chiyome-*sama*. "My lady, we of course consider it a privilege to enter your home and will also leave our swords in our camp."

With simultaneous bows, the three Matsudaira samurai and the four Takeda withdrew, leaving their lords momentarily unattended.

"My lords," said Lady Chiyome, giving a demure bow, "I appreciate your delicacy and vouchsafe your safety in my home. We would not want my young girls to be frightened of your weapons."

I could not help but notice the steel-tipped chopsticks in Hoshi's hair, the slight bulge of the knives at Mieko's forearms, the garrote wire disguised as a bracelet on Mitsuke's wrist, and the fan with the retracted blades behind which Sachi was hiding her face.

Lord Matsudaira nodded and turned to Takeda-*sama*. "You are truly well met, my lord. I have been growing concerned for our timetable."

"Precisely why I suggested we meet here, my lord."

"Well, my lords," chirped Chiyome-*sama*, gesturing toward the Great Hall, "I am sure you are hungry. And I'm just as sure that the cooks have something ready. Come join me for a mid-day meal."

———

When we entered the kitchen, the scent of pork soup filled the air, spiced with tension.

Kee Sun was muttering in Korean while Kumo fumed at a short, dour man who was standing in the doorway. "We aren't going to *poison* your master, Torai!"

"Just as well," grunted the small man, his accent flat and nasal, sniffing at the soup. "I wasn't going to let you."

Kee Sun glared as he slopped *kimchee* into serving bowls.

Emi raised her eyebrow at me; Kee Sun would never have let us serve out good food like that.

"And don't let that pickled fire get anywhere near the head table, Kee Sun, you hear? Takeda-*sama* may think he likes that stuff, but it doesn't like him."

"My lady likes my *kimchee*, Shorty," Kee Sun growled, "and it likes her just fine."

"Well," said Kumo before the two cooks could come to blows, "it's just as well that these lovely young ladies are here to carry out the food. Kee Sun, why don't you help Torai go and get all of the supplies he brought settled in the storerooms, and we'll make sure the meal is served properly, yes?"

Kee Sun and Torai stared at each other—for a moment I thought they might break into laughter as Kumo and Kee Sun had the day before. However, the Takeda cook snarled at us, "Don't let me hear that you've let Takeda-*sama* eat any of that stuff, do you hear me, children?"

We all looked to Kee Sun, who ground his teeth but nodded. Then, with a bang, the two cooks were off.

"Well," sighed Kumo, "I thought you girls handled that very well. So gather up the bowls and start serving, will you?"

7—Startled

There were fewer people in the Great Hall than there had been the night before. Only the officers seemed to have been invited. For the rest of our guests' stay, the soldiers ate in their camps.

The Takeda officers took the tables to the left while the Matsudaira sat to the right, with the doors at their back.

The *kunoichi* had scattered themselves among the men, who all looked torn between being happy to have female companions and being annoyed at the other clan's presence.

Emi was pouting as we served out the soup. I whispered, "I think Aimaru and the Little Brothers are helping the Takeda set up."

She shook her head. "It's Mai. It's funny seeing her acting like this."

I glanced to where Mai was standing before a Takeda officer with a pointed beard. She was giggling and blushing as she served him *kimchee*. Giggling. And blushing. Mai.

"You look like you tasted something bad," said Jolalo.

"No, Jolalo-*san*." I filled the bowl that Emi had placed before him. "I was . . . This humble servant's hands are still raw. From climbing."

"Oh." He scowled at me, but nodded. The scowl, I realized, meant that he was trying to understand something.

The Portuguese priest, whom I was now serving, murmured to him in their singsong language.

Jolalo sat up straighter. "Thank you very much, it is."

Emi smirked.

I shot her a look that I hoped would keep her quiet.

It did—for a while.

"Ugh."

"Now you're the one who looks like she ate something disgusting."

She wrinkled her nose and I followed her eyes to where Mai was talking to another man—the Matsudaira lieutenant with the scar she'd flirted with the night before. She hid her mouth behind her hand, tittering at something he was saying.

"Someone looks as if she's been taking your lessons too well," Hoshi muttered to Sachi.

"Or not well enough." Sachi said with a wink, and laughed.

The two Matsudaira to her left laughed along, though I am certain they had no idea what they were laughing at.

I was about to ask Sachi-*sensei* about Mai's behavior when I noticed Lord Takeda lifting a helping of bright green *kimchee* into his bowl. I whispered to Emi through clenched teeth, "Should we—"

But it was too late. Takeda-*sama* plopped some of the spicy pickled cabbage into his mouth and began to chew.

I felt as if I were watching someone fall from the top of a tree.

As Chiyome-*sama* talked with Matsudaira-*sama*, Lord Takeda's face slowly turned bright red.

"Oh, dear," Emi gasped. We both turned away from the head table, determined not to be caught staring.

I filled a bowl that Emi had laid in front of one of the Matsudaira. "Do you think the cook, Torai, will—"

"I hope not." She laid down another bowl, and I filled it.

Not able to stand it any longer, I dared another glance at the head table.

Lady Chiyome was grinning at Lord Takeda, whose face was sunset red. She handed him a cup of wine.

He drank it down. His face was just as red. But he was smiling. Mopping his face with a napkin. But smiling.

Mai had no idea what a disaster she'd nearly caused by leaving the bowl of *kimchee* at the head table.

Even though she was only a few steps away, she was back flirting with the Takeda officer, who was grinning even more broadly than his lord.

On the other side of the room, the Matsudaira lieutenant she'd been flouncing at earlier glowered into his soup.

—————

The meal ended not long afterward when the two lords rose and their retainers rose with them. Lord Takeda's face was still flushed, but he seemed to be smiling.

After a moment, he and Matsudaira-*sama* strode shoulder to shoulder out the front door. The officers streamed out, glancing at each other uncomfortably.

One of the Matsudaira, Captain Tokimatsu, stood unmoving. He stared as he had done throughout the meal at Mieko, who bowed demurely. "What does the honorable captain wish that this humble servant may provide?"

He frowned, a look that did not seem to fit his face. "Have . . . Are you . . . " He shook his head and smiled. "Takeda-*sama* has a nephew named Masugu. Do you know him?"

Though her eyes were downcast, Mieko gave a small smile and nodded. "Masugu-*san* has been a guest at the Full Moon."

"I had hoped that he might come with Lord Takeda's party."

Mieko's eyes were still down, but being small I could see them flash. "I am sure that Masugu-*san* will be sorry when he hears that he missed the captain."

"I'm sure." Now Tokimatsu-*san*'s grin came back. "He and I were . . . *guests* of the Imagawa together when we were young."

"Ah."

Guests. The great families exchanged children—hostages, in fact—to seal pledges of peace.

So Tokimatsu-*san* too was one of the children that Lord Oda ordered Emi's, Toumi's, and my father to kill.

Which they had refused to do.

The Matsudaira captain gave a laugh and smiled at Mieko. "Well, I can see why Masugu would want to spend time here." He bowed. "I must attend my master. I look forward to speaking again, Miss . . . "

For the first time, her eyes flicked up, measuring him. His smile did not falter.

"Mieko is this humble servant's name."

"Mieko-*san*." Tokimatsu-*san* bowed again and departed.

When he had left the hall, I whispered, "Mieko-*san*, do you and the captain—"

Her gaze filleted me. My question evaporated.

"Go help clean up, Risuko," Mieko said. "Perhaps we can discuss this tonight?"

A thrill passed through my body at the thought of another lesson. "Yes, Mieko-*sensei*."

The kitchen sounded as if a pitched battle were being fought inside. I entered, laden down with bowls and serving trays, worried that blood might be shed and that it might not be only a pig's. Only.

Using my leg to open the door, I slid carefully in.

"After everything," shouted Torai, "your idiot girls *fed* him that trash?"

Kee Sun looked ready to explode. Kumo stepped between them. "You should not speak so about these lovely young ladies. They are doing the best they can."

"And it wasn't one of us," growled Toumi. "It was Mai."

Kee Sun's hands flew up. "That *byeong-shin!*"

Emi added, "She got to the general before we had a chance to tell her not to serve him."

"*Byeong-shin!*" Kee Sun repeated.

Torai gave a disgusted growl, and the three cooks began clearing leftover food from the preparation table. Some was placed in leaves or jars to be reused. What little couldn't be salvaged was dumped into baskets.

"Bright Eyes, Smiley," Kee Sun grunted. "Take that out to the rubbish pit."

"Yes, Kee Sun-*san*," we said, and happily escaped the kitchen.

———

As we stepped out into the sunlight, we heard a giggle. Mai was by our dormitory, talking to the Takeda officer with the pointed beard she had been flirting with during the meal. She leaned against the corner of the building, and he was loomed over her, grinning.

Emi and I fairly ran out the back door of the compound.

No sooner had the door closed behind us than we both began to laugh. The fact that we were both trying desperately not to only made it worse.

Once we had finally caught our breath, Emi said, "I wonder if he knows she has a garrote wire hidden in her hairband."

That set us off again.

We stumbled out toward the rubbish pit, which was on the east side of the ridge from the Full Moon. Mitsuke, who was arranging piles of rocks between the rows in the garden, shot us a disapproving look, but we couldn't stop. Our eyes were streaming, and it was only partially from the smell of the offal we were carrying.

When we had dumped our loads and turned around, we both looked up at the cliff as if we had agreed to do so.

"So," Emi said, "did you get all of the way to the top?"

I shook my head. "When it started hailing, I was about two-thirds of the way up—see that ledge?" I pointed.

She nodded.

"Now see that dark crease over there to the left?"

She squinted, her frown deepening. Again, she nodded.

"It's a cave." Staring down at my still-raw hands, I whispered, "There was a monster inside."

"A monster?"

"An ogre. With huge tusks and sharp teeth."

"An . . . ogre?"

I nodded, waiting for her to doubt me.

Her eyes grew large. "Did it . . . chase you?"

I shook my head. "Just stared at me with those huge, black eyes."

"Could it be a friendly spirit?"

"It didn't look friendly."

"But it didn't come after you?"

"No." Obviously not, or I wouldn't have been standing there.

"Maybe it was . . . " She scowled. "Maybe it was . . . sleeping or . . . dead?"

I thought about it. The stillness, the dryness of the cave. The sunken pits of its eyes. "Maybe."

I wasn't sure that made it any less terrifying.

We both stared up at the cave for a moment. Then a cloud passed over the sun, and we both shivered. "Come on," I said. "It hasn't ever come down the mountain before now. I'm sure it will stay put, dead or not."

Emi nodded. "Yes. Let's go back in."

The ogre had stolen our thoughts so thoroughly that when we got back to the door and heard shouting, neither of us had any idea what it could possibly be about.

As we came back in, we saw Mai standing between two men—the Takeda officer and the scarred Matsudaira she'd been flirting with the night before. The men were screaming words at each other that I hadn't heard even during the week of traveling with Lieutenant Masugu's lancers months before.

Though they dwarfed her, Mai seemed to be doing a remarkably good job of pushing them apart.

Kumo came lumbering out of the kitchen with Torai, Kee Sun, Toumi, and Aimaru behind him. "What do you think you're doing to that young lady?"

The Takeda soldier growled. The Matsudaira shouted and pointed at the other samurai. "This piece of filth was trying to—"

The Takeda lunged again, and Mai looked like a puppy trying to separate two wolves.

"*Stop!*"

The courtyard became still.

Lady Chiyome strode into a patch of sunlight. "Gentlemen, I am certain that you both have duties elsewhere. I am quite certain that your duties do not include pestering any of the maidens of the Full Moon. Your commanders will be hearing of this, I promise you. If I were you, I would go attend to those duties you were shirking. *Now.*"

Faces warring between fury and shame, the two men marched stiffly toward the main gate.

"Clearly, Mai-*chan*," said Chiyome-*sama*, her tone lower but no less sharp, "you still need to learn a lesson in decorum. I think perhaps some chores for Mitsuke would do you some good." She spun on her heel and swept back toward the front courtyard.

Mai's eyes looked venomous. However, she bit back whatever it was that she wanted to say and bowed at Lady Chiyome's retreating back.

"There, there," Kumo said, and started to put an arm around Mai as if to support her.

She held a hand up; I could see her holding back the impulse to punch the big cook. "I'm fine. I'll go find Mitsuke-*sensei*. To help with her *chores*." She stomped past me and Emi out the back gate.

We all stood there, the three cooks, the three kitchen maids, and Aimaru. After a moment, Kee Sun shook himself and said, "Falcon-girlie, Moon-cake, you show Smiley and Bright Eyes there what's left to clean. These lads and I'll go make sure all of the Takeda supplies are properly sorted." Nodding solemnly, the three men strode off toward the storehouse.

uietly, the three of us made our way back into the kitchen. It was spotless.

"Great timing," Toumi said, her face twisted.

"Murasaki saw an *oni* in a cave up on the cliff," Emi said.

The other girl stared in shock, first at her, then at me.

"I . . . " I stammered. "I think it was . . . dead?"

"Still," said Toumi, staring at me in a manner suggesting she wasn't sure she believed a word. "An *oni?*"

"Huge tusks," Emi whispered. "Claws like meat cleavers."

Toumi's eyes stayed on me. "But . . . dead."

I shrugged. I was trying to think what to say when a bang announced the opening of the big front door in the Great Hall.

Lady Chiyome's voice snapped, "My lords. Thank you for honoring me with your presence."

A second bang masked two low responses.

"My lords, may this humble widow assume that my lords' officers have reported this afternoon's incident?"

Again two low voices answered.

I felt a tap on my shoulder. Blinking, I turned my head. Emi and Toumi were both pointing up toward the grate that divided the kitchen from the dining hall.

I shook myself, then leapt onto the cutting table and up into the rafters that ran the width of the room. Stepping carefully over the herbs that Kee Sun had hung there, I made my way toward the grate, ducking low so that I could not be seen.

"Lady Chiyome," said Matsudaira-*sama*, "I have already disciplined Sakai Tadashige. He will not bother your ladies again."

"On behalf of my girls, my lord, I thank you."

"And I shall do the same with my lieutenant, Torimasa Noritada," murmured Lord Takeda. "My lady, I should like to drive the point home to all of my troops. May I bring them in here to speak with them?"

"Of course, my lord." I heard her shift. "I have, naturally, disciplined my girl. However, if your lordships wish, I can have her executed."

After a moment of silence in which I was unable to breathe, Lord Matsudaira said, "Surely not."

"That won't be necessary," grunted Lord Takeda.

"Thank you, my lords. We humble servants appreciate your lordships' forbearance." I heard a rustle that had to be Chiyome-*sama* bowing. Before she straightened, she added, "My lords, I wish to inform you that my teachers and I know that in their service to the gods, our students will be forced to walk through a dangerous world. Though it is against their nature, we have trained them to defend themselves. We have trained them well. I hope that you will inform your men so that they should endeavor not to . . . startle the young women of the Full Moon. In their innocence, my girls might react so as to cause some *embarrassment*, and I believe my lords will agree that none of us would wish this to occur."

"No," said Takeda-*sama*.

Now it was Lord Matsudaira who grunted. "We can indeed agree on that. I believe we understand each other." After a pause, he added, "My physician is at the young lady's disposal if she requires care."

"My lord governor of the Three Rivers is too kind," Lord Takeda rumbled. "Yet this young lady is a Takeda subject. My physician is at her disposal."

"You are both too kind," said Lady Chiyome. "I do not believe that she was injured; I would not waste such generous gifts needlessly."

I heard the lords shuffle and mumble and thought how strange it was that two of the most powerful men in all Japan were having so awkward a conversation about Mai.

Finally, Lord Matsudaira said with more customary authority, "I shall gather my men."

Lord Takeda grunted in agreement.

"My lords, you honor my household." Another rustle marked Lady Chiyome's standing.

"Chiyome," said Lord Takeda, "I will gather my men and bring them in here. My lord governor of the Three Rivers, please feel free to use the meeting area as your own for now. Perhaps we can reconvene our discussions at the Hour of the Goat?"

"My lord governor of Worth, at the Hour of the Goat it shall be."

With that, the two lords marched to the front door. When it had closed, I began to sidle my way back to the floor, but Chiyome-*sama*'s voice stopped me. "You can get down now, Risuko, and inform all of my servants that they are needed in the Great Hall immediately. And yes, you can tell the girls I bragged about them." Then she added, "Oh, and you might tell Mai how close she came to a very messy end."

8—The Lesson

It took no time at all to get the girls and women of the Full Moon into the hall. Most of them were already in the kitchen courtyard discussing what had happened. When Mai and Mitsuke came in from the garden, eyes followed them. Mitsuke looked as bland as always. Mai looked sweaty and uncomfortable, not surprisingly.

I decided that I wouldn't pass along Lady Chiyome's warning to her. I did, however, make a point of whispering to the girls what our mistress had said about our training.

Soon, we were all lined up behind the head table with Lady Chiyome. Eighteen women, five girls.

Lord Takeda's men stood at attention between the tables, where we had served them just a little while before.

Takeda-*sama* himself took Lady Chiyome's usual spot in the center of the head table just in front of us. Once he was seated, his troops too sat on the floor. "Our hostess, Lady Chiyome, has reminded me of something of which none of us should need to be reminded. These young ladies, beautiful as they are, are not here for our entertainment."

Some of the men began to chuckle, but something in Takeda-*sama's* expression stopped them immediately. "Lord Matsudaira is telling his men to show the ladies of the Full Moon all due respect because they are virtuous young women and servants of the gods." He leaned forward, resting one elbow on the table. "I am telling you that, yes, that is so, and yet there is a greater reason to show respect to the servants of Mochizuki Chiyome. For, as all of you should remember—though others may never know—these lovely young ladies are being trained to do far more than dance and play and serve food to you and to the gods. They are trained too in the arts that you practice. Though they may not look it, these women are your fellow soldiers."

In the front row, one of the officers—the lieutenant with the pointy beard who had been fighting over Mai, in fact— rolled his eyes.

Lord Takeda's head tilted to the side, and then he glanced back at Lady Chiyome, who smiled and said, "Perhaps a demonstration is in order." She extended two fingers toward me and Emi, then at the shrine behind us.

We opened the doors and heard a murmur behind us as we revealed the statues of the goddess Benten, the warrior-god Bishamon, and the Buddha-to-Come—but also four steel practice swords and the battered armor that had decorated the pig the day before. Mieko nodded to us, stepped forward, and took one of the swords.

In the first row, the lieutenant who had rolled his eyes now snorted.

Her smile fixed, Mieko slowly raised the tip of the sword into the pose of the Two Fields. She looked to Lady Chiyome, who tipped her head.

With one long stride, Mieko leapt to the top of the head table; she swung the sword behind her as she took one more long stride toward the kneeling lieutenant, whose eyes flew wide. With an animal growl, she brought the sword straight down as she landed—the Key to Heaven—stopping as close as she had with me the night before, a finger's breadth from the top of the lieutenant's head.

The soldier's eyes remained wide, but his posture didn't change at all.

"Lieutenant Torimasa," said Mieko, the blunted blade held steady over his head, "this humble servant begs your forgiveness. I have caught you unprepared. Perhaps you would like to attack me?" She flipped the sword, catching it by the blade, and offered the handle to the lieutenant.

He scowled, started to say something, and then flicked his eyes toward his commander.

Takeda-*sama* said, "Take the sword, Torimasa."

His scowl now colored pink, the lieutenant stood and took the practice blade.

Mieko stepped back and bowed to him.

"I cannot attack a woman. An unarmed woman."

"Torimasa." The commander's relaxed posture did not change at all, but his tone was cold.

From her sash, Mieko drew her fan and fluttered it open. "Now I am not unarmed, Torimasa-*san*."

Several of the soldiers sniggered. I looked to my right. Mitsuke's expression was as neutral as ever, but the other women and the girls grinned like hungry wolf pups.

Lip rising in a sneer, Torimasa flicked the flat of the practice blade at her.

Mieko slapped the sword away with her fan. The maneuver would have snapped a normal fan, but this one had steel ribs—and more.

Torimasa frowned, standing at last. With a look of bored annoyance, he swung his sword one-handed—negligently—aiming the dull edge now at Mieko's head.

She deflected the cut easily and slapped his cheek with the now-closed fan.

It drew blood. Flushed with rage, the lieutenant lifted his hand to his cheek, glaring at Mieko.

She danced away, flipping the fan open once more. "Perhaps this humble servant must give the lieutenant more reason to treat this exercise seriously?" Pressing a button set into the fan's hinge, she released gleaming blades from hiding. Her lovely fan now looked like the deadly weapon that it truly was.

It was a sight that few outside of the Full Moon had seen—and lived to tell of.

"These are envenomed, Torimasa-*san*, with the juice of a lovely berry. I dipped them in the poison just this morning. The death that they bring will be long, but you will be unable to defend yourself within minutes. And you will remain fully aware of your body's slow failure, right up until the moment of death."

With a bellow, Torimasa now feinted at Mieko's left leg, switching to a vicious attack at her neck.

As if in a dance, Mieko smoothly shifted her weight, catching the slash between the blades of her fan, shredding the lovely silk with its lovely flowers. With a snap of her wrist, she yanked the sword from the lieutenant's hands, sending it sliding under the table, not far from Takeda-*sama*'s feet.

Continuing her dance, she spun behind her opponent and let the tips of her fan blades press against the back of his neck. From a sheath in her hair, she pulled a thin blade and held it against his uncut cheek. "Do I have your attention now, Lieutenant Torimasa?"

Unable to move, he grunted, "Yes," between clenched teeth.

"Then please, listen. I have ended the lives of one hundred and forty-three human beings. One hundred and eight men, many of them fully armed, and thirty-five women. Sixty-one of them I killed with knives. Eight with swords and three with glaives. Twenty I shot with arrows. Twenty-three I strangled, four with my bare hands. The other twenty-eight I poisoned. I have not enjoyed killing any of them, as I would not enjoy killing you." She smiled grimly at the line of us standing behind Lord Takeda. "Yet I would kill you, Torimasa-*san*. Nor am I the only woman here at the Full Moon trained in the Way of the Warrior. Risuko-*chan*?"

"Mieko-*san?*"

Keeping the fan's poisoned blades against the back of his neck, she lobbed her knife toward me. It was a careful, easy toss so that I was able to catch it by the handle. And yet gasps of surprise exploded from the assembled soldiers. Mieko smiled, an acknowledgement that I had done well. "Come here, Risuko."

Feeling a hundred pairs of eyes on me, I walked out from behind the table. As I did, I sensed all of those Takeda soldiers staring at me. I felt tiny and enormous, both at the same time. The reason for her choosing me blossomed in my understanding: I was the smallest, least imposing of the girls there.

And so I was not completely surprised when she asked me, "How would you kill the lieutenant, Risuko-*chan?*"

Torimasa's eyes were narrow now with rage but also something I hadn't expected to see there: fear. His jaunty pointed beard trembled, as did the blacks of his eyes, which were small as poppy seeds.

"I do not wish to hurt you, Torimasa-*san,*" I said. Only after the words had left my mouth did I realize that I had echoed Mieko herself just before she killed the two Imagawa guards at the Mount Fuji Inn the previous autumn. I glanced toward my teacher.

Her eyes were almost kindly. "Yet if you had to, Risuko, how would you go about it?"

With a gulp, I walked next to her, behind the lieutenant. Hand trembling, I placed the deadly tip of the knife next to her fan's blades. "I would slip the tip of the blade beneath the skull, severing the spine."

The hall was silent.

I was close enough to Torimasa-*san* to smell his uneasy fury—which for some reason brought to mind nursing Masugu-*san* after he'd been poisoned.

"Thank you, ladies," said Lord Takeda. As when we first met him, the warmth of his smile did not reach his eyes. "That will be all."

Mieko and I lowered our weapons and bowed, then returned to our place with the other girls.

"I believe," continued Takeda-*sama,* "that I have made my point. These are your comrades in arms. They go places no soldier could go and do things no soldier could do, and yet they are every bit as vital to our winning this war as any of you. Any of you. Do I make myself clear?"

As one, the soldiers called, "Yes, my lord!" and bowed to him—though it felt as if they were bowing to us.

Torimasa prostrated himself before his lord. "My lord, I have dishonored myself in your eyes."

"Perhaps, Lieutenant. And perhaps it is just as well that we have forgone wearing our swords in this house. I forbid you to punish yourself, do you understand? Your punishment will be simply to attend to your duty rather than distracting these lovely if deadly young ladies. Do I make myself clear?"

"Yes, my lord," said Torimasa, still flat on his belly on the polished wood floor.

"Now, gentlemen, remember: the Matsudaira do not know this school's true purpose nor these ladies' true . . . abilities. Let us see that that remains the case."

"Yes, my lord!" called the assembled horde.

———

Dinner that night was almost silent. The Matsudaira and the Takeda never even looked across at each other—aside from Jolalo, who looked around like a kitten that knows someone else is in trouble but not him.

"Mieko, Sachi, Hoshi, Mitsuke, Rin," barked Chiyome-*sama* as soon as the soldiers had left the hall, "come. We need to talk." She turned and climbed the stairs to her apartment.

Mieko shot me a sad smile; we could not meet that night for another lesson.

And so instead, after we novices had cleaned out the tubs, I sneaked back into the kitchen and took down the *wakizashi*. Holding the knife against the base of Lieutenant Torimasa's skull had felt . . . awful. And awesome. Somehow it felt better holding a sword rather than one of Mieko-*san's* daggers.

I returned the short sword to its shrine and tiptoed my way back to our dormitory. It had been an endless, exhausting day, and so I expected everyone to be asleep.

They all were—all except Emi.

"Where have you been?" she asked as I slid into my bedroll.

I considered lying, telling her that I'd gone to visit the King, as Kee Sun called it. But it seemed as if truth was a better idea. "I went to the kitchen. To . . . to make sure the sword Masugu gave me was safe."

"Oh," said Emi, snuggling up behind me. "That makes sense. It is a beautiful sword."

During the coldest part of the winter—which had lasted a bitterly long time up there in the mountains—we had slept like that, bundled together for warmth but also for comfort. And of course it made whispering back and forth easier. Toumi wasn't easy to wake, but when she did, she was as irritable as a hibernating bear.

"So, have you thought any more about the ogre?"

I shivered. "No, I was trying to forget about it."

"Can't blame you." Emi held me tight. "I'll protect you, don't worry."

"Fine. Thanks." Not certain whether she was teasing or not, I gave her ribs a gentle poke with my elbow. "I've been thinking about what you asked, whether it could have been dead. I don't know. I didn't see or hear it move. But I could feel it, watching me . . . "

We shivered together, though the night was not cold.

When I was young, my mother used to tell me and Usako stories as we went to sleep—stories of monsters and demons that had us trembling in our bedrolls. Of course, they always ended with the Peach Boy or the Sword Girl or whoever outwitting the creatures and bringing back a magical treasure. Even so, those stories gave me nightmares.

Somehow none of them seemed as terrifying as whatever I had encountered up in that cave.

"What are you thinking about, Murasaki?"

"About my mother. She used to tell my sister and me all of these terrifying stories about ogres and such."

"Hmm. My mother used to tell me stories about rich lords and ladies. All love stories. Mostly sad love stories."

"Huh." I turned to face her. "Do you think of your mother often?"

She shrugged her top shoulder. "Every day. I go to sleep telling myself those stories."

I snorted. "You go to sleep before your head hits the pillow."

She rolled her eyes, then looked over my shoulder into the darkness. "Murasaki?"

"Yes?"

"Do you think I'm . . . pretty?"

"What? Yes, of course I think so. Especially when you smile. What on earth makes you ask that?"

She shrugged, her eyes meeting mine again. "Those men fighting over Mai, I guess."

"Well, I never thought she was pretty." I whispered it, even though I could hear Mai's distinctive whistle of a snore through the wall.

"Torimasa-*san* and the Matsudaira officer certainly seemed to, though."

"Well, I think they've learned their lesson."

"Let's hope so. Good night, Murasaki."

"'Night, Emi." I turned away from her again, and we went to sleep, peacefully oblivious to the fact that the morning would bring us a dead body facing our front door.

9—The Rising Sun

The first sign of something amiss was Shino's shrill scream, which woke all of us in the initiates' dormitory and probably everyone else in the valley.

Shino wasn't given to screaming. Grumbling, growling, snarling, yes. But I'd never heard her cry out like a hawk. Not for any reason.

More to the point, she was almost never the first person in the dormitories to wake.

As Toumi, Emi, and I stumbled toward the front door, there was another scream—Mai this time.

The scene we came upon as we stepped out into the dawn light was an oddly serene one.

Mai and Shino stood swaying like wind-tossed pines on either side of a kneeling figure: Lieutenant Torimasa. His head lolled to one side, and his hands gripped a short sword thrust through his belly. Blood streamed down from the wound over his bright blue robes, pooling between his shins.

A part of me noted that his blood was thoroughly gelled; the blood in the vat the previous day had still been mostly liquid when I'd hewn the pig an hour after Emi killed it. So Torimasa had been dead longer than that.

A part of me wanted to scream as Shino and Mai had done. But I didn't.

I had seen dead men before, obviously. I'd seen blood. Lots of it. We all had.

Looking around at Emi and Toumi, I could see that they felt as I did that something was wrong about Torimasa-*san's* death.

Before I could think about it or talk to the other girls, a thunder of feet on gravel announced the arrival of the Little Brothers, who skidded to a stop after rounding the corner of the Great Hall. Aimaru slammed into the back of the smaller one just as Hoshi, Sachi, and Mieko sprinted up from the Nunnery, the older women's dormitory, with some of the younger *kunoichi* at their heels. Kee Sun and the other two cooks stumbled out of the kitchen.

We all stared at the body. Sitting there in his bright blue jacket and trousers, he looked almost at peace, as if he'd gone out for an evening stroll and were surprised to find himself dead.

Lady Chiyome stepped out from behind the cooks and took in the tableau. She muttered a series of words that made Kumo, the Matsudaira cook, turn white. Then she turned to us initiates.   "What a lovely way to greet the new day. One of you . . . " At first she looked at Shino and Mai, who still stood there stunned, and then turned to me. "Risuko. Go find Lord Takeda and tell him that his lieutenant is dead."

———

wasn't thinking as I sprinted toward the front of the Full Moon. If I had, I would have realized that, of course, the gates were closed. It took both Little Brothers to open them.

Doubling back to use the rear gate would have forced me to run through the crowd assembled around the body, and that idea made my empty stomach churn. I didn't want to see the body again—but it was more the idea of having to run back past Lady Chiyome and the other girls that made me ill.

And so I did what I do naturally: I climbed.

Using the half-timbers set into the walls of the Guest House (where Masugu-*san* had nearly died the previous winter), I flew up to the roof, sprinted to the front wall of the compound, and leapt over.

I've fallen and jumped out of trees more times than I can count. I've twisted my ankles and skinned my elbows and knees nearly as often.

Even so, blindly jumping from the top of a wall that was over three times my height was probably not the wisest thing I've ever done.

Fortune favored me. The earth immediately outside the front wall of the Full Moon was covered in thick spring grass, still damp from the previous day's rain. The impact knocked the breath out of me, but I rolled to the side and sprang to my feet. Nothing felt injured.

I looked up, gasping for air, and saw the red *torī* gate a step away from the wall. I would have laughed—if I'd had the breath for it. I could have slid down the slanted scarlet pillars and climbed back up without launching myself into space.

Next time.

There were two sentries stationed near the gate—one with a four-diamond *mon* and the closer one bearing the emblem of the three ginger leaves. As soon as I landed, both turned toward me and began to run.

The eyes of the Matsudaira sentry were wide as an owl's. "You . . . Are you all . . . " He frowned. "You're . . . a girl."

"One of the Full Moon girls," murmured the Takeda sentry with a grim smile.

"I'm fine," I said, dusting the grass off my pants. I turned to the Takeda soldier. "Please, I need to speak to Takeda-*sama*. It's urgent."

He raised his eyebrows but nodded. To the Matsudaira soldier, he said, "Aosagi, you think you can keep all of your pals from breaking down the gate?"

The Matsudaira soldier blinked and then snorted. "And all of your pals too, sure, Yukishiro."

Yukishiro led me away from the gate.

The two armies had set up camps on either side of the road—blue Matsudaira flags marked the tents to the right while Takeda red marked those to the left. Both camps seemed to be largely still, though the smoke from several campfires rose into the silver-blue morning sky.

I followed Yukishiro into the heart of the Takeda camp. We stopped at the entrance to the largest tent, and Yukishiro addressed the two guards outside. "Our comrade in arms here says she has urgent news for the Mountain."

I bowed quickly.

One of the guards shot me a sour look, but the older one held up a hand. "What news, miss?"

At first, I thought to insist on giving the news only to Lord Takeda himself. However, it suddenly occurred to me that the news I was carrying was unlikely to make the general happy. "Lieutenant Torimasa . . . is dead."

That surprised all three of the guards. The youngest reached for his sword; Yukishiro stopped his hand.

A voice rumbled from inside the tent. "What's this?" The door flap to the tent flew open, and Lord Takeda stalked out. "What did you say, girl?" His face was rumpled and his bald head rough with stubble. But his eyes were narrow, and his voice was low with anger.

I knelt and touched my forehead to the matted grass. "My lord," I said, "Torimasa-*san*, we found him, in the Full Moon. He . . . He is dead."

"By whose hand?" growled the general.

"It looks . . . " I dared a peek up at Lord Takeda and immediately regretted it, lowering my head back to the ground. "It appears that he, um, that he took his own life, my lord."

"*Appears*," he snarled. Then he barked at his guards. "Tell Baba and Hara to meet me inside. We'll see how this appears."

———

By the time we made it back to the Full Moon, the Little Brothers had opened the front gate. Yukishiro split off and took up his post once more opposite the Matsudaira sentry, Aosagi.

Lord Takeda and his guards followed me to the kitchen courtyard, where the inhabitants of the Full Moon had gathered—all, it seemed, but the cooks and younger girls. A finger of smoke rising from the chimney above the kitchen let me know that I was missing breakfast duty, a fact that Toumi would no doubt grumble about for days.

The women parted before Lord Takeda like trout before a bass. The only figures not moving were Lady Chiyome, Shino, Mai, and (of course) the late lieutenant. The two older girls stood before Torimasa, hardly seeming to have breathed since I had left.

Lord Takeda strode between the two initiates, breaking the spell. They backed away as Takeda-*sama* stared down at the body.

As he stood there, glowering at his lieutenant's corpse, a cloud swept down from the mountains and covered the rising sun.

No one breathed.

Just as quickly as it had appeared, the cloud floated down the valley, and the courtyard was filled with golden morning sunlight, quite at odds with our mood.

Lord Takeda's eyes flashed up to mine. "You told me the lieutenant *appeared* to have committed *seppuku.*" He gestured down at the body. "Tell me, girl: why did you say, 'appeared?'"

There are moments in life when one has no thought of being anywhere but where one is. At that particular moment, however, I would gladly have been back in the demon-haunted cave or strung up by my wrists in a bandit camp rather than standing there before one of the most powerful men in the realm and all of the women of the Full Moon, trying to think how to answer.

My dry mouth opened and closed. I looked to Lady Chiyome, who was stone faced. Sachi, the music teacher, nodded minutely when I caught her eye, however, and so did Mieko, and so I took a deep breath. "It looks like *seppuku*, my lord, but I don't believe it is."

"No?" He bared his teeth at me. I think it was a smile of sorts, the kind a tiger might give a rabbit. Or a squirrel. "Why not?"

"Because . . . " Again Mieko nodded. "Because, my lord, the blood . . . "

"The blood?"

"If . . . It seems to me, my lord, if . . . " *Don't speak the name,* I thought. Don't invite his ghost to stay close by. "If he had been alive when the sword pierced his flesh, the blood would have, um, sprayed. All over. It didn't. It just flowed straight down to the ground."

"I see," he grunted. "And if the sword didn't kill him, how, girl, do you claim my lieutenant died?"

"Um . . . " I pointed at Torimasa-*san's* head. "It looks as if someone broke his neck." Like one of the many chickens Toumi, Emi and I had slaughtered over the months. "And then they arranged him so that it would—as this humble servant mentioned, my lord—so that it would appear that he had taken his own life."

"Is that so?" He crossed his arms.

Two older men—Captains Baba and Hara—came running up to either side of me. Each stopped, hissing in surprise at the sight of Torimasa-*san's* body.

"Gentlemen," said Lord Takeda, "this child here was just telling me why she thinks the young lieutenant didn't commit suicide."

"Didn't?" said one of the captains.

"Yes," Lord Takeda growled. "What is your name, girl?"

Though they did not actually move, all of the Full Moon's women seemed to take a step back.

"I . . . " I knelt and touched my head to the rough gravel. "Kano Murasaki is this humble servant's name."

There was a brief silence, then Takeda-*sama* barked, "Kano?"

Not sure how I was supposed to answer, I peered up. But the general wasn't looking at me. He was gawking at Lady Chiyome, who gave a pursed-lipped smile and a small, self-satisfied bow.

I wasn't sure what the point of that exchange had been. It didn't look as if any of the *kunoichi* had any idea either.

"So, Kano Murasaki," Lord Takeda continued, and I dropped my face back to the dirt. "Since you seem so knowledgeable about such matters, who would you say murdered my officer?"

"Um, I do not know, my lord."

"No?" His feet scattered gravel as he walked closer to me. "Perhaps you yourself committed the crime? You told us all last night you were capable of killing him." The gravel crunched as he stepped above my head.

"No, my lord! I—I couldn't have done it! Whoever did this must have been taller." Inspiration flamed through me. "I do not believe any of us were tall enough to break his neck that way."

"No?" He walked away from me now, and I heard all of the women of the Full Moon answer that, indeed, they couldn't have done it. He stalked further away. "Not even if he were . . . lying down?"

A gasp forced me to raise my head. Lord Takeda was standing extremely close to Mai, who was weeping, her face hidden against Shino's neck. Shino threw her arms around the other girl; standing tall, she said, "No, my lord. Mai and I share a sleeping pallet. We had no visitors. And she could not have left the bed without my knowing."

I am not sure who was most surprised: Lord Takeda, because Shino had stood up to him so assertively, or the women of the Full Moon, because Mai and Shino usually couldn't discuss the weather without it turning into a competition. It taught me a lesson I have had to learn many times in my life: the glaze is not the cup. Appearance should not be taken as truth.

Lord Takeda scowled at the two girls; Shino scowled right back. For a moment, I feared that he would cut her down where she stood for her impudence—but then, he wasn't wearing a blade.

With an angry snort, Lord Takeda turned to Chiyome-*sama*. "What about those enormous carriers of yours, Chiyome?"

The old woman inclined her head. "They are certainly capable, my lord. However, I believe they would only have done so to protect me or one of the girls. And I can't imagine they would have bothered with this ridiculous stage-play sham of a suicide. They'd simply have come and told me. Which they didn't."

"Bah!" He strode away from Lady Chiyome now and back toward the body. "What I want to know, Chiyome, aside from who killed my soldier, is what my nephew Masugu's sword is doing buried in this man's belly."

10—A Boiling Pot

Lady Chiyome grunted. "That, my lord Takeda, is an excellent question." She turned to me, still prostrate on the gravel. "Tell me, Risuko, what *is* Masugu-*san's* sword doing here?"

I spluttered that I hadn't stabbed the lieutenant.

"Yes, yes," the old woman tutted. "I suppose the person who wielded the sword must have been the person who broke the soldier's neck. Fine. No, I was asking how it was that you ended up with the sword at all. I saw you carrying it the other day. Drop off of Masugu's horse, did it?"

"No, my lady!" I could have sworn that I heard Mai and Shino sniggering at me—but in fairness, Mai was most likely still weeping.

A quiet footstep crunched near me. Mieko said, "Masugu-*san* left his short sword in Risuko-*chan's* care while he was on his mission. It is such a fine weapon, and it bears the Takeda diamonds. He felt that it would too conspicuous for the ride he was making." She knelt and touched me on the shoulder.

"Is this so, Kano girl?" Lord Takeda rumbled. "Did my nephew leave his *wakizashi* in your keeping?"

"Yes, my lord."

Mieko squeezed my shoulder.

"And where were you keeping it, that it came to be embedded in my soldier's gut?"

Hoshi, the calligraphy teacher and body guard, stepped up on my other side. "My lord, our cook Kee Sun had her keep it in a rack in the kitchen. We all saw it there."

"Is this so?"

All of the Full Moon's women murmured together, "Yes, my lord."

"Hmm." Lord Takeda's sandals stomped away from me.

Mieko whispered, "Get up," and helped me to my feet.

Lord Takeda and Lady Chiyome were both standing with sour expressions, staring at Torimasa's corpse.

Looking at him from behind, I noticed for the first time that the bottoms of his trousers were stained. Streaks of dark red colored his shoes and his blue trouser legs.

Blood? No. Paint.

"So," grunted Lord Takeda to his captains, "if none of these ladies did this, and those two oxen didn't"—he jerked a thumb toward the Little Brothers—"it must have been someone from outside." He glowered at the captains Baba-*san* and Hara-*san* and then at all of us. "How did the killer get in? For that matter, how did *he* get in?" Now he scowled down at his dead lieutenant. "You, girl," he said to Sachi, "go tell the guards at the front gate to come immediately and report to me. You," he said to one of the guards from his tent—the oldest one—"go and see if the back gate is still locked. Hara, go and inform my lord governor of the Three Rivers that we need to speak urgently with his lieutenant, Sakai—the boy who got into a fight with this one." He nodded at the corpse.

Mai sniffled again, and Takeda-*sama* looked at her and then the rest of us with a sour expression. "And the rest of you—I am certain that Lady Chiyome here has many duties that she expects you ladies to be attending to."

"Yes, my lord," we all murmured.

"Then go attend to them," he ordered. As we began to disperse like frost on a spring morning, he pointed at Mai. "Except you."

Mai still looked ashen, but when Shino tried to stay with her, Hoshi grabbed her by the elbow and pulled her away from the scene of the murder.

———

When I entered the kitchen, six faces turned on me with owls' eyes—three cooks, two initiates, and Aimaru. "Well?" asked Toumi. "Please tell me they figured out he didn't off himself."

"Toumi!" Emi scowled while continuing to scoop fermented soy beans into a huge bowl.

"Yes," I said, slipping between Emi and Aimaru and helping to shell the beans. "And Lord Takeda recognized Masugu-*san*'s sword. Hoshi-*sensei* told him everyone saw it in here."

Kee Sun swore in Korean and Torai in Japanese. "Gentlemen!" Kumo huffed. "Remember there are young ladies present!"

"We've heard worse," muttered Toumi.

"Either way," barked Kee Sun, "it's nothin' to do with us. Everyone's goin' to be hungry, murder or no."

"We need more rice," said Torai, the calmest thing I'd ever heard him say. "I'll go get a bag—"

"No, Shorty," Kee Sun answered. "We need yeh here. These two can grab a sack of rice from the storerooms." He flicked his head toward me and Aimaru. When Torai started to argue, Kee Sun just held up his cleaver and stared at us. "Get."

We got.

———

As we scurried out the kitchen door, the guard was informing Takeda-*sama* and Matsudaira-*sama*, who had arrived with his entourage, that, indeed, the back gate was still locked.

Lord Matsudaira shot a sword-sharp look at Mai. Kneeling, she repeated for the second lord's benefit that she had not gotten out of bed, had not arranged to meet the lieutenant, and had not let him in.

Lord Takeda called for his physician, and Lord Matsudaira did the same.

When we turned the corner, Aimaru whispered, "Do you know, you're right. The dead man didn't look like he'd done that himself. It looks wrong."

"If he'd stabbed himself, there would have been blood splattered all over the courtyard in front of him. Also, I doubt he could have done it in one thrust. And his neck was broken, which he couldn't have done himself."

"Huh." Aimaru peered at me, his head tilted, his usually open face thoughtful.

I stared out the now-open front gate to where the bright red *tori* arch stood, the two guards back in position at its feet. Now that the thought had occurred to me, I itched to climb it.

When we arrived at the storeroom, Aimaru immediately began to wander around the piles and shelves overflowing with food and supplies. I had to call him back from a dark corner to help me pick up the rice. "Why are you wandering off?"

He shrugged and smiled. "I don't get in here much." Then he picked up the sack of rice, and I trailed after him, feeling even more useless than usual.

As we stumbled our way back toward the kitchen, Aimaru said, "So Kee Sun keeps his accounts in the storeroom?"

"Huh?"

"I found a scroll that looked like it was keeping count of things in there. On the shelf all of the way at the back."

"Uh, no." As far as I knew, Kee Sun kept track of the supplies and what had been spent on them on a slate in the kitchen pantry that he went over with Chiyome-*sama* every month. "What were you doing back there? That corner should be spare bedding and uniforms and such."

"Oh." We shuffled along for a moment before he said, "But there was a scroll back there with a bunch of numbers."

"Numbers?" When he didn't answer, I asked, "What was written next to the numbers? Maybe it was . . . I don't know. Did it say what the numbers were about?"

His gaze suddenly searched anywhere but toward me, and for once, he wasn't smiling.

"Can . . . " I walked in front of him. "Aimaru. Can you not read?"

"I . . . " Now the poor boy looked thoroughly miserable, though I didn't know why. "I can. A little." His round face, usually sunny, suddenly twisted into an Emi-like pout. "Not very well, though."

"That's all right," I said. "Almost nobody in my village could read or write at all except my family, and my father was a scribe. Did Lady Chiyome test you?"

"Yes," he said, and his eyes, though still downcast, took on a glint. "I tricked her. I just wrote the symbols that were over the gate of the big temple, back where I grew up. Something about a net and jewels."

"'The flowers of enlightenment lie like a net of gems, each reflecting the others' brilliance like clouds of thought.'"

"Is that what it says?"

I nodded, grunting. "It's from a sermon. The Sermon of the Flower Wreath. Hoshi had us copying it today. It was one of my father's favorite passages."

"Your father the scribe?"

"Yes. So you just copied that from memory?"

He nodded.

"I don't think I could have done that before I came here. That's impressive."

We rounded the corner of the Great Hall to find the eerie tableau had shifted once again. Lord Takeda, his captains, and his guards were standing at the entrance to our dormitory, while Lord Matsudaira stood by Lieutenant Sakai—who was sporting a maple-purple swollen eye from the previous day's fight. The young soldier was shaking his head, but he couldn't take his eyes off of Torimasa's body.

Lord Takeda's expression was as imposing and as unmoving as the cliff rising behind the wall. Captain Baba stroked his beard.

Lady Chiyome held Mai's hand in a surprisingly caring fashion. Under her breath, however, our mistress was muttering, "Say nothing. Keep quiet. Don't be silly." She then said something about "bedroll" that made the already pale girl go white, then pointed to the opposite rear corner of the compound and muttered, "Retreat."

Mai shuffled away with a blank, down-turned face and a silent tread that even our teacher Mitsuke couldn't have made less noticeable.

Begging their pardons, we pushed through the kitchen door. Inside, Kee Sun was just checking the large rice pot to see whether it was boiling. Except for him, the kitchen was empty.

"Sent the lot of 'em off to get mustard greens from the garden. Couldn't stand the yammerin', Fatso and Shorty goin' on about the dead lad outside. Shorty sayin' it's Foxy-girlie's fault, Fatso sayin' she's just a poor, innocent victim. *Innocent*. Bah." The cook shuddered, then waved a hand toward the pantry. "Now get that rice into the barrel in there, then bring a measure for me t'cook once the water boils."

"*Hai*, Kee Sun-*san*." I pulled Aimaru with me back toward the barrel. Once we'd emptied the rice sack, I pointed to the big, flat piece of slate leaning against one shelf. "See," I told him, "this is where Kee Sun keeps his accounts."

"Is that writing? Can you read it?"

I laughed. "No, it's Korean. But the numbers are the same, see?" I pointed to the smudged Chinese numbers that Kee Sun was constantly updating.

"What are yeh jabberin' about in there? Where's my rice?"

I filled the huge scoop we used to measure out rice and brought it to the cook. "I was showing Aimaru your accounts."

He snorted. "You plannin' on being a merchant, Moon-cake?"

He shook his head, smiling. "I was just telling Risuko about the scroll with all the numbers I found back in the storeroom."

"Scroll?" Kee Sun squinted at him.

"He found it near the bedding at the back, isn't that right, Aimaru?"

He nodded. "It had a list with lots and lots of words and numbers."

Pouring the rice into the bubbling pot, Kee Sun scowled. "Why'd a body . . . " He covered the rice and looked at Aimaru. "Did yeh know any of the words?"

He shook his head, looking down again with shame. "Some names, maybe, but none I knew."

"And yeh saw numbers?"

Aimaru nodded. "Big ones, uh-huh." He shot me another sly grin. "I'm good with numbers."

Kee Sun shook his head. "Rice paper back there—I'd never put something in that corner the rats are like to find tasty." He stirred the pot and then looked at us both, his brows bristling like caterpillars. "Come on, yeh two. I want to see this scroll."

As we left the kitchen, the Matsudaira lieutenant was saying, "I shared the tent with my soldiers; ask any of them. And the gates were closed and guarded—how could I have gotten in?"

Lord Takeda and his captains didn't seem convinced.

When we got to the dim back corner of the storeroom, there was no scroll.

"Yeh're sure yeh saw it here, Moon-cake?"

He nodded emphatically. "It was right on this shelf, under that bedroll. I thought it was a weird place to put a scroll, so I looked at it."

I could see that the bedding was somewhat askew—not placed as neatly as the older women usually demanded they be stored. "It does seem like a funny place for a scroll. And it does look like someone's been moving these around."

We searched the whole storeroom but didn't find so much as a scrap of paper, most of which was kept in the Tea House.

As we walked back into the courtyard, Kee Sun swore under his breath. "Not right. Somethin's not right."

11—Numbers

When we got back to the kitchen courtyard, the lords and their captains had gathered in front of the well while two men with white beards poked and prodded at the body. The Matsudaira physician was muttering something about "fixed blood" while the Takeda physician muttered back something about "lividity" and "rigor." They peered at each other and nodded, and the Matsudaira physician said, "Sometime around midnight, my lords."

The Takeda doctor nodded and added, "During the Hour of the Rat, definitely."

While the generals conferred about this new piece of information, Kee Sun walked up to Chiyome-*sama* and whispered into her ear.

The lady shot me and Aimaru a sour look and then strode over to us, Kee Sun in tow. "Come, children. Show me this scroll that doesn't exist."

As we walked back to the storeroom, Aimaru tried hiding in my shadow, which was amusing, given that he was twice my size.

The warmth of the morning sun warred with the cool mountain air that pooled in the compound, and I truly felt as if I were standing between worlds. Turning back toward where Torimasa-*san*'s body still rested, I saw the cliff looming over the rear wall of the Full Moon, saw the black slash that marked the cave two-thirds of the way up, and suddenly felt the black gaze of that ogre on me once again. I shivered.

"Keep up, Risuko!" barked Lady Chiyome.

I did, with Aimaru shuffling beside me. I could feel him peering at me as we entered the storeroom.

———

We showed Lady Chiyome the corner where Aimaru had found the scroll. Sighing, she asked Aimaru to tell her what he'd seen.

When he looked uncomfortable, I said, "Aimaru had a hard time reading it."

"A hard time?" Lady Chiyome's eyes narrowed. When he just gulped, the old woman snarled, "Child, you copied out a passage from the Flower Wreath Sermon without hesitation. Are you trying to tell me you *can't read?*"

"I can," mumbled Aimaru, trying unsuccessfully to hide behind me. "A little."

"You read the characters I wrote for you well enough!"

"Numbers," he whispered. "I'm good at numbers." He slashed the characters in the air. *"Nine in one."*

Ku. No. Ichi.

Chiyome-*sama* scribbled 十二 with her toe in the dust of the floor. "What does that say?"

"12."

"How about this?" She wrote 四百三十二.

"432."

"And this?" Chiyome-*sama*'s foot scraped 八千弐百六拾七 into the floor. Again Aimaru answered without hesitation, "8,267."

"What about this?" Lady Chiyome knelt down and wrote with her finger:

などて君むなしき空に消えにけん
淡雪だにもふれIばふる世に

"I . . ." Aimaru stammered. "It's . . . something about . . . the air?" His wide, usually happy face was turning bright red.

Sighing, Lady Chiyome looked at me.

I read aloud, "How could you disappear into the blank, blue sky? Even the delicate white snow falls where I can touch it." I cleared my throat. "It's a poem by Izumi Shikibu, about the death—"

"Yes, yes," said Chiyome-*sama*, standing again and swiping the knees of her robes. "Thank you, my little literary critic." She turned back to Aimaru. "So. You're a genius when it comes to numbers but an idiot with words." Before Aimaru could do more than shrug miserably, Chiyome-*sama* said to Kee Sun, "Serves me right for recruiting an oaf who spent his childhood watching bales of rice go in and out of a Capital warehouse."

The cook's eyes narrowed. "Yeh're a thief, Moon-cake?"

"*No!*" The poor boy was looking so miserable I found myself trying—and failing—to think of some way to come to his aid. "This was before I went to the monastery, when I was little! I just . . . kept an eye on Lord Ashikaga's warehouse. And . . . told some of the older boys when there'd be enough just come in that the foreman wouldn't notice if a few bales went missing."

Kee Sun grunted.

"Well," said Lady Chiyome, "I don't mind how you kept yourself alive before. Some of the girls here started out doing much worse. But I need you to be able to read and write if you're going to be able to put your peculiar talents to use." She smirked. "Just for interest, how many tents are there in Lord Matsudaira's camp?"

"Seventeen, my lady. Nine eight-man tents, seven four-man tents, and the big one for the boss."

"Yes, yes, very good, but you're no use to me illiterate. You must learn to read and write words better."

Unable to watch Aimaru crumple in on himself further, I stepped next to her. "I can help him learn, my lady."

"Yes. Yes, Risuko, you can. And will."

Aimaru was once again looking down, muttering.

"Do you hear me?"

"Y-yes, Chiyome-*sama*."

I was preparing myself to step in on his behalf once more, but Chiyome-*sama's* thunderous expression softened slightly to her habitual sour smirk. "So. Let's get back to this vanishing scroll, shall we? Numbers. How big were those numbers?"

"Well," wheezed Aimaru, "mostly between about five hundred and a thousand or so—and every five or ten lines, they'd be totaled up." He wiped his nose. "And then they were all added up at the bottom. It looked like the old warehouse ledger. Kind of. Which is why I thought it might be how Kee Sun-*san* kept track of what's in here."

Lady Chiyome's face was suddenly grave. "And what was the grand sum?"

"83,482." He spat the figure out without blinking.

Kee Sun and Chiyome-*sama* shared a look. In a flat voice, she asked, "And did you recognize any of the names next to these numbers? At all?"

"Well," Aimaru said, shifting uncomfortably. "Up at the top, there was . . . " He began to move a finger through the air again. He drew a *kanji* ideogram I recognized immediately: 武 (*take*).

"War," I said.

"And then . . . " Aimaru sucked in his cheeks and drew a square with a vertical cross inside of it: 田 (*da*)—the sign meaning rice paddy.

"Takeda," Lady Chiyome and I gasped together.

Kee Sun swore elaborately in Korean.

"Watch your tongue, Kee Sun." Lady Chiyome led us back out into the morning sun. "Go, the three of you. Get breakfast ready before two whole armies descend on us in a ravenous rage. I need to speak to Takeda-*sama*."

———

As we approached the kitchen, we saw that a monk and two helpers had arrived. The monk, clad in orange robes, was muttering a prayer—a sermon that I vaguely recognized about entering the Pure Land—and burning a stick of sweet, dusty-smelling incense as the helpers wrapped Torimasa-*san*'s body in a shroud. On the gravel beside the body lay Lieutenant Masugu's short sword. When I began to pick it up, Kee Sun pulled me up by the neck of my jacket and whispered gruffly, "Don't yeh be messin' with that, Bright Eyes. Don't want the lords thinkin' yeh had nothin' to do with that soldier's killin', now, do yeh?"

I shook my head.

"Besides," he continued with a shudder, "needs to be purified before it comes back in my kitchen."

12—The Tori Arch

"Bosses," grumbled Kee Sun to the other two cooks as we reentered the kitchen.

Kumo and Torai both shrugged and nodded; Kee Sun winked at us.

Aimaru raised an eyebrow at Kee Sun for a moment but then followed me as I pulled him toward the work table, where we cleaned and chopped the greens that the rest had gathered.

Once the chopping was done, Aimaru meandered off to the Great Hall with a shrugged apology.

Breakfast that morning was rice, mustard greens, and fermented soy beans. Sticky and smelly, the gloopy beans were my least favorite of Kee Sun's specialties—but I was one of the only people who felt that way. Most of the women of the Full Moon treated them as a delicacy; I thought—and still think—they smell and look like cat vomit.

If we had in fact served hair balls that morning, the mood in the Great Hall could not in fact have been chillier than it already was. Both the Takeda and the Matsudaira ate in understandably solemn silence. The *kunoichi* were equally somber; even Sachi-*san* abandoned her usual jokes.

At Torimasa-*san*'s spot at the table, one of the other Takeda officers placed his chopsticks sticking upright in a bowl of rice.

As I was filling the teacup of the Portuguese priest, Jolalo-*san* peered over toward the Takeda table with a puzzled look on his face. Frowning down at his bowl of rice, he began to place his chopsticks straight down into it.

"No!" Aimaru and I both gasped.

He stopped, blinking at us like a newborn puppy.

"You can't do that," Aimaru said. "It's . . . unlucky."

"Why?" asked Jolalo.

When Aimaru just gawped at the other boy, I tried to answer. "It is a ritual for the dead. We leave a bowl of rice out with their chopsticks placed so. To do so yourself is considered . . . bad luck."

Jolalo started to ask another question but then looked across at the bowl at Torimasa's place. "Someone . . . died?"

Surprised that he had not already heard, I looked at Aimaru, whose usual open smile dimmed. "One of Lord Takeda's officers. It's being investigated."

"Oh," said Jolalo with a frown. Then he looked back at his chopsticks. "You have many thing that you cannot do with chopsticks, yes, it is? You cannot point with them. You cannot hold them in your fist. You cannot spear your food with them. You cannot wave them."

"Well," I said, "yes." Who didn't know these things?

He nodded as if I'd actually said something and then turned to the priest, speaking in their twittering language and demonstrating all of the taboos he'd just mentioned.

Aimaru's smile dimmed even more.

I was about to move on to the next Matsudaira guest when Jolalo asked, "These . . . beans, it is? Are they . . . supposed to taste good?" He gestured with his chopsticks at the *nattō* in exactly the manner that he'd just acknowledged one wasn't supposed to.

"Well," I said, "many people think so."

"Many people, it is?" He cocked his head and looked at me. "You do not?"

"While I am not fond of them, no, many people find them delicious."

He leaned forward and whispered, "I think they smell like something died."

In spite of myself, I giggled. "I think so too."

———

At the end of the meal, Matsudaira-*sama* and Takeda-*sama* conferred for a moment with Lady Chiyome. She bowed to them, and Lord Matsudaira strode out of the hall, followed by all of his soldiers.

At a word from Takeda-*sama*, the *kunoichi* and his soldiers also left—all except his captains. As Toumi, Emi, and I cleared the tables, Lord Takeda sat with Captain Baba and Captain Hara, watching us.

"Children," said Lady Chiyome, "stop. Aimaru, Risuko, come tell Lord Takeda what you found this morning."

Suddenly Aimaru looked ready to bolt, and I couldn't blame him. But we both knelt in front of the head table and recounted what we'd found.

"*Che,*" grunted Captain Hara.

"Oh!" whispered Emi. "It sounds like a list of the Takeda forces!"

Toumi hissed at her to shut up.

Lord Takeda shot her a grim smile. "Yes, girl. That is indeed what it sounds like. Though what it was doing in your storeroom is a question almost as pressing as finding my lieutenant's murderer." He grimaced and pointed at me, there on the floor before him, and then up at Emi. "So, Chiyome, you told me who this one was. Who's that, some long-lost descendant of Empress Jingu?"

Though still solemn, our mistress's face took on the round expression of a satisfied cat. "Emi. Toumi." She gestured next to me on the polished bamboo floor. When they'd knelt beside me, Toumi more than a little stiffly, Chiyome-*sama* said, "My lord, allow me to introduce two more of my young ladies, recruited at the same time as Kano Murasaki, here: Tarugu Toumi and Hanichi Emi."

Captain Hara whistled while Captain Baba's eyes flew wide, and he gasped, "Kano, Hanichi, and Tarugu!"

Lord Takeda stared down at the three of us for a long time, to the point where I began to sweat and Toumi to twitch. At last, he turned to Lady Chiyome. "Well, well, my dear. You are playing a long game, aren't you?" When she bowed her head in pleased acknowledgment, the general turned back to us. "*Mukashi, mukashi*—long, long ago, Kano Kazuo, Hanichi Benjiro, and Tarugu Makoto were all great samurai. Are you three truly their daughters?"

"*Hai*, Takeda-*sama*." We touched our heads to the floor.

"Hmm. Well," grunted Lord Takeda, "in any case, Chiyome, I hope you know what you're doing."

She bowed to him.

"Be that as it may," he sighed, "we seem to have a murderer and a spy on our hands. For now, I think it's safe to assume that they are one and the same."

As the two captains nodded in agreement, Lady Chiyome whispered, "Girls. Finish clearing."

We got up and began to take away the dirty bowls and dishes.

Emi kept staring at me.

When I came back into the hall to get more bowls, I heard Captain Baba say, "Yes, yes, but how did the lieutenant get in! The guards both swear the gate was closed and barred all night, and we can see the back gate was as well. He can't have flown in."

I looked up and then swallowed what I was going to say. I needn't have bothered.

"Come, Risuko," Lady Chiyome said. "I know that look. Spit it out, girl, whatever it is."

"Paint," I rasped. When all four sets of eyes narrowed, I spluttered, "On Lieutenant . . . on his trousers. Red paint. It must have been . . . from the *torī* arch."

Captain Hara gaped at me. "The arch?"

"He . . . " I pointed to the insides of my knees, where the lieutenant's trousers had been stained. "He must have climbed up and jumped to the wall."

Lord Takeda peered at me appraisingly. "Is that even possible?"

"I—I think so, my lord." I stared down at a knot in the bamboo floor. "I was thinking after I jumped from the wall to get you that climbing up and down the arch would have been easier."

"Jumped from the wall?" Captain Baba coughed. "Climbing the . . . Nonsense!"

"One way to find out, my lord," said Lady Chiyome. "If Risuko there can't do it, it can't be done."

———

We all walked out to the front gate, where the guards Aosagi and Yukishiro were back at their posts.

"Did anyone climb up the arch here last night?" barked Lord Takeda.

"No, sir!" they both answered. Aosagi, the Matsudaira guard, pointed at me. "That skinny girl there jumped down, though."

Captain Baba gave a huff of surprise.

"Yes, yes," said Takeda-*sama*, waving his hand at the Matsudaira guard and then pointing up. "Kano-girl. You say you can climb that?"

I nodded and then, thrilled at the opportunity to do the thing I most enjoyed, I ran toward the closest pillar and leapt. Wrapping my arms and legs around the painted wood, I quickly shimmied upward.

It was easy climbing. The beam was about as thick as one of the pine trunks from home but smooth. Though the paint and the morning's dew made the surface a bit slick, I could gain enough purchase with my feet and hands to keep myself moving upward.

Just below the first lintel, I stopped.

"Too hard, Mouse-*chan?*" called Toumi. The teasing was just to keep up the tradition, I knew.

I shook my head. "Scuff marks. Fresh." Looking down, I saw Lord Takeda and his officers staring up at me, mouths open. The sight made me smile even as the fact that Emi still wasn't looking at me made my stomach clench.

I reached the first crossbar and threw my leg over it. Where it met the pillar, a nail stuck out; from its head, a bright blue thread fluttered in the morning breeze. I plucked the thread free and let it fall to the watchers below. "I think the lieutenant was here."

Aimaru caught the thread, but I was already making my way to the upper crossbar, throwing my arms over, and pulling myself up. The arch, which looked so stable from the ground, swayed slightly beneath my feet. Still, it was steadier than a tree top. And I had made it to the top.

I looked out over the hillside—the two camps, marked with red flags to the left and blue to the right, wisps of smoke rising from campfires into the sunlit morning air over the valley, all gold and green, and the white and grey mountains above. The blue sky and golden sun.

I truly had never felt more alive.

Remembering why I was there, I looked down at the top of the huge crossbar. On either side of my foot were two large footprints—clear, fresh ones, unwashed by the rains of two days before. "Footprints!" I called out.

Looking down at the small sea of astonished faces, I smiled and waved, then turned and jumped the two paces to the wall of the Full Moon.

I had to spread my feet to avoid landing on the sharpened bamboo stakes that pushed up from the wall like broken teeth. Some loose gravel on the top of the plaster wall made my left foot skid slightly, giving me a moment of terror, but then I grabbed one of the spikes to steady myself and was able to stand. I walked along the wall to the roof of the Guest House and then clambered down the half-timbered wall to the ground.

I walked back out the gate, bowed to Takeda-*sama*, and nodded. "That's how he got in." And then I pointed to the inside of my trousers, which were stained with red paint just as Torimasa's had been.

"Well," Lady Chiyome sighed, "it seems that I'm going to have to move that arch farther from the wall."

Lord Takeda, however, rounded on the two guards, his face like mountain thunder. "You swore that no one approached this gate last night."

Both guards fell to their knees, horror twisting their faces. "We saw no one, my lord!" said the Takeda guard, Yukishiro.

"We would have seen anyone who did *that!*" gasped the other guard, Aosagi, gesturing at me.

Captain Baba came up and glowered down at the two miserable men. "And when did you come on duty?"

"At the nine bells of midnight, my lord," said Yukishiro.

Aosagi nodded. "The Hour of the Rat."

I looked over at Aimaru, who nodded at me.

That was when Torimasa-*san* had been murdered.

"And who," asked Captain Baba, "were the guards on duty before you?"

Shaking, the two soldiers—soldiers of different armies, now thrown together—looked at each other. His voice low and thin, Yukishiro said, "Sato and . . . "

"And Kobayashi, my lord," finished Aosagi. "When we arrived last night, they were . . . asleep."

"Asleep?" growled Lord Takeda.

"Drunk, my lord," both guards whispered.

"And you did not think to report this?"

Through gritted teeth, Yukishiro said, "We have been on duty all this time, my lord. We meant to report it to their superiors when our shift ended."

"And you have done so now," the general grunted. "Get up. You have acted well." He turned to the older of his personal guards. "Kotoku, go and inform my lord of the Three Rivers that we wish to speak to his soldier Kobayashi regarding circumstances touching on my lieutenant's death. Tadashi," he continued to the younger one, "I did not see Sato at breakfast. Go to his tent and drag his drunken carcass back here at once."

13—Guards

We waited there at the foot of the *torī* gate.

The sky was just as blue and the sun as bright as before. A fresh, mild breeze sang through the grass, making the white wildflowers dance.

Yet somehow, as I stood there with the furious lord and his angry captains, it did not seem as delightful as it had up on top of the arch. Indeed, delightful was precisely what it was *not*.

Even so, one of the virtues that the months at the Full Moon had taught us was patience. If you can spend a blizzarding afternoon carrying rocks from one side of a courtyard to another, then waiting for two soldiers to arrive with two other disgraced soldiers in tow is . . .

Well, not nothing. It's just not as hard.

I found myself thinking about the two guards, Sato and Kobayashi. It was clear that they were in real trouble. They had failed in their duty. They had allowed not only Lieutenant Torimasa into the Full Moon but most likely his killer as well.

Would they be whipped?

Beheaded?

I tried not to think about it, but even though I had never met the men, I found myself worrying about them. Did they have families? Did they have children?

I looked over at Emi, who was frowning ferociously—no surprise. Toumi had the smile on that I always interpreted as a threat that she might bite.

Aimaru was standing at awkward attention.

Tadashi, the younger of Lord Takeda's personal guards, returned from the Takeda camp ashen faced and prostrated himself before his lord.

"Well?" snapped Takeda-*sama*. "What is it?"

"Sa— The soldier that you sent me to find . . . He is dead, my lord."

"Dead?"

"At his own hand, my lord." When the general met that statement with a snort, Tadashi murmured, "The other members of his squad witnessed it, and Lieutenant Itagaki honored him by providing the death blow."

Takeda-*sama* gave a low growl. Captain Hara said, "We should speak with Itagaki."

The general shook himself. "Yes. Later. But did he say why?"

The guard answered, "Yes, my lord. When the squad came back from the morning meal, he was still asleep, and so they poured water on his head. When he woke, he realized what he had done—abandoning his post. He knew that he had earned a traitor's death. And so he asked your forgiveness, my lord, and yours, my lady."

Lady Chiyome tsked.

"And then he killed himself, my lord."

"Yes, well, Itagaki killed him," said the general. "Still, he took the honorable path. We will see that he is shown the proper rites along with the late lieutenant."

The guard stood and bowed. "I will let the soldiers know, my lord."

"Do it."

The man left at a run.

Lady Chiyome murmured. "I am sorry, my lord, to have shown you and your men such poor hospitality."

"Nonsense, Chiyome," said Takeda-*sama*. "We are sorry to have brought our troubles to you."

The two captains murmured in agreement. "Something smells of week-old carp," said Captain Baba.

At that moment, the other guard, Kotoku, returned—not with Kobayashi but with Lord Matsudaira and his officers.

"My lord governor of Worth, greetings," Lord Matsudaira said, as if they had not just shared a meal.

Takeda-*sama* answered with equal formality, "Greetings, my lord governor of the Three Rivers. We hope to speak to one of your soldiers, Kobayashi, about events while he was on guard duty yesterday evening."

Matsudaira-*sama* gave a *hmm* of irritation. "To be honest, I would like to speak to him about the same thing." He indicated Kotoku. "Your messenger here informed me of what happened last night. Lady Mochizuki, my apologies that a man under my command left your home undefended."

"My lord," she answered, deflecting the apology with a bow of her head.

"Unfortunately," continued Matsudaira-*sama*, "Kobayashi is not to be found. There was evidence that he slept in the tent last night, but he was not there when the men awoke this morning. They did find this *sake* bottle." He gestured to his young captain, Tokimatsu, who held up a porcelain wine jar.

It looked a lot like one from our kitchen.

"Captain," said Lady Chiyome, "may I see that bottle?"

Tokimatsu-*san* handed it to her; she sniffed at the contents.

"So," grunted Lord Takeda, "my guard has killed himself, and your guard seems to have deserted more than his post."

"So it seems."

"My lords," said Chiyome-*sama*, "I cannot be sure, but it smells as if this wine has been tampered with. Our cook is a master herbalist; may I have him inspect the bottle?"

"Certainly," said Matsudaira-*sama* with a back-handed wave. "In the meantime, shall we send a joint search party out?"

"Certainly. Chiyome, where is he likely to have got to?"

"You are best to start by looking in the valley, my lord. He wouldn't last long up in the mountains. And either way, he can't have gotten far on foot."

Takeda-*sama* peered up at the cliffs above the compound and sniffed. "True. Hara, work with Tokimatsu there to set up a mounted search party. We'll make sure he hasn't left the valley first."

"My lord," said the Takeda captain, striding off with his young Matsudaira counterpart into the camps.

At that moment, the Buddhist monk came through the open gate, followed by the two helpers carrying the shrouded body of Torimasa on a plank. The monk bowed to the two lords.

Aimaru watched them pass, a rare frown on his face.

"What a morning," grumbled Takeda-*sama* to Captain Baba. To the holy man, he said, "Take the body out to the open field past the camp. We will set up the pyre there. And, as it happens, there will be another body to attend to."

"Oh?" For a moment, the holy man looked almost excited. He quickly pulled on a solemn expression. "Of course, my lord. I would be honored to deliver their souls to the next life."

"Yes, yes." Takeda-*sama* dismissed the man with another back-handed wave. As the monk and his helpers took their gruesome cargo away, he looked up at the sun. To the other officers, he said, "Gentlemen, as pressing and as sad as all of these affairs have been, we are here for a purpose of far greater import. The Hour of the Dragon is well upon us. May we adjourn to the meeting tent?"

"My lord," agreed Matsudaira-*sama*. He turned to Lady Chiyome and to us. "Ladies."

"My lord," we said, and bowed deeply.

———

As the men left, Lady Chiyome watched them. "Mieko," she said, "gather the women together in the hall, will you?"

I started. I wasn't sure when the eldest *kunoichi* had arrived.

"Yes, my lady," she said, and strode off toward the stables, where the women were going through the Sixty-four Changes, as we did most mornings.

"Girls," Lady Chiyome muttered, "I am going to inform the others of what has happened. I want you to bring Kee Sun this." She handed the *sake* bottle to Emi. "Ask him if he can tell whether someone has added poppy juice to the wine."

"Yes, my lady," Emi said, but as Lady Chiyome walked off toward the stables, she looked at me and Toumi, and we all shuddered.

Outside the gate, eight riders—four Takeda, four Matsudaira—thundered away from the compound, down into the valley. They were searching for the missing guard, Kobayashi.

"Come on," Emi murmured, staring as we all were at where the riders had disappeared over the ridge's edge. "Let's bring this bottle to Kee Sun."

As we all walked back toward the kitchen, a thought occurred to me. "Do you think we should let the other cooks know?"

"Why not?" asked Toumi.

"Because," Emi said, "if this was done by a Matsudaira soldier, Kumo-*san* might tell the killer. And even it's done by a Takeda, we don't want Torai-*san* tipping him off too soon."

We reached the kitchen door. Masugu-*san*'s sword leaned, still bloody, against the stand that held the gong, with the scabbard lying on the ground beneath it. I gazed at it for a moment and then shook myself. "Well, how are we going to get Kee Sun out here?"

Aimaru beamed at us. "You wait here. I'll get him."

He was gone just long enough for Toumi to snort something about the three cooks filleting him.

Kee Sun came out the creaky kitchen door, scratching his beard, with Aimaru in his wake. "Moon-cake here tells me yeh wanted to know if it's all right for yeh to clean off Masugu's blade now they've decided it didn't have nothin' to do with the murder."

I nodded. "Yes, Kee Sun-*san*. But there's something else." I indicated the bottle in Emi's hand.

She held it out to the cook. "Lady Chiyome wants to know if someone drugged two of the guards last night, like . . . that girl did with Masugu-*san*'s *sake*."

Once again, Emi and I shuddered.

I knew that she and Toumi and the others had been at the bottom of the tree while I had clung to the very top.

I knew that they'd heard Fuyudori scream as she fell and had heard her hit the icy ground.

I may have had nightmares about the sight of the white-haired girl falling backward into the snowy night, but I knew Emi had had some of her own, always ending with that sound.

Kee Sun sucked air in through his teeth. Taking the ceramic bottle from Emi, he ran the open mouth under his nose. He gave a low groan and closed his eyes. "Does someone need my tonic?"

We looked at each other. Toumi said with a smirk, "Well, one of the guards offed himself. For real this time. So I don't think he'll need it."

"Toumi!" Emi said.

"The other one ran away," I added. "I suppose he might need the tonic, but we don't know. And, to be honest, if they find him, I'm not sure he'll need it either."

Toumi sighed. "Yeah. He'd probably be happier to still be drugged."

Aimaru was staring at the bottle. "Was it really poisoned?"

"Well," said Kee Sun, "what do you girlies think?" He passed the bottle to Emi, whose eyes got wide. "Oh!"

She passed it to Toumi, who sniffed and then passed it to me, sticking out her tongue. "I hate that stuff."

I took the bottle from her and ran it under my nose. I recognized the scent immediately—it was the smell that had filled Masugu's room that day when Fuyudori had almost killed him. Under the tart, flowery smell of the *sake* was the sickly, cloying odor of poppy juice. I fought down my rising gorge. "Do we think this is from our stores?"

Kee Sun grunted and plucked the bottle from my fingers, turning it over so that the last of the wine dribbled out. He pointed at the mark on the base. "See there? That's the mark of Karoku, the potter up in Highfield I bought most of these from. Mind, just about anyone who's eaten here could have grabbed one."

"Yes," I said, thinking out loud, "but doesn't it make sense that they'd have taken the wine and maybe even the poppy from our stores? That's where the killer got the sword from, after all."

"True," grumbled Kee Sun. "But it's also true that the kitchen is open. So maybe the killer took the wine and poppy juice and the bottle, drugged the guards, sneaked in—"

"Over the arch," said Aimaru, nodding at me.

Toumi grunted. "And then the dead lieutenant just happened to sneak in the same way on a late-night love call, and the killer just happened to break his neck?" She looked up at the roof of the Great Hall. "Maybe he fell and broke his own neck."

"And then the spy just happened to find his body and just happened to pose it in front of our dormitories?" I shot back. "Besides, I didn't see any marks on his face or head. His hair wasn't even out of place. If he'd fallen headfirst from the top of the Guest House, he'd have been a mess."

"Maybe the lieutenant found the spy after the spy sneaked in and hid that scroll," mused Emi.

"Then they got into a fight—no weapons, so the killer breaks the lieutenant's neck . . . " I ground to a halt. "But . . . "

"What is it, Bright Eyes?"

"Well, Kee Sun-*san*, how did the spy get out?"

We all looked at each other. Peering toward the gate, Emi said, "Maybe he got out the same way you did, Murasaki. He jumped."

"Well, sure," I admitted. "I did it. But I think a man might have had a harder time—that's a big fall."

"Maybe he's a mouse like you," said Toumi with a snort.

"Then how was he big enough to break the lieutenant's neck?"

"Maybe he stayed in the storeroom until after the gate was opened this morning," Emi said. "No one would have noticed one more person coming or going then."

"And . . . maybe he forgot the scroll and then came back for it?" I suggested.

Kee Sun shook his head. "Maybe. Sounds awful complicated to me, and I'm never fond of complicated. Now, yeh four, yeh're not to stick yehr noses in this, yeh hear? The lords got officers investigatin'. Don't want the four of yeh getting trampled underfoot, right?"

We looked at each other and nodded. "Right, Kee Sun-*san*."

"Now, Bright Eyes, about that blade, yeh already know how to clean it. Just like after the pig. But it was used to kill a man, and that's a different kind of stain on it, and so—"

"I need to purify it, I know. You said."

He nodded, scowling at the sword. "And do you know the rites for doin' that? 'Cause I don't. I'm just a cook, after all."

"I . . . " I thought about my father. About how he had brought his swords up to the spring above our village every New Year's Day. "I think . . . Yes. A waterfall?"

"Ayup." Kee Sun scratched at his beard again. "Sounds right. Movin' water's what's needed for sure."

"Is there a waterfall anywhere near here?"

Toumi flashed the most genuine smile I'd ever seen from her. "Is there a waterfall?" She smacked Emi on the shoulder. "Come on, let's show them!"

14—Fathers

cleaned the sword off, first with straw to get rid of the clotted blood and then with a rag soaked in clove-scented oil that Aimaru fetched for me from the kitchen.

Toumi watched with greedy fascination and Aimaru as if I were going to ask him to repeat the actions himself. Emi looked lost in thought.

When the blade once again gleamed in the morning sunlight, I sheathed it and slipped the scabbard into the back of my sash.

Kee Sun shooed us away, saying that he needed to check to see if anyone had been dipping into the poppy juice.

Lady Chiyome was talking with the older women. The generals and their men were all engaged in whatever it was that they had come to talk about.

For one of the very first times since Lady Chiyome had called me down from the pine tree that first day near my family's home in Serenity, I had been given permission to go off on my own. It felt as if a breeze had blown a veil of cobwebs from me; it also felt as if I were standing naked. I looked around at the others.

"Come on, Mouse-*chan*," Toumi barked. "Let's get out of here." She and Emi had retrieved their bows and arrows from the armory.

As we walked to the back gate, I could just see Mai sitting in the shadows of the doorway to the Retreat, her arms wrapped around her knees. Until then, I had never actually felt sorry for the older girl. I whispered as much to Emi.

She didn't respond.

"What do you think you're doing coming along, Moon-cake?" Toumi said to Aimaru.

"Well, Kee Sun told me to go away. And since that's where I am supposed to be, it seemed like a good idea to stay with you three."

Toumi made a dismissive *pff* sound. "You could stay and bother Mai."

Aimaru smiled blandly. "I don't think she would like that very much."

"Sure. She'd probably kill you. But then we wouldn't have to bother with you anymore." Toumi gave a laugh that sounded more than a little like an angry pig.

Aimaru, being Aimaru, laughed along.

We walked through the rear gate and out into the gardens at the back of the Full Moon. Birds were singing in the trees, but the cave two-thirds of the way up the cliff intruded into my thoughts.

"Stop teasing him, Toumi," I said. When Toumi laughed again, I observed, "You seem in a good mood."

"Yeah, well, men with swords make me nervous. It's nice to get away from them."

Aimaru asked, "A girl with a sword doesn't make you nervous?"

Toumi snorted. "It isn't the sword that makes me nervous, it's the men. I know Mouse-*chan* there wouldn't have the guts to kill me."

I sighed. "My father made me promise . . . not to do harm."

"Oh, sure," chuckled Toumi. "Whatever helps you sleep at night."

"I *don't* sleep at night," I muttered back. When that brought another derisive snort from Toumi, rather than snap back, I turned once more to Emi. "What are you thinking about?"

"Hmm?" Her scowl seemed deep but abstracted, as if she were contemplating something on the other side of the world. Her eyes flicked to me. "I was thinking . . . about what Lady Chiyome told Takeda-*sama*."

"What, about the *sake?*"

"No," Emi said. "About our fathers."

"About—? Oh."

"What about your fathers?" Aimaru asked, and for once, I agreed with Toumi: in that moment, I would have been happy to leave him behind to pester Mai to explosion.

Emi looked me in the eye for the first time since Lady Chiyome had told the general and his captains our family names. "Your father is the reason my father is dead."

My stomach suddenly felt full of the rocks that Mitsuke and the others made us carry. From what little I knew about what had happened all of those years before, that didn't seem entirely fair. But still . . .

"Why didn't you tell me?" she asked, her voice even, her face blank—aside from her habitually downturned mouth.

"I thought you knew."

"Thought she knew what?" Aimaru asked.

But Toumi turned around with another bray of laughter. "You mean you didn't, Frown-face? Ha! I knew. Knew the minute I met you, Kano-mouse—the minute Mieko told us your name. Wanted to kill you right there."

"I remember," I whispered.

"Me too," said Emi. I reached out to touch her, but she held up her hand. "I'm angry, Murasaki. And most of it's not with you. Most of it's with your father. And my father. And yours, Toumi. But I'm still angry."

"I—I'm sorry." I honestly didn't know what else to say. We walked on in silence for a bit. We were on a trail I'd never taken that led between the base of the cliff and the tangled forest that tumbled down the hillside to the west of the Full Moon. We were gradually climbing.

Eventually, predictably, Aimaru broke the silence. "What happened to your fathers?"

I looked to the other girls, but neither of them seemed to want to talk. Emi was lost in thought again, and Toumi was staring straight ahead, leading us up the mountain. I sighed. "Our fathers . . . were all samurai of Lord Oda. Oda-*sama* ordered them on a mission. They refused. He then offered them a choice: suicide or life with dishonor. Emi's and Toumi's fathers committed *seppuku*. My father chose dishonor."

"Oh."

We trudged on, climbing now alongside a stream that gushed down out of the mountains, white and musical and absolutely at odds with our mood.

"I watched my father kill himself," Toumi said. I could only see the back of her head, but I couldn't imagine that her expression was a happy one anymore.

"I'm sorry."

"Why are you sorry, Murasaki?" Emi asked. "You weren't the one who gave the order or the one who refused the order. You're just like us."

"Except she grew up with parents," Toumi snarled, and I was glad that she wasn't facing me. "She grew up in a house."

"I'm sorry."

Now Toumi spun, and I was shocked to see tears flowing down her cheeks. "Don't be. I watched my father stab himself. I watched that samurai cut my father's head off. I'm tougher because of it." She swiped at her face with her sleeve. "I survived, and I don't owe anyone anything, least of all you, Mouse."

I fought back an urge to reach out to her. "When my father died, we never knew for sure what happened, just that he was summoned by Lord Imagawa

and that he never came back. I always wished I could know for sure what happened, wished that I could have been there with him. But . . . I don't know if
I could have watched."

"Like hell you could have," Toumi growled and turned away. She did not
start walking again, however.

Feeling tears pushing up in my own throat, I turned to Emi. "Did you?
Watch your father?"

She nodded, eyes searching the mountains on the far side of the valley.

We all stood there in silence—me looking at Emi, Aimaru looking at me,
and Emi and Toumi looking emphatically anywhere but at me.

Finally, Toumi grunted, "So, are we going to this stupid waterfall or not?"

"Yes," I said, "Let's go."

———

We climbed in silence for a while.

The little valley we were climbing was wet and green. The trail,
such as it was, crossed the rushing blue stream several times, and we had to
walk carefully across the slick rocks.

"Murasaki," Emi said, as we were waiting for Toumi to ford the creek,
"when did your father die?"

It was a perfectly reasonable question, but I felt as if she had punched
me in the stomach. The threatening tears, which hadn't completely subsided,
began to close my throat once more. "Three . . . No. I guess four years now. It
was spring. Maybe a little earlier than now."

She nodded. "You know the date."

Again, I felt as if I'd been punched. "The fourteenth day of the Month of
the Blossoms."

Again, Emi nodded.

When I could breathe again, I asked, "Do you? Remember the date?"

"Yes," Emi said. Then she stopped and bent forward, grabbing at the bow
over her shoulder.

Aimaru rushed to her side.

"Emi?" I found myself grabbing for the sword at my back, worried that we
were under attack. "Are you all right?"

"I remember." She looked at me, her eyes wide. "Murasaki. Toumi. I
remember."

"Remember?" Toumi spat, not turning.

"You. Both of you. It must have been. Picking wineberries." She pointed
at me and then at Toumi. "Kiki. Tutu." Now she was the one crying, tears

dribbling down the length of her nose and along her downturned mouth. "We were picking berries, smearing them all over our faces. There was a woman, laughing." She blinked at me. "Your mother, Murasaki."

"My mother?" I couldn't remember my mother ever laughing.

Toumi growled and turned, her bow clutched in her hands. "I don't remember any stupid mothers or any stupid wineberries, and I sure don't remember any stupid girls." Then she growled again and sprinted away from us up the trail.

I started to follow but Emi put a hand on my shoulder. "I think she just wants to be alone for a bit. I know the way to the waterfall." She wiped the tears from her face with her sleeve.

Right. The waterfall. I had completely forgotten it and Masugu's sword at my back.

With Emi now in the lead, we resumed our climb along the banks of the stream.

I had no memory from before we arrived in Serenity. As for Toumi, the time before—with friends and honor and a mother who laughed—might as well have belonged to a different life. The thought didn't make me angry, so much. Just very, very sad.

Still at Emi's elbow, Aimaru asked, "So your fathers were friends?"

I answered, "I guess."

Without turning, Emi said, "Toumi's father and mine both served under Kano-*san*. But I think the families were close."

All of this seemed like a story from a book. It sounded right, but . . . "Do you have a lot of memories from . . . from before?"

Emi shook her head, tiptoeing her way back across the stream. "Mostly, my mother told me about it. But I remember the wineberries and another time, a little girl crying. That must have been you, Murasaki."

I wondered what I had been crying about. What could there possibly have been to cry about? Remembering Usako, I realized it could have been about nothing at all.

"So their fathers killed themselves, but yours didn't? What happened?" Aimaru prodded.

"We moved to Serenity. My father took work as a scribe—mostly for Lord Imagawa."

"So what were they ordered to do that they refused?"

Now Emi stopped and turned. "Nobody knows."

I gulped. "Actually . . . I do. Some. Lady Chiyome and Masugu told me some of it."

Emi stared at me. The tears were no longer flowing down her cheeks, but her eyes remained puffy and red.

"Can I . . . " I wanted to reach out to her, but she didn't look as if she wanted to be touched. "When we reach Toumi, I'll tell you both. All right?"

She nodded, turned, and continued up the trail.

Aimaru looked as if he were about to ask another question, so I beat him to it. "What about you?" I asked. "What happened to your parents? Do you know?" I imagined, I think, that his story must have been something like mine—a disgraced samurai or a murdered noble.

He shrugged, grinning. "No idea who my father was. My mother worked in a brothel in the capital."

"Oh."

"I grew up there. It was nice. There was food. The women and the older girls played with me. One winter, though, when I was about six, *Okā-san* got the pox and died. That was hard. And Hiromi-*san* kicked me out because I asked too many questions and made the customers uncomfortable, and because I was a boy."

I could imagine that.

"And I lived on the streets for a few months, watching the warehouse, like I told you and Lady Chiyome, Murasaki. That was hard too. But then a monk found me and brought me to the monastery, and then, last autumn, Lady Chiyome found me and offered to take me on to help the Little Brothers. So that was good."

"Ah."

He wrinkled his nose. "Does the stream smell funny to you?"

It did—like eggs that had gone bad. I said so.

Emi called back, "You'll see why at the waterfall."

———

As we approached what looked like a little valley, a small cleft in the mountainside above us, Emi came next to me and tugged on my sleeve. "I think someone is out there."

I stopped short. "Where?"

She kept looking up the hill. "Behind us. Keeping in the trees."

"Man or woman?"

She sniffed thoughtfully. "Well, not in the red and white robes the older women wear. And I guess it could be Shino or Mai but probably a man."

Aimaru, who had stopped, muttered, "Do you think it could be that guard, Kobayashi?"

"Maybe." Emi shrugged. "It's just a shape."

We walked along for a moment.

I was suddenly aware of every shadow beneath every tree.

"Do you think Kobayashi is the spy?" I asked.

Emi grunted, "Spy?"

"You know, the person who left the scroll in the storeroom. Or who picked it up."

Shrugging again, Emi said, "Well, they're probably not the same person, right?"

"Oh." That made sense: one person sneaks in and leaves a document in a place where no one would look for it; the other comes by later and retrieves it. That way neither of them looks suspicious, and no one connects the two. "So do we think they're both Matsudaira, the spies, or is there a Takeda traitor?"

"There'd kind of have to be a traitor," mused Aimaru. "If Matsudaira-*sama* had someone who already knew how many soldiers Takeda-*sama* had, he wouldn't need a spy, would he?"

That too made sense.

I found myself thinking out loud. "I don't think Kobayashi can be the spy, though."

"Why?" asked Emi and Aimaru together.

"Well, he'd have to be a pretty stupid spy, to drug his own fellow guard when that would make him the obvious culprit. Also, if the dead guard had been drugged and the traitor came to drop off the scroll, why not just hand it to Kobayashi instead of hiding it in the Full Moon?"

"Maybe the traitor doesn't know that Kobayashi is the spy?" Emi said.

"Maybe, but it still seems like, if there'd been an easier way to pass the document along, they would have done it that way. Also, if the spy is working for Lord Matsudaira, why did he point the finger at Kobayashi?"

"Sure," Emi agreed, sounding much less lost in the past. "But maybe Kobayashi . . . " She shook her head like a dog stepping out of a pond. "No. You're right. It doesn't make sense. And I didn't get the feeling that Matsudaira-*sama* was hiding anything."

Aimaru said, "He seemed pretty angry to me. And we traveled with him for over a week. He doesn't get angry a lot."

We digested all of that as we reached a place where the slope began to level.

"Emi," I whispered. "Do you still see someone behind us?"

She nodded. "It's open here, so they're staying back."

"See those rocks on either side of the stream ahead?"

She nodded.

"Maybe we could hide behind one of them and then see who's following us."

"Good idea, Murasaki."

The rocks stood like broken doors through which the sulfurous stream rushed. When we reached the rock on the right, we turned quickly behind it. Emi pointed at Aimaru and then at the far side of the rock, which folded into the steep hillside. "Up there. Look if you can see who's behind us. Don't let him spot you."

"'Course not." Aimaru seemed offended at the suggestion. He slinked along the back side of the rock, his bulk low to the ground. Through a kind of chink in the side of the rock, he peered. Turning back to us, he smiled and mouthed, "Jolalo-*san.*"

Why was he up there, stalking us? It made me uncomfortable.

"What should we do?" I asked Emi.

"He's your friend," she said with something like a smirk.

"He's not my friend! He's just a strange boy I'm trying to be polite to!"

"Well, he's not being very polite right now," Emi answered, definitely smirking now. "I say we stop being polite to him."

There was a quiet scuffle of feet in loose gravel from just on the other side of the rock.

I nodded to Emi.

As Jolalo tiptoed past our hiding spot, Emi tripped him with the end of her bow, and I drew my sword and had it at his throat before he could move. He said something in his soft-edged language—something rude, I had to assume.

"Why are you spying on us?"

His voice came out a high squeak. "Spy?" Understandably, he seemed to be more focussed on the deadly tip of my *wakizashi* than on what we were saying.

"Watching us. Following us. Listening to us."

He blinked his round eyes and looked up at me along the length of the blade. "Not listening. Not watching."

"You followed us. Why?"

He frowned. When Emi smacked his boot with her bow, he grunted, "Wanted. See where go you. Where you go."

I looked at Emi. She said, "We are going up into the hills to conduct a ritual." That was true enough.

I added, "One that strangers are not allowed to see." That wasn't exactly true, but I didn't exactly care.

"With sword?" he asked. "And bow?"

"Yes," I grumbled. I couldn't think of a better way to explain the fact that we were walking through woods armed.

He laughed, which only annoyed me more. "You can use sword?"

I hesitated. We weren't supposed to tell outsiders that we knew how to use weapons—except perhaps to be cute.

My hesitation made him laugh more.

"Yes!" I growled. "Yes, I can use this sword. Quite well." Emi tried to get me to stop, but I couldn't, angry as I was. I lifted the blade into the Bamboo Bud, the preliminary to a sweeping diagonal cut that could remove his head. His eyes grew wide. "My father was Kano Kazuo, one of the most famous swordsmen in the empire. Emi, Toumi, and I are all the descendants of great samurai. We are trained in the Way of the Warrior to defend ourselves, and so yes, I am quite capable of using this sword. Please do not make me!" Again, all of these things were true, although they did not go together the way that I wanted him to think.

Smile gone, he stared up at me. "Not make. It is."

I stepped back into the Eight Phases, sword on my rear shoulder, pointed straight up—ready to strike in any direction.

Not taking his eyes from mine, Jolalo stood unsteadily and dusted off his embroidered black jacket. Then he gave an odd bow: one foot out in front of the other, back leg bent, his hand on his heart. "Risuko-*san*."

I nodded my head, feeling the aftermath of my anger flowing through me.

He turned and without another word walked back between the two rocks and down the hillside.

When he disappeared into the trees, I lowered my sword, and relief flooded through me.

Emi and Aimaru, of course, laughed.

"Come on," I grumbled, resheathing my sword. "Let's find the stupid waterfall."

15—The Waterfall

E mi sniggered. "I think he likes you."

"Likes me?"

She repeated his strange bow—only where his expression had been one of humiliation, if not fear, she fluttered her eyelashes at me. "Risuko-*san*."

"I don't care!" I found myself blushing, and it was only partly because I was still furious.

That just made Emi laugh again, which made Aimaru laugh too.

They stopped as we approached the pool.

It was a pond whose dark blue center suggested that it was nearly as deep as it was wide. Steam rose from it, bearing an even stronger smell of spoiled eggs. On the far side, a hot spring spilled down over a cliff face in a waterfall that looked as white and fluffy as snow. The whole valley seemed smaller there, swaddled in mist, and the sound of the falling water masked any birdsong. The noise made the place seem strangely quiet.

Toumi squatted, facing the waterfall. Her bow was on the ground by the water's edge, her empty quiver beside it. Her head was bowed.

A knot of snow monkeys peered glumly at her from the other side of the pool. They were half-submerged, their little red faces just above the water, like a group of old men in the hot tub at the bathhouse.

"Toumi?" said Emi as we approached the pool.

"First thing I remember is my father's head bouncing on the *tatami*. Don't remember his voice. Don't remember his face. Don't remember my mother, 'cause she died when I was born. Just that. And the smell of blood." Toumi was staring down at the water, chewing on a fingernail.

"I'm sorry," I said again, though I realized there was no point.

I might as well not have said anything. She just stared into the steaming pool. "Servant dragged me around the city, looking for other Tarugu kin to take me in, but there weren't any. Least we couldn't find any. And then he . . . just sort of gave up. Left me alone where the Jizo statues are."

"I'm sorry."

"Got hungry. Stole an apple. Got chased. Stole some more. Stayed alive. For *ten years*. And why? 'Cause your dad chickened out. So I'm the last stupid Tarugu."

I almost argued with her, but I knew Toumi: she was ready to bite someone's head off, and I didn't want it to be mine. We had too much else to talk about. "At least your father redeemed your family's honor," I said.

"Lot of good that did." She started chewing on the next nail.

Emi crouched next to her. "Hey. What happened to your arrows?"

"Shot 'em at the waterfall." She sniffed. "Thought about shooting the monkeys, but that just seemed stupid."

"So you shot them at the waterfall?" Emi asked.

Standing, Toumi shrugged.

"Um. I have to go and purify the sword," I said. "I can get the arrows."

She shrugged again.

I walked away from her, Emi, and Aimaru, who was gazing up at the woods above.

The valley rose steeply to either side—a wooded mountain slope to the left, a sheer wall of rock to the right that my fingers itched to climb. Between them, above the waterfall, thick steam rose, marking the spring that fed the waterfall and the pool.

It was a magical spot. A spot where I could sense the *kami* of the place watching. Not a friendly spirit exactly but not a hostile one either.

I made my way around the steep shore at the base of the rock cliff, inching my way to the edge of the waterfall. I'm not certain why I went that way—it was probably the harder way around the pool. Perhaps I wanted to take the more difficult path. That sounds like me. Perhaps I just wanted to climb. That sounds like me too.

But no climbing yet. First, I had to purify the sword and retrieve Toumi's arrows.

The smell grew stronger as I approached the waterfall. It wasn't pleasant—not at all—but there was something cleansing about it. Something alive and healthy and earthy, like new-turned soil.

When I reached the cascade, there was no easy place to stand or kneel—just a scrabble of small boulders and gravel washed by the mist. At least it was warm—where the air on the hike up had been mountain cool, there by the waterfall it felt like a hot, close, humid summer day before a thunderstorm.

Resigning myself to getting wet, I drew the sword and laid it on the rock away from the water. My sash, the scabbard, and my jacket joined it there. I rolled up the bottoms of my pants.

Still standing on the edge of the pool, I turned toward the waterfall and bowed deeply and thanked the spirit of the hot spring for welcoming me there. I knelt and picked up a handful of water from the pool, first in my right hand to wash my left, then in my left to wash my right. After bowing again, I turned, picked up the sword in my left hand, and walked into the water until the spray from the waterfall wetted my face and fogged the mirror of the blade and I was close enough to touch the crashing stream.

Looking back across the pool, I saw Toumi and Emi, both staring at the monkeys on the far side of the waterfall. They were squatting side by side, silent.

Aimaru continued scanning the woods above the spring, occasionally shooting a glance toward me.

With a sigh, I reached into the flood, filled my right hand with the hot water, and then dribbled it along the length of the blade. Switching hands, I repeated the gesture on the other side of the sword. Then I knelt in the water, holding the sword before me across my palms in the crashing torrent, and recited the prayer of purification, inviting the gods to open the cave of heaven and clean away all pollution, all impurity, like the holy wind that clears away the threatening clouds.

It's a long prayer.

I had watched my father go through this same ritual every new year with his *katana* and *wakizashi* at a small cataract in the hills above our village. It was cold—freezing—yet he would wade into the water and let the stream cleanse the swords—and him, I realized.

It was one of the only times I saw the swords every year.

Why, I wondered, did the swords need spiritual cleansing if they had not been used?

Perhaps they had been used so much that *Otō-san* felt the need to continue to purify them. And himself.

As I recited the prayer, thanking the eight million spirits—the spirit of the springs among them—for cleansing the world and maintaining balance, I watched a mother snow monkey with a baby on its back wade under the waterfall. Then, as I was inviting the gods' blessing and protection, I watched the mother monkey wade back out—without the baby. Strange.

When I had completed the prayer, I rested the sword across my thighs and bowed deeply, letting the water flow over my head. Then I straightened, clapped twice, and stood, the sword in my right hand.

I splashed back to my jacket and the scabbard. I used the jacket to dry off the sword—water and steel do not mix well. Once I had removed the water (making my jacket now wet, but no matter), I took out the oily cloth and, as I had outside the kitchen, rubbed a protective layer over the blade. When it gleamed, I sheathed the sword and looked once again across the pool.

Emi and Toumi still crouched next to each other, still looking at the pack of monkeys, who seemed to be staring back at them.

Aimaru waved at me, and I waved in answer.

I was about to start making my way back to them when I remembered Toumi's arrows. Looking at the cataract, I wondered if there were a space behind the falls. If there were, I might be able to find the arrows there. If not . . . Well, if not, I was about to get soaked and was unlikely to be able to retrieve much of anything.

Only one way to find out.

I waded into the pool and stuck my arm through the waterfall.

Space.

Taking a deep breath, I walked into the falls.

The weight of the hot water rushing down nearly knocked me flat. I had a moment of terror, imagining myself being crushed, swept underwater, drowned—but then I pushed through to the air behind.

Gasping, I looked around to find myself in a blue-green world.

The waterfall fell over a stone ledge that leaned like the eaves of a roof over an open space. The pool churned behind the falls, but a stone wall angled up at the back.

Through the falls I could make out the barest shadows of what was on the other side. The sky at the end of the valley was a bright wedge. The trees on the mountain slope were a wash of dark green to my right. Emi and Toumi were a single blob in the center of the valley. Aimaru flickered, a tall grey shadow beside them.

Turning back toward the space behind the waterfall, I saw a small clump of moving shadows. As my eyes adjusted to the strange light, I could make out that it was a trio of baby snow monkeys, playing with . . .

Playing with Toumi's arrows.

"Hey!" I shouted—but I couldn't hear myself, and so I wasn't surprised when they didn't react. Stepping up onto the slanted back wall so that my head almost touched the overhang, I made my way toward the monkeys. They stared up at me, backing away as I approached, but their retreat was cut off by the rocky wall at the far side of the falls.

There were five arrows. I knew that Emi and Toumi usually carried closer to a dozen, but I imagined that the rest had been swept down into the depths of the pool. I picked up three of them, but two of the little monkeys held the others, banging them on the rocks and snarling at me in a manner that would probably have been menacing if I could have heard them.

Tucking the three arrows into the waist-tie of my trousers, I reached out to try to take the other two. I managed to grab one and pull it away from a displeased monkey. While I was doing so, the other scampered past me, up toward the top of the slanting wall where it joined the ceiling.

And then the monkey disappeared. I squeezed up to where the roof of the space met the sloping wall and saw that there was a crease, a black hole, dark as the space between the stars. There was no way to know how deep it was, how far down the little monkey might be hiding, or if there were any dangers waiting for me.

I thought about chasing after the monkey and the stolen arrow anyway—but then I realized that Emi and the rest were still waiting for me on the other side of the falls. Grumbling, I slid back down into the pool behind the waterfall.

Once I got close to the falling torrent, I saw a shape through the greenish-white curtain of water and heard a voice calling, though I couldn't make out what it was saying. I realized that it was Emi, calling my name. "Here, Emi!" I shouted. "I'm in the space behind the cascade!"

After a moment, the shadow grew—Emi approached the waterfall and stepped through. Her face looked bloodless, her eyes wide. Her mouth shaped my name. "Murasaki."

"Emi!" I panted. "I found—"

But before I could say what I had found, Emi punched me in the stomach.

16—Out of the Woods

bent over, feeling the morning's eggs threatening to explode all over Emi's sodden shoes. Blind and shocked, I shoved Emi away with me and yelled, "*Why did you* do *that?*"

Emi slipped on the slick slope and slid into the water behind the falls. Her face red and wet, she shouted something back at me.

On guard, I walked closer and shouted over the roar of the cascade, "*What?*"

"*I thought you were dead!*"

"*What?*"

"*You went into the water and you didn't come out!*" she screamed into my ear. "*I thought you were dead!*"

Oh. "*I'm not!*"

She punched me again—in the shoulder this time and not as hard. Then she pointed back out to the edge of the waterfall.

We made our way back through the flood. I handed the five arrows to Emi, who once again wasn't looking at me, then picked up my jacket and sash and put them on, becoming soaked through almost immediately.

I held the sword in its scabbard.

"Sorry, Murasaki," mumbled Emi.

"I'm sorry." I tried to shoot her a smile.

Emi, however, was scowling across the pool at Toumi, who was facing in the opposite direction, an arrow nocked and her bow drawn. Aimaru stood behind her. Both were staring into the woods. "What are they looking at?" she mused.

"I don't know." I looked up into the trees myself, but I couldn't see anything. "Come on, let's go see what's happening."

Water streamed from our clothes as we made our way back to the others.

"So where were you?"

"There was an opening at the very top—"

"Sure, I saw you sliding down from there."

"Well, did you see the little monkeys?" When Emi nodded, I said, "One of them slipped down into a gap at the top. I couldn't see the monkey down there at all. I couldn't tell, but it felt as if the gap went a good ways into the hill."

"Oh." Emi leaned down and picked up her bow and deposited three arrows in the quiver. The other she nocked as she walked up to Toumi. "What is it?"

Aimaru whispered, "I saw someone out there."

"Probably a deer," Toumi grumbled.

"No, it was a man."

"Could it be Jolalo again?" I began scanning the woods where they were looking.

"Don't think so. Jolalo was wearing black. This one's wearing blue."

"One of the cooks, maybe?" Emi said.

"Maybe," Aimaru admitted, his focus sharp as I hadn't seen it since the attack on the Mt. Fuji Inn.

A flash of blue. In a cedar some way up the hill. A brighter blue than the color we wore—or Kee Sun. And a face. At first I thought it might be a snow monkey, droop cheeked and sad, but the face was pale, not red, with a scraggly beard and surrounded by black hair. "Aimaru. Do you see someone in the closest cedar?"

"Cedar?"

"Big, fluffy tree, darker green than the others?"

"Oh." He sniffed, tilting his head. "Yes. That's him."

Emi whispered, "Where?"

But Toumi didn't wait; she loosed her arrow straight at the figure in the tree.

His eyes widened and he disappeared behind the trunk of the cedar. The arrow whistled through the space where his face had been.

"Toumi!" I gasped. "It could be a hermit! Or a farmer from the valley!"

She loosed another arrow on the other side of the tree. "Or a spy or a murderer or a nasty old man who likes watching girls at the hot springs!" She grabbed another arrow from Emi's quiver, but Emi took hold of her wrist before she could draw it. "I think he's gone. We should go look."

And so the four of us walked toward the trees. With my sword in my hands, I approached the place where we'd seen the figure. He may have been a mountain holy man, but Toumi was right— he could also have been someone much more dangerous.

Bows drawn, Toumi and Emi scanned the woods above us for any sign of movement. Aimaru kept looking up the hill, sniffing like a bear seeking honey.

A soft breeze picked up, carrying away the rotted scent of the spring and bringing the rich scent of the forest above us. It was wonderful to be under tall trees again. It had been months—the previous autumn—since I had had pines and cedar swaying overhead, blue sky peeking through between the tops. I wanted more than anything to drop the sword and scabbard and scamper up into the beckoning boughs.

I didn't, though. Because there was a man somewhere in the woods. And because Toumi might have been right.

She and I had been grabbed by men in the woods once before. I had no desire for it to happen again. Ever.

When we reached the cedar, there were signs that the man had dropped out of the tree and run uphill into the woods. Broken underbrush showed that he was nowhere nearby.

"There's your arrow, Toumi," Aimaru said, and shuffled to where the bolt had planted itself in the mulch-covered ground.

"Do you see any sign of the man?" Emi asked.

I pointed at the snapped bushes up the hill. "I think he's long gone."

"Che," Toumi grumbled.

"Maybe he was a farmer after all. Good thing you didn't hit him." I wasn't surprised when Toumi glared at me, but I didn't flinch. She had glared at me a lot, and I knew that she was sure to do so again.

Emi stepped between us. "Murasaki, why don't you take a look up in the tree—see if you can find out who he was."

I didn't need to hear more than that. I sheathed the sword and tucked the scabbard at my back, then scrambled my way up the cedar's rough bark into the lowest branches. I could see scars in the bark that showed he had climbed farther. Shimmying up one more level, I reached the spot from which he had watched us.

I had a clear view of the bottom end of the pool steaming below me. I could see the scuffed gravel where Toumi and Aimaru had been. A pair of monkeys had wandered out of the water and were poking in the gravel, perhaps looking for dropped food.

Food. I could smell a familiar, spicy scent. Sniffing, I looked around until I saw a grimy cloth caught between two twigs. I grabbed it and held it to my nose. The scent of clove oil.

I dropped down through the branches and out of the tree as quickly as I could.

All three of them stared at me.

"What's wrong, Murasaki?" Emi asked. "Are you all right?"

"We need to get out of here," I gasped, holding up the cloth. "He's not a farmer. He's a soldier."

"*Che,*" spat Toumi—but she ran with us out of the woods.

Aimaru stayed at the back of our pack, glancing over his shoulder the whole way down to the Full Moon.

———

"So let me get this straight," grumbled Toumi as we returned down the path by the stream. "You know he's a soldier 'cause you found a stupid cloth that smells like the stuff Kee Sun uses for *toothaches?*"

"Yes," I sighed. "Oil of cloves. We use it to clean swords, to keep them from rusting."

Toumi gave a dismissive snort. "I still say we could have taken him. Whoever he was, he was clearly scared of us, the way the *baka* ran away."

"Or he just didn't want to be found," Emi said. "I wonder if it was Kobayashi."

I nodded. "That's what I was thinking."

Aimaru piped up for the first time since we had left the spring, "I didn't recognize the face, but he could have been one of the Matsudaira soldiers."

"Right," I said. "I forgot you traveled with them. All of the way from Three Rivers?"

He nodded.

"So should we tell Lord Matsudaira?" I asked.

"Lord Takeda," said Toumi.

Emi grunted, still holding her bow in one hand and an arrow in the other, ready to draw and shoot if the strange man were to jump out of the trees. "I think we should probably tell Lady Chiyome and let her decide."

We all agreed that that was probably the best idea. Even Toumi.

———

While we walked, I shared what Lady Chiyome and Masugu-*san* had told me about how Lord Oda had ordered our fathers to attack a group of Lord Imagawa's children—as well as two young hostages: Lord Takeda's nephew Masugu, and Lord Matsudaira's nephew Tokimatsu.

Aimaru gave a whistle of surprise.

Emi frowned, but nodded.

Toumi stared at me. *"Kids?"* She spat on the path. "He wanted our fathers to kill a bunch of *kids?*"

"Yes." I shivered, remembering Fuyudori's crazed laughter as the snow fell around us. "The girl who tried to kill us all—she said so too."

"Why would Oda-*sama* want them to do that?" wondered Emi.

When I had no answer, Toumi just spat again. "Bastard."

We made our way silently back to the Full Moon's rear gate.

———

We knelt in front of our mistress in her apartment above the main hall. "So, what were you doing up on Ogre Mountain?"

"Ogre Mountain?" I asked.

The old woman arched an eyebrow at me. "Yes, girl. Ogre Mountain." She pointed through the wall toward where the cliff loomed over the Full Moon. "You know, the one you were climbing up the hard way the other day."

"Oh. I . . . " I looked at Emi, whose eyes were wide.

Emi finished for me. "We brought Murasaki up to the hot springs so that she could cleanse Masugu-*san's* sword."

I gasped. "I know why it's called Ogre Mountain!"

Now both of Lady Chiyome's eyebrows were up. "What?"

"When I climbed up the cliff, there was a cave. And I saw . . . an ogre. Or a dead ogre, at least."

For one of the first times since I had met her, Chiyome-*sama* stared at me, speechless. Then she closed her mouth, gave her grey head a quick shake. "Hmph. The stories I was told said that the path to the *oni's* lair was behind the waterfall, not up the cliff."

Excited, I began to tell her about going behind the falls, about how I'd seen the monkey disappear down the crease up at the back.

But she stopped me with a raised hand. "I see. In any case, Risuko, that explains why you're still wet. So what were the rest of you doing while she was playing mole?"

"Picking our teeth," Toumi said with a grimace.

"I was watching the woods," said Aimaru. "I had a feeling someone was up there."

Emi mumbled, "I was watching Murasaki. And the monkeys. They were . . . funny."

"Oh, yes, very funny," Chiyome-*sama* said with a smirk, "until they steal something from you."

"That's how I found the crease," I said. "In the space behind the waterfall. Toumi had fired some arrows—"

"Target practice," she muttered.

"—and there were some baby monkeys back behind the falls, playing with the arrows. I got most of them back, but when I tried to grab the last one, the monkey got angry at me and ran down this chute up at the top. I wonder if it leads to the cave where the ogre is."

"Ogre." Toumi rolled her eyes.

Lady Chiyome tapped a finger on her writing desk. "You'll have to show us this ogre, Risuko."

I was both frightened and excited by the thought. "Yes, my lady. Um. It might be a bit difficult for you to get up and down the chute."

"I might surprise you." The old woman's eyes glittered. "In any case, Toumi, I take it you saw the intruder. While you were picking your teeth."

"Uh, yeah. Yes. My lady."

"He was up in a tree," Aimaru added, shrugging. "Watching us."

"Was he?"

"Yes, my lady," he said.

Toumi huffed. "Wasn't much else to look at up there."

Lady Chiyome shot her an irritated glare. "I have always found it quite scenic up at the hot springs, girl. What about you, Emi—did you see him?"

"No, my lady," mumbled Emi. "Murasaki had disappeared behind the water for a long time. I went to make sure that she was all right."

"I see. So, Toumi, Aimaru. What did this intruder look like?"

"A man," said Toumi. "Scraggly beard, maybe."

"Yes," Aimaru agreed. "A beard. I think a scar over one brow. And he was wearing a blue jacket and pants."

"You mean like Kee Sun's?"

"Lighter," I said.

"So you saw him too, Risuko?"

"Yes, my lady. For just a moment. Before . . . " I glanced at Toumi. "Before he ducked behind the tree he was in."

"I see." The old woman smiled at Toumi. "Got a shot off at him, did you?"

Toumi looked down. "Would have hit him between the eyes if he hadn't ducked."

"No doubt." Lady Chiyome gave a tart laugh. "Did any of you recognize him?"

We all shook our heads.

"I found this, though." I handed her the cloth.

She sniffed it. "Ah. Clove. Sword oil."

Emi interjected, "When Murasaki told us it was a soldier, we came back here."

"So four of my servants—trained servants of the Full Moon—ran away from one soldier?" Lady Chiyome poured herself a cup of tea.

Aimaru winced.

"Well," murmured Emi, "we weren't sure it was just the one."

Which was true, though I hadn't considered it.

"Fair enough," the old woman said with a smirk, and sipped from her tea-cup. "Had you considered the possibility that it might be Lord Matsudaira's missing guard, Kobayashi?"

We all nodded.

"Hmm. And you felt it was best to bring this to me first. Good. I shall bring this to Lord Takeda's attention. Now, it is almost time for the midday meal. You children might want to get changed so that you don't serve the meal looking like a raiding party."

I looked at the other girls. Toumi and Emi both still had their bows and I my sword. We were all covered in dust, but Emi and I were particularly dirty, still wet from the sulfurous spring. The front of my jacket was brown with cedar bark. "Yes, my lady."

17 — Pretty

The midday meal was quiet. It felt like after an earthquake has hit and all you can do is wonder when the next one is coming.

During the meal, Captain Tokimatsu was looking only at Mieko, an expression on his face like a cat's that's trying to decide whether the raven in the tree is something he should hunt—or whether it might be hunting him.

Next to him, the Matsudaira samurai who had fought with Torimasa-*san* the previous day, Lieutenant Sakai, was covertly scanning the room as he slurped his noodles.

When I pointed that out to Toumi, Shino's flat face warped. Teapot in hand, she marched over to the lieutenant. "She's not here."

Lieutenant Sakai blinked up at her. "I beg your pardon?"

"Mai has been confined to quarters." Remembering who she was talking to, she softened her posture. "As it pleases our lords."

Bewildered, the samurai shrugged. "Of course."

Tokimatsu-*san* shot him a smirk—the first smile I'd seen in the hall that whole meal.

As we were clearing the tables, the orange-robed monk glided into the hall and back toward the kitchen. Uncertain what to do, we just shared confused looks until Torai, the Takeda cook, intercepted the holy man, his flat voice calm. "No, no, Excellency, not in here! Let me show you—" And he led the monk back out toward the hall's front door.

"What do you think that was about?" asked Emi.

"I don't care!" snarled Shino, and that was the last we spoke of it.

———

After the kitchen was cleaned, we all trooped back into the Great Hall. Hoshi-*sensei* informed us that all of the women of the Full Moon would be having a lesson together.

Not Mai. She was still in the Retreat. I assumed she'd been ordered to stay there, but we didn't know.

Not that we didn't talk about it.

When we joined the older women, I saw that there was one man there— or rather one boy: Aimaru, dressed in heavy padding, with a helmet we used to practice sword fighting.

"Hey, Aimaru," Emi whispered.

He answered back, though we couldn't hear him through the padded helmet and the mask.

Sachi-*san,* the music teacher, clapped her hands together rhythmically, quieting us all. "So it's clearly time for us to remind you how to deal with unfriendly advances."

The women—and us girls—all groaned. "We know how to defend our-selves, Sachi-*san,*" complained one of the *kunoichi.*

Hoshi spoke up. "Still, it's always good to refresh our memories."

Mieko appeared in the midst of the group, her voice low as always yet car-rying. "As with many arts, it is important to approach it anew with a novice's eyes. To be ready, we must be prepared. To be prepared, we must practice. Danger strikes when we least expect it."

And, as usual, Mieko quieted all objections.

"So," said Sachi, sashaying up to Aimaru, "who can tell me the three best ways to escape an armed man?"

———

But in the courtyard, we helped Aimaru remove the last of his padded armor. "Are you sure you're all right?" Emi asked, looking concerned.

"Fine," he croaked, having taken dozens of punches, chops, and elbows to his shielded throat.

"You might want to have Kee Sun take a look—" she added, but he cut her off, unusually gruff.

"Fine," he repeated, stumbling back into the hall, shedding the padded armor.

Emi pouted after him.

"He'll be fine." I was trying to reassure myself as much as her.

Toumi snorted. "Seeing as Frowny-face here got some of the best shots in, I'm sure he'll be walking and talking funny for a while."

Emi frowned and looked as if she were about to say something. Before she could, we saw Captain Baba and Chiyome-*sama* coming our way.

The captain nodded in our direction and muttered something to Lady Chiyome. She nodded back, though her expression looked anything but agreeable. Baba-*san* stroked his bristly beard and mustache and strode away.

"Well, girls, lucky you—you've got an assignment."

Toumi's eyebrows shot up; she looked happy for the first time in days. "An assignment?"

"Oh, yes." Lady Chiyome chortled. "Thrilling. We're hosting a double funeral tomorrow. Captain Baba wanted me to get some of the girls to gather up the dead men's effects, get their finest clothes."

Toumi's manic grin turned to a positively Emi-like frown.

Aimaru emerged from the hall, rubbing his neck.

Chiyome-*sama* gestured him toward us, and then, leaning forward, she whispered, "And if you should happen to find anything—if there should happen to be a love letter from Mai in the lieutenant's tent, or if the guard should happen to have a bag full of gold coins marked with the Matsudaira crest . . . Well, I expect you to keep your eyes open—and your mouths shut. Report to no one but me. Do you understand?"

"Yes, Chiyome-*sama.*"

———

Someone had lit incense in the tent that Sato, the Takeda guard, had shared with three others. The scent brought me back to the previous winter, with Mieko burning pellets of *mogusa* against drugged Masugu-*san*'s feet.

The tent was small but neat. It reminded me a bit of our dormitory.

Two soldiers stared glumly from the opening, Aimaru standing between them. It suddenly struck me that our friend was, in fact, taller than either of the Takeda warriors.

As Emi and I looked through the late soldier's pack for a clean kimono, Toumi looked through his weapons and then poked a toe into the *tatami* on which Sato's bedroll lay rolled.

"So little," I whispered as we pulled out a brown robe, which was made of silk but looked to have been mended many times. From the sleeve slid a small amulet woven from straw, just like the ones that Usako and I had made for our parents. "Did . . . Did he have any children?" I asked the soldiers by the entrance.

They both grimaced, but then one nodded.

"Please," I found myself saying, "sirs, please make sure that the dead one's family learn how he died. Please."

They both flinched back, their eyes wide. "*Aiiiii . . .* "

Emi rested a hand on my shoulder. "Please, sirs. We are all orphans. We understand what it's like. We understand that they are better off knowing."

Not startled now but still looking deeply uncomfortable, they both nodded.

As we put the robe and the amulet into a basket, one of the guards shot us a grim smile. "So is it true you girls're all training to fight? I mean—"

Aimaru nodded at me. With a lazy smile, he said, "Risuko there climbed to the top of the big tree in the compound in the middle of a snow storm last winter to defeat an assassin." Then he flicked his chin at Toumi. "I saw her hit a bullseye with an arrow at over a hundred paces. And Emi could rip your throat out with her bare hands."

Emi and I both blushed, hiding our faces. Toumi, of course, looked pleased.

The soldiers laughed, but it wasn't scornful. "Never thought I'd serve with a fellow soldier looked smaller than my little sister," one said, but they bowed to us.

We bowed back and left the tent.

"You can't say things like that, Aimaru!" muttered Emi.

He grinned again and shrugged. "It's all true."

"Sort of!" I groaned.

"Mouse-girl, the assassin's assassin!" said Toumi, chuckling even harder when I shot her an annoyed look. "Come on. Let's go turn over the lieutenant's quarters."

———

Torimasa-*san*'s tent was the same size as the one we had just searched, but he had had it to himself.

It was a pigsty.

When the guard waved us in, we saw clothes strewn across the floor, scrolls scattered across his traveling desk and onto the *tatami*, and four bottles that looked suspiciously like the poppy-laced *sake* they'd found in Kobayashi's tent.

The tent stank of sweat and rice wine. It wasn't a pleasant scent, as Toumi made sure to point out.

I sighed. "The faster we find some clean clothes, the faster we can get out of here."

We all began to look around the floor for a pack or chest, but everything seemed to be topsy-turvy. "Do you think someone's searched here?" I wondered.

"No," said Aimaru. "He was just a slob. Someone searching wouldn't have made this much of a mess, would they? Stuff would have been pulled out and dropped where the searcher found it, not flung ankle deep all over the tent."

All of us considered that, looked around the room, and nodded. When he put it that way, it was sort of self-evident.

I peered under the traveling desk. "Here's a clean kimono." It was white, folded neatly (most likely by someone other than the lieutenant), and laid atop a pair of matching trousers. I pulled them out. "I think this was his funeral outfit."

"Well," Toumi snorted, "looks like he'll get to wear it to his own."

There were three torn pieces of paper on top of the robes. Turning my head, I squinted at one. *T owes H 7 monme.* The next one read *T owes T 12 monme.* The last read *T owes T 3 koshukin, 5 monme.*

Looking over my shoulder, Toumi whistled. "That's a lot of silver and gold for a dead man to owe!"

"I guess," observed Aimaru, "it would be awfully hard to collect from a dead man. Maybe he did commit suicide?"

"No," said Emi, mouth bowing down even more than usual, "Murasaki was right. He was dead when he was stabbed."

I turned my head, looking at the notes, then turned it again, trying to peer as if through a reflection in a pond's surface to see the depths beneath. "So . . . what are these?"

The others all blinked at me.

"It's an IOU," said Aimaru.

"An . . . "

Emi pointed at the unevenly torn edges of one of the notes. "See that? The two parties tear a piece of paper in half, then write the debt on both halves. If the edges match and the numbers match, then it's a binding debt."

"Huh." I looked down at the three notes—promissory notes. Then at the debris scattered around the room. "And these are just the ones that were easy to find. Bet he had more."

Now that we had something specific to look for, we sifted quickly through the late lieutenant's belongings, discovering a draft of a letter to his father asking (not surprisingly) for money, an embarrassing sketch of a woman with nothing but a fan to hide her honor, and a few more notes like the ones we'd found. In each case, the debtor's initial was 𝒯—and in most, the lender's name began with the same letter. I pointed this out.

"Do you think that the lieutenant could have been the lender for some of these?" asked Emi. "Perhaps he was killed by the person who owed him money?"

I considered this. It made a kind of sense, but . . . "Has there been any money in all this mess?"

The others all shook their heads—and then we all looked methodically (or as methodically as we could in all of the chaos) for any coins. Through pouches, bags, and boxes, in jars and even in dirty socks we searched. Not a single silver *monme* or gold *koshukin* was squirreled away. We did find a few scattered brass coins—I had to keep Toumi from pocketing them—but nothing like the amounts named in the notes.

"So," Emi mused, "the lieutenant owed a lot of money."

"To at least one person whose name begins with 𝒯." When Aimaru frowned at the notes in Emi's hand, I pointed at the *hiragana* と, and he nodded, his ears coloring. To Toumi and Emi I said, "Can you think of anyone whose name begins that way?"

Emi shrugged. "Well, Torimasa-*san* himself, of course."

"But he can't have been the lender," I reminded her.

"No." She pouted.

Toumi clicked her tongue. "The Matsudaira captain? What's his name?"

"Tokimatsu," Aimaru said.

"Yes," agreed Emi, now chewing on her lip, "though he and the lieutenant would have only just met." Then she turned to Toumi with what was, for her, a wicked smirk. "And, of course, there's you."

Toumi glared at Emi and threw the piece of paper with the draft letter on it at her. I knew that if she'd seriously been angry, Toumi would have thrown something a lot harder than a piece of paper.

Emi laughed and started to crumple the letter to throw it away. But on the back . . .

"Wait," I said, and held out my hand.

Toumi barked a derisive laugh. "Want to read about the brave lieutenant boldly begging Daddy for coin?"

I shook my head and unrolled the paper, turning it over. "Look."

In a sloppy hand that looked to match that on the draft letter, someone—Torimasa-*san* most likely—had written two long columns: one of barely legible words, the other of numbers. And the numbers were added up at the bottom.

"Aimaru," I whispered, "what was the big number at the bottom of the list you found in the storeroom?"

Emi and Toumi both blinked at me, but he answered, once more without a pause, "83,482."

I pointed to that very number at the bottom of the scrawled column of figures. Emi and Toumi's eyebrows shot up. Aimaru's contracted.

"I think," I said, "we need to bring this to Lady Chiyome. I think we need to show it to her right away."

18—Connivers

"So," I said to our mistress, who was peering at the pieces of paper we had brought her, "we think that the late lieutenant must have copied down the numbers to give to someone—maybe to the person he owed all of the money to, my lady."

We were kneeling in front of the writing table in her chamber—the map was still there, the colored stones and pins arrayed across the islands of Japan. Lady Chiyome had one of the smaller red stones in her fingers.

Red for the Takeda, I remembered. Blue for the Matsudaira. White for the Oda. Yellow for the Uesugi and orange for the Hōjō . . .

Chiyome-*sama* breathed out a sound between a sigh and a growl. "I see." Her nostrils flared as if she smelled something foul, and she held up the red stone. "You see this?"

We all nodded.

She placed the stone on the map, on top of where the Full Moon was marked by a small white circle. Then she picked up a blue stone. "Each of these represents the troops commanded by a general or a captain. Part of what I'm training you girls to do is to find the locations and approximate strengths of each of these forces." She placed the blue stone—Matsudaira—next to the one painted Takeda red. "Big stones are armies of a thousand or more. Small stones like these, just a few hundred men. Now, my *kunoichi* are very, very good at discovering whose troops are where. And some are even wizards, like this one apparently is"—she flicked a backhand gesture at Aimaru—"at estimating how large those forces are."

Still looking down, she lifted the paper. "But a complete, accurate tally like *this* . . ." She glanced up at Aimaru. "Captain Baba tells me that the number you remembered, my large monkey, is the precise count of the number of troops that Takeda-*sama* has in the field at this very moment. Such information, which would take my girls months to discover, would be worth far more to our enemies than a few paltry pieces of gold and silver." And now she held up the IOUs. She muttered, "Ruffian," and tossed the slips of paper down again as if they dirtied her fingers.

I looked at the blue stone and the red resting on the Full Moon. "Forgive your humble servant, my lady, but are the Matsudaira our enemies? I thought they were our allies."

"Allies? Hmm." Lady Chiyome's face took on the coy smile that always reminded me of a cat about to pounce. She grinned at the girls on either side of me. "Emi, Toumi, what do you think? Are the Matsudaira our allies or our enemies?"

Toumi stared down at the map and shrugged. "Don't trust 'em."

Emi blew out a stream of air that fluttered her bangs. "I think we would like them to be our allies. Their allegiance would help Lord Takeda counter Lord Oda."

When that name made all three of us tense, Lady Chiyome grunted, "Lord Oda. Yes." Then the cat smile returned. "And you, Aimaru?"

The boy's broad face seemed to turn in on itself. "Well. The Matsudaira soldiers all seemed to think their lord was wonderful. But I know the Takeda think the Mountain is too. So I don't know."

Lady Chiyome's smile showed more teeth, and she spread her hands, gesturing at the jumble of factions scattered across the map. "Precisely. One doesn't know. Today's allies may be tomorrow's enemies and vice versa. One cannot simply trust—as what you have found shows us. Even our own cannot be completely trusted without question. The ruffian lieutenant was clearly selling Lord Takeda's secrets—but to whom?" When none of us seemed to have an answer, she continued, "I want you four to keep your eyes open. I will tell Takeda-*sama* we are continuing our . . . investigations. I won't tell him about this, however. It may implicate another Takeda traitor, and I do not wish to approach our lord with anything less than proof." She looked back down at the battle map, waving her hand at us. "Go. And if you can find any evidence of the dead man's co-conniver, tell me at once."

———

As we left the Great Hall, looking to give the dead men's clothes to the monk, who would lay the bodies out on the pyres, Aimaru asked, "What's a co . . . co-con . . . "

"Conniver," I muttered. "Conspirator. Fellow criminal."

"Oh."

We walked out through the gate, and a thought occurred to me. "If the other conspirator, the person he owed money to, was a, you know, *Takeda*"—I mouthed the last so that the guards couldn't hear what we were talking about—"why would he have had to sneak into the Full Moon last night?"

Toumi rolled her eyes. "Silly Mouse. It's because . . . " Then she frowned, looking down at the lieutenant's clothes, which she was carrying. "I don't know. Good question."

"Hmm," agreed Emi. "Yes, it is. If he was trying to get the paper to a fellow soldier, he could just have brought it to the other man's tent. Or given it to him."

"But they wouldn't have wanted to be caught with the list, would they?" I asked.

Aimaru grunted, "That's why they used a dead drop."

"A . . . dead drop?" I gawped at him, as did Emi and Toumi.

He nodded. "Sure. When you want to get a thing to someone—like that piece of paper, or something, um, stolen—and you don't want anyone to know what's going on or who's doing it, you use a dead drop. The first person leaves the package in a place no one's going to look. Like a lantern in an old shrine. Or a knot in a tree."

Emi nodded. "Or a shelf at the back of a storeroom."

Aimaru nodded back. "Yup. The second person maybe knows when the drop's supposed to happen, so they check there sometime later—and if the package isn't there yet, they just check back again the next day."

"And that way," I mused, "no one will know what's happening or who's involved—maybe not even the two people doing the exchange?"

"Yup."

Toumi reached up and ruffled Aimaru's hair. "Why, you little conniver."

He scowled as we walked past the last row of tents and into the meadow at the tip of the ridge overlooking the valley, his shoulders bunching. Emi laughed.

There two men were setting up stacked piles of wood—pyres, I realized, to burn the two dead men's bodies. In front of the pyres, Torai-*san*, the Takeda cook, was talking with the Buddhist monk. When he saw us coming, he waved his hands and shouted in his flat voice, "No! We don't have any wine to spare!"

"But *sake* is important for the rituals," the monk wheedled.

His workers both stared at us as we approached, each holding a log in what looked like an overly casual manner.

"I've told you no," growled Torai-*san*. "Now stop asking." Then he stomped back toward the front gate.

The monk held up his hands apologetically. "The rice wine is terribly important," he said. "Now, lovely ladies, sir, how can I help you?"

I handed over Sato-*san*'s clothes while Toumi all but tossed Torimasa-*san*'s at the monk, who stood there in his orange robes, beaming at us. "Bless you, my children," he said, and we left.

As we wandered back toward the kitchen—it was time for us to be helping with the evening meal—Emi whispered, "Aimaru, did something seem strange about that monk?"

Toumi gave a snort. "He likes his wine, that's for sure."

Aimaru, however, was staring forward as we walked, his eyes moving back and forth as if he were reading. "I don't think he's from here."

"Not from here?" I asked.

"From the valley. I've visited the local shrines with the Little Brothers, and I don't remember seeing him. Or the two men working for him, now that I think of it." He chewed on his lower lip.

"Come on," I sighed, "before we can solve any more mysteries, we've got an army to feed."

As we approached the gate, eight horsemen galloped up—the search party. As they dismounted, I heard young Captain Tokimatsu say, "No luck. Kobayashi's not in the valley."

No, I thought, *he's up in the hills*. And as we entered the Full Moon, I looked to the others, and I could see they were thinking the same thing.

———

Dinner was beef—butchered by the farmers, thankfully, and delivered while we had been up at the hot springs. The recipe was Kumo-*san*'s, a bland stew that made me think of Kee Sun's complaints that Japanese tastes ran to *sweet and brown*.

The Matsudaira and Takeda entered the Great Hall, once again silently. Where the silence had been uncertain at midday, this time there seemed to be an inaudible rumble of anger—the Takeda angry for the death of two of their own, it seemed, and the Matsudaira angry for being accused.

As we began to serve, Kee Sun pulled a bowl together with some rice, covered it, and handed it to me. "For Foxy-girlie," he murmured.

Mai. "Yes, Kee Sun-*san*."

"And bring her some wine, why don't yeh." He handed me a bottle exactly like the ones we'd found in Torimasa-*san*'s tent. He slipped a cup on top and waved me away. "Get."

I got.

The door to the Retreat was closed. I slid it carefully open and called in, "Mai-*senpai?*"

A snort came from the far, shadowed end of the small building: *"Senpai."* I saw her look up from a low table. "What do you want, Mouse?"

I held up the bowl and the bottle. "Your supper."

I could see her bite back the urge to snarl. She turned again to the length of paper she was drawing on. "Thank you." Politeness was never Mai's natural mood, but at least she tried.

I knelt next to the table and placed the food to the side. As I poured her wine, I happened to glance at the drawing she was working on. Hoshi and the other teachers trained all of us on our brushwork. Lady Chiyome felt that the ability to draw an attractive and accurate picture might come in handy in our *kunoichi* duties. However, I would say that none of us were what I would think of as artists.

I had seen Mai's calligraphy and one or two decorative flourishes, but I had never actually seen her attempts at drawing anything. What she was producing made my mouth fall open.

"What are you gawping at?" Mai grumbled around a mouthful of beef.

"Your drawings," I said. "They're beautiful."

She frowned and grunted.

On the strip of creased paper, she had been sketching a series of figures in motion. Each was suggested by a few simple lines of ink, but I could recognize who it was immediately: Shino. And while I had never thought of the other senior initiate as elegant, here, in Mai's sketches, she was. On the back of a used piece of much-folded paper, with just a few splashes and squiggles of ink, Mai had managed to bring Shino to life.

I turned my head. "Is it . . . It's the Sixty-four Changes, isn't it?" As soon as I said it, I knew that it was true—she'd drawn the first eight of the forms in the exercise that we did every morning and that I now did with a sword whenever I got the chance.

She looked down and snorted. "I guess." She placed her bowl over the paper, covering and smearing the drawings, and scowled up at me, daring me to . . . I'm not sure what. I think she was waiting for me to make fun of her or insult her.

While I did not like Mai, I didn't feel any urge to tease. "It really is lovely."

Now her scowl became Mai's more typical foxy grin. "Yeah, yeah. Sure. So. Anyone else died out there yet?"

"I hope not!" I realized that, in fact, I had been waiting for the next tree to fall. "Though one of the guards committed suicide."

She shrugged. "Yeah. I heard." She gulped down a mouthful of wine. "And they don't know who . . . who did it?"

I shook my head. "I don't think so. I mean, obviously someone knows, but I don't think Lady Chiyome or the lords do." I didn't tell her that we were helping to investigate—I knew Mai wouldn't like that.

She growled. "They'll probably blame it on me, anyway."

"I don't think so. They know you couldn't have done it—broken his neck like that. And even if they tried, Lady Chiyome wouldn't let you take the blame." When she rolled her eyes, I asked, "So . . . you really hadn't agreed to meet the lieutenant, had you?"

"That *baka*?" Her face twisted in scorn.

"And Sakai-*san*?"

Her eyes narrowed to slits, and she slurped some more *sake*. "I was just *flirting*, Mouse, like Sachi-*san* always does. It was fun. Well, at least until the two of them started fighting over me like a pair of *oni* over a goat leg."

"Hmm." I peered down again at what I could see of the beautiful drawings. Stains from the stew showed the ranks of writing from the other side, but Mai's sketches still brought the other senior initiate breathtakingly to life. "I don't think Shino liked watching you, though."

"Yeah." Mai's expression usually stayed in a tight range between cunning—conniving—and malicious, but she now looked almost regretful. "She gave me hell about that. It's what we were arguing about this morning when we . . . "

When they went outside and found Torimasa-*san*'s corpse on our doorstep.

When I saw that she had finished her meal, I took the bowl. I started to reach for the bottle of wine, but she stopped me. "Leave it."

I nodded, stood.

As I reached the door, Mai called out, "Hey. Tell Shino she's an annoying *busu*, and if she doesn't like it, she can come here, and I'll tell her to her face."

"Uh." I blinked, trying to imagine what Shino would do if I called her ugly. Really, their relationship was strange. "Good evening, Mai-*senpai*."

"*Senpai*," she growled again, but if she said anything else, I don't know—I was out the door.

———

When I got back to the Great Hall, the soldiers had almost finished their meal. Emi whispered that they'd all been drinking heavily, but it didn't look as if the *sake* had lightened their moods at all. The Takeda were glaring across at the Matsudaira, who were glaring right back. Even Captain

Tokimatsu, who always seemed ready for a joke, was frowning—though his eyes continued to flick across to where Mieko was seated, pretty but mournful, at the head table. Beside her, Chiyome-*sama* and the two lords also looked grim.

As we cleared the last of the bowls from the tables, but before anyone had a chance to stand, Matsudaira-*sama* raised a hand, and the hall fell into an even deeper silence.

"My lord governor of Worth has informed me that funeral rites will be held tomorrow morning for the fallen. This evening, the monk holds a wake, and since we recognize that it would be both difficult and disrespectful to the dead to hold further conference this evening, we both invite all of you to join us out where the pyres have been prepared to offer prayers in honor of the departed."

Both sets of soldiers bowed in acknowledgement, and the hall soon emptied.

The kitchen seemed to have been infected by the hall's foul mood. Even Kee Sun's humor was dampened, Kumo-*san* chewed on his lip, and Torai-*san* grumbled under his breath. Emi, Toumi, and I looked at each other and silently began cleaning up. Just as I was about to take the scraps out with Emi, Sachi-*san* came into the kitchen and pulled me aside.

"Risuko, Lady Chiyome wants some of us to play at the wake this evening. Suzume and Aoki"—two of the other older women—"are off having fun up in Estuary, so I need you initiates to help. Shino can play the *koto* and the bells, and I'll handle the flute. I'd have Mai on the *samisen*, but she's off—"

"In the Retreat." Dread weighted my stomach. "You . . . want me to play?"

Sachi tapped my nose with her finger and laughed. "Lucky girl." Seeing my expression, she laughed again. "You'll be fine, Risuko. I've heard you play. Your fingering's not quite as polished as Mai's— you and your little fingers— but your phrasing's better. It'll just be 'Cherry Blossoms' and a few other old favorites."

I looked over to Emi, who was peering questioningly at me, and Toumi, whose expression accused me of abandoning them. "Um, Sachi-*sensei*, do you need me right away?"

"I'm afraid so. We should be set up out there before the wake starts. I've already got Aimaru grabbing the instruments from the Tea House."

"*Hai,* Sachi-*sensei*." Turning once more to the others, I grimaced in apology. Emi shrugged, and Toumi, naturally, glared.

Taking that for an answer, Sachi led me gently by the elbow out of the kitchen and toward the gate.

9—The Departed

When we reached the place where the pyres were, Shino was already there, grumbling at Aimaru as she placed her *koto* on its low stand in the trampled grass. "You could have at least tried to carry the thing flat, *baka*."

"I'm sorry, Shino-*san*." It sounded as though Aimaru had been saying that for a while. He held up Sachi's long flute and my *samisen*. "But I had the other—"

"How I am I supposed to play without my picks?" Shino snarled.

"Calm down, Shino," said Sachi, who had begun cleaning out her flute. "You can tune with your fingers. Aimaru, there are finger picks in the top shelf of the cabinet right by the door in the Tea House. Would you be a dear and bring those to Shino here?"

"Yes, Sachi-*san*." Aimaru sprinted off.

"And if you see the ones you dropped, don't step on them!" Shino yelled after him.

Sachi snorted and then began playing a deceptively simple tune, "The Deer's Call," while Shino and I began to tune our instruments.

I struggled—it's difficult making the tiny adjustments to the pegs necessary to properly tune the strings of the long-necked *samisen* when your fingers are trembling and moist. It's even harder when you're sitting a dozen paces from two neatly stacked piles of wood, each the bed to a body covered in a white sheet. I may have seen death. But I have never been comfortable being near it.

And so I took a deep breath and listened to our teacher's playing for a moment.

It always astonished me that Sachi could turn a few puffs of air blown through the long hunk of bamboo into such achingly beautiful, seemingly effortless music. It reminded me, if I'm honest, of nothing so much as the feeling I get sometimes when I'm climbing, where I'm not making the climb happen but rather, the climb is lifting me, if that makes sense.

As she took a breath—the breath as much a part of the music as the notes— Sachi winked at me.

I smiled in response and went back to tuning. It wasn't exactly easy now but easier than it had been.

Next to me, Shino was muttering as she adjusted the bridges on her wide *koto*.

I remembered the rude greeting that Mai had passed along to her pal-let-mate. "Mai-*senpai* sends her regards."

Plucking at one of the strings while she tapped the bridge beneath it with a knuckle, Shino raised an eyebrow at me. "Sends her regards."

I blushed and glanced back down at my own strings. "Um. She also told me to tell you you're annoying and ugly."

I could hear Sachi cough into her flute.

Shino plucked three strings loudly; they now sounded in tune. When I glanced up at her, her eyes were narrowed and her cheeks red—but she was also smiling.

I didn't understand those two at all.

Aimaru jogged back with two sets of finger picks. "Found the ones that dropped by the storeroom as I was coming back."

"Fine." Shino rolled her eyes and held out a hand. "Let me have the ones that aren't all covered in dirt."

Aimaru handed them over with his habitual cheer, and Sachi-*san* had us play a few easy songs to warm up.

The sun had passed behind the mountains some time before, but the sky was only now beginning to show the flame of sunset. Aimaru took some wood left over from the pyres and created several bonfires to illuminate the wake once it was dark.

As we finished playing, the monk came up, wearing white robes. "How lovely you look," he said, smiling.

I bowed my head and did my best to smile back, though I couldn't help thinking it was a strange thing to say. Shino rolled her eyes, but Sachi, naturally, smiled, tilting her head to one side as she cleaned out her flute. "So, how are things up north in Estuary?"

The monk's smile thinned. "Up north?"

"Oh, I'm a Seashore girl myself. I know an Estuary accent when I hear one."

"Ah!" His grin relaxed once more. "I'm from Middlemanor, not Estuary itself, but yes, I am from Armory Province! You have a good ear, my dear."

"Well," said Sachi with a wink, "I am a musician!" She gave a sparkling grin and a giggle like a summer shower, and he laughed along before nodding to us. "Ladies."

"Your Reverence," we answered as he walked off.

Sachi's smile remained, but I could tell that she was thinking as she watched him approach the shrouded bodies. When I began to ask a question, she shook her head slightly. Then she said, "Let's run through 'Cherry Blossoms' again. Shino, keep the beat steady—and Risuko, follow her, not me." She fluttered the fingers of her free hand and intoned in a singsong voice, "I am the butterfly. Shino is the branch. You are the flower. Stick to the branch, or you'll tumble to the ground."

"Yes, Sachi-*sensei*."

She winked again and counted us in.

As we played, I worked to keep the beat, but I was watching the monk talking to the dead. He seemed most concerned with Lieutenant Torimasa.

A part of me, however, was thinking of the straw amulet that we had tucked back into the guard Sato's jacket. Thinking about the child who had given it to a father who would never return.

———

Lady Chiyome and the two lords led a solemn, sullen procession out to the field, while Sachi played "The Empty Sky" with Shino and me beating small, muffled drums beneath the haunting tune.

Each group of soldiers drifted toward the side of the ridge on which their camp stood—Matsudaira to the west and Takeda to the east. Lady Chiyome and the ladies of the Full Moon, dressed not in their fine kimonos but in their white and red *miko* garb, separated the two armies at one end while the monk and we musicians provided a buffer at the other end.

Aimaru and the Little Brothers lit the bonfires around us, making the falling night feel somehow darker.

As we played through the song for the third time, the lords and Lady Chiyome all knelt. Sachi gave us a nod, letting us know that it was time; we stopped together at the end of the refrain.

The silence thickened and held.

Then the monk stood and mumbled something—it sounded like a part of a sermon—and approached Lieutenant Torimasa's pyre. Carefully, he peeled back the shroud, revealing the Takeda officer's face, which still looked surprised, though his eyes were now closed. With a brush and a small bowl of water that had been placed on the pyre, the monk painted the dead man's lips with water—the last drink before the soul departed the body. Murmuring on, he took the water and the brush to the other pyre, leaving Torimasa's astonished face there for us all to see. He uncovered the guard Sato's face and repeated the lip-washing ritual.

Sato's face bore not surprise—he had known his death was coming. Instead, his expression was one of sorrow and, not surprisingly, pain.

From where I was seated, I could see that his head had been separated from his body. Though the monk and his assistants had done their best to clean the body, blood still stained the wood on which he was resting.

People like to say that the dead look like they are sleeping, as if they are resting after having put down the struggles of life. This is a lovely image.

I have never found it to be true, however. A dead body looks nothing like a sleeping one. In a sleeping body, there is always a spark of the soul, seeking and alert like some tiny mouse, sniffing, ears swiveling to detect pain or pleasure. It is subtle. I would not have been able to say that such a restlessness was present in someone sound asleep.

Yet once I had seen death, I knew. It is a stillness beyond stillness. It is a silence beyond silence.

Whatever it is that departs when we die, it takes everything that is essential to the person with it and leaves a husk.

That was the sermon that the monk was now reciting to the assembled nobles, soldiers, women, and girls. "I," he intoned, "am not my body, nor is my body me. I am that which shall be reborn, while the body returns to the earth from which it arose. The body is merely food. The spirit is eternal."

He looked to the two lords and to Lady Chiyome. "Wise and pious lords and ladies. The wisdom of the Buddha and of his servants teaches us that just causes lead to just actions, while evil intentions give birth to evil results. Just as an acorn can only grow to become an oak and an arrowroot seed can only grow to become a *kudzu* vine, so our thoughts give birth to our actions. Ill thoughts pile up so easily, even in men of virtue." He gestured to the two dead men before him. "We are all of us prone to evil thoughts. Let them go! For they lead only to evil ends. Think good. Do good. Your *gō*, your *karma*, your actions, will follow you from this life to the next. The unwise believe that all events result from present causes. But *karma* is the invisible cause that weighs down or lifts up your spirit from one life to the next."

As the sermon went on—all that he said was familiar—I gazed around at the crowd. Lord Matsudaira and his officers, including Lieutenant Sakai, sat solemnly, as did their soldiers around them and even Jolalo and the

Portuguese priest. On the opposite side, Lord Takeda and his captains were just as serious.

The faces of many of the Takeda soldiers, however, were twisted with some other spirit—restless and uncomfortable. Lieutenant Itagaki, who had been the dead soldier Sato's commander, was glaring in the direction of the Matsudaira officers.

Behind him in the shadows, a face appeared—it looked familiar, but I couldn't place it. I knew that Mieko would be disappointed in me since she was always training us to use our memories. It was a pale, sunken face with a thin beard . . .

As soon as I tried to look closer, however, the face disappeared among the gathering shadows.

As the monk's sermon meandered toward its conclusion, Sachi held up a finger, letting me and Shino know that we should be ready to begin playing once he stopped. I picked up my instrument, and Shino put her picks back on—she had been fidgeting with them for the whole of the monk's talk.

When he bowed, first to the two bodies and then to the assembled mourners, we struck up "Cherry Blossoms," slow and sad.

Takeda-*sama* stood and walked to the two shrouded bodies. He placed a length of twisted paper—a *shi-de*—onto a branch that bridged the two pyres. Baba-*san* and Hara-*san*, solemn as owls, repeated the ritual offering. Once they had stepped away, the other officers and soldiers on that side began to move forward.

Before the other Takeda soldiers could make their way up to pay their respects, however, Matsudaira-*sama* stood, straight as an ash tree, and strode to the pyres. He bowed and placed his own zigzag of rice paper on the branch. His captains, too, repeated the gesture of respect.

As they stepped away, Lady Chiyome invited the lords and their senior officers back to the compound for some refreshment—I assumed she meant rice wine.

We played on, the three of us, running back through the songs we had already played as both sets of soldiers began to come up and pay their respects, some offering a prayer, many leaving a paper offering.

The crowd was thinning and Mieko and the others approaching to make their own offerings when the Matsudaira lieutenant, Sakai-*san*, went up to add an offering. From our right, the remaining Takeda gave a growl, and Lieutenant Itagaki shouted, "No! Not you!"

Sakai looked up, eyes wide. "What? I didn't—"

"Don't you dare!" growled Itagaki, storming up with his hand on his sword.

I had gotten used to the soldiers going unarmed in the Full Moon. It came as a shock to realize that we were sitting between two heavily armed, unhappy groups of men.

The monk, who had been kneeling on the other side of Sachi-*sensei*, stumbled to stand, but Sachi found her feet with her usual grace. "Gentlemen!" she said, her voice high and birdlike. "I think this has been a trying day for you all." She touched Sakai-*san*'s elbow. "Perhaps my friend Hoshi and I"—she gestured to the tall *kunoichi*, who was striding up with the other women—"can bring you and our other guests from Three River Province back to their camp and entertain them."

Mieko walked in front of Itagaki, fluttering her fan (which I could see he recognized as a lethal weapon). "And Mitsuke, Rin"—the two *kunoichi* appeared at her shoulder—"please take our guests of Worth Province to their camp and help them forget the day's sorrows as well."

"Yes, Mieko-*san*." The two women bowed. Mitsuke might have been forgettable to look at, but she was an excellent dancer, as was Rin. Though Rin was also the teacher who had shown us how to use a garrote to strangle someone. A kind of dance, in a way.

As the soldiers were led back to their camps, Mieko turned to the monk. "Will Your Reverence need any further assistance, or may I take these young ladies back to their dormitory?"

The monk's broad face was covered with sweat—not that I could blame him. Even so, he managed to force a smile. "Of course, of course. I will stay here and watch the night, saying prayers for the safe passage of the dead."

"Of course," Mieko said, bowing. "Girls?" As we gathered our instruments—Shino complaining at having to carry the long *koto*—Mieko asked the monk if he needed us to send a guard. He assured us that there was no need, and we returned to the Full Moon, our arms heavy with musical instruments, our minds heavy with the events of the day.

20—Night Lightning

Once we had returned our instruments to the Tea House, I helped Toumi and Emi finish cleaning the bathhouse.

When Toumi complained that I'd been off "on another cushy job," I asked if she'd have rather been playing in front of all of the soldiers. She responded to that offer with all the pleasure of a kitten being lowered into one of the tubs.

We returned to our dormitory, and I wasn't surprised when Emi and Toumi both fell asleep as soon as they lay down. It had been a long, draining day—even longer and more draining than days at the Full Moon usually were.

Just like two nights before, however, I couldn't fall asleep. Images from the day kept flashing through my mind like reflections off a rippling pond: Torimasa-*san's* stunned expression, the serene view from the top of the *tori* arch, Emi's tears and Toumi's snarls as we'd talked for the first time about our fathers, the little monkey tossing the arrow into the crack behind the waterfall, and, strangely, Mai's lovely drawings of Shino dancing the Sixty-four Changes. That image kept floating across my mind's eye—the drawings but also the folded paper, the stains from Mai's meal showing the ranks of script on the back of the page.

Resigned to the fact that I wouldn't be able to fall asleep though I was weary to the bone, I slid back out of my bedroll and sneaked out of our room. I knew Mai was still in the Retreat, and though I couldn't hear Shino's usual snore when I listened at their door, I assumed I was alone as I stepped out into the moon-frosted kitchen courtyard.

I was not surprised, however, to see Mieko standing by Kee Sun's gong, holding both Masugu's short sword and one I had seen her practice with.

"I thought perhaps you might like another lesson," she said.

"Yes, please."

And so she once again led me through an exhilarating, exhausting session with that shard of frozen lightning in my hands. The Sixty-four Changes, yes—I could see the lines of Mai's drawings as Mieko and I mirrored the opening stances of the dance. Then she taught me a drill of what she called parry and riposte—that is, blocking the opponent's cut and counterattacking. The idea was to use the smallest, most efficient motion possible. She showed me how to tap the blade away with the back of my sword and then slice at her wrist with the tip. I could see that even a small cut from a sharp *wakizashi* could discourage any but the most frenzied attack.

"I . . . I don't want to hurt you," I said when she first asked me to practice the riposte—the return cut.

"No," she said, smiling warmly, "of course you don't. But I promise: you won't touch me. I've been doing this a bit longer than you have. And you need to get used to fighting with a real blade."

I didn't like that idea at all.

Seeing my uncertainty, she bowed her head. "However, I don't want you to be worried about me when you should be focussed on your sword." Reaching into the sleeve of her kimono, she withdrew a square of thick leather and a long leather tie. "Kuniko made this for me when I injured my wrist once."

As she secured the leather bracer around her wrist, I realized that it was the first time since the Mount Fuji Inn I had heard her use the dead woman's name.

We took up the swords and practiced the back-and-forth of the parry and riposte: she'd thrust her sword at me, I'd beat her point to the side—*tik*—and flick the tip of my blade at her wrist—*tak*.

At first, I couldn't get over the fear that I was going to cut Mieko even through the leather, but soon I saw that the only way to actually do any harm would be to miss terribly, and I was determined not to do that.

Soon we were running through the combination at speed: *tik-tak, tik-tak*. Without warning, Mieko added a parry of her own and a counterattack: *tik-tak-tok*. I leapt back in surprise, throwing my arms up—and leaving myself completely defenseless.

Her smile now was anything but kind as she touched the tip of her *wakizashi* to the middle of my chest. "A swordsman—or -woman—must anticipate surprise."

"How am I supposed to do that?"

"An excellent question," she answered. And then she started the attack once more.

I blocked and countered—but when she parried and riposted this time, I was ready with my own combination.

"Good!" she said, and continued. Back and forth we went, cutting and warding, until I was breathing hard and even Mieko's face was bright in the moonlight.

"I think we've earned some water, Risuko-*chan.*" Mieko led me over to the well and pulled up the bucket.

The water was cold and sweet, and I reveled in it as it cooled me from the inside out.

"May I ask you something, Mieko-*sensei?*" I said when we had both drunk our fill.

"Of course."

"Have you really killed that many people?"

She gazed down into the well, dabbing frigid water on her temples and either side of her throat. After a long silence, she said, "One hundred and forty-three. Yes."

"Does it . . . Does it ever get easier?" I was pretty sure I knew the answer but needed to hear it.

"No, Risuko-*chan.* It doesn't."

I nodded. She nodded. I held up my sword. "And . . . when a weapon has been . . . part of someone's death. Does it ever get easier to pick it up again?"

She gazed into my eyes. The moon was behind her, and so hers were shadowed, but I could still see their knife-sharp intent. "The weapons do not cause tragedy, Risuko. They do not wound or kill. It is we who do that. Masugu does not blame that blade for his grandmother's death. I believe that the purifying rituals we undertake are meant to rinse the stain not from our weapons but from our souls."

"Oh." Washing the *wakizashi* that morning hadn't cleansed the blade, since I'd already done that thoroughly. Yet it had helped me take up the sword again without discomfort. "Yes, that makes sense."

Mieko nodded and began to stand.

"Another question, if I may?"

"Go ahead, Risuko-*chan.*"

"The young Matsudaira captain—"

"Tokimatsu-*san.*"

"Yes. Why is he always staring at you?"

"Ah." She peered down into the well again, but whereas she had seemed to be cloaking herself in its shadows before, now she seemed to be enjoying seeking out memories in its depths. "One of the first missions I undertook for Chiyome-*sama* was to silence an Imagawa commander who was trying to convince his lord to break their alliance and attack while Takeda-*sama* was focussed on the Uesugi."

"Oh." Lady Chiyome had talked, looking at her map, about the dance of swirling colors, of alliances and betrayals. Another thought occurred to me. "Was Masugu-*san* a guest there then?" *A hostage, in fact.*

"Indeed," said Mieko, a small smile and faint color warming her moon-pale face. "It was when we first met. He helped me and . . . and Kuniko escape the castle." Now she looked up at me, her smile less warm but just as bright. "And Tokimatsu-*san* was a hostage there too. He is one of Masugu's oldest friends. I can see that he is trying to place where he met me before."

"And you don't want just to tell him, of course."

"Of course." Her smile showed her teeth. "Where would the fun be in that?"

We both laughed and stood. I felt as if I were finally ready to go to sleep. I handed Mieko-*sensei* my sword and began to thank her for the lesson.

But before the words had left my mouth, a growl erupted from behind the Great Hall, and both of us turned toward the sound. I suddenly regretted giving up the protection of Masugu's blade.

Shino burst out of the shadows. Her jacket was awry, the sleeve torn. She was holding something in her hand, and her flat face, never sunny, promised lightning and thunder. *"Baka ama!"*

Mieko stepped in front of me, both swords raised slightly, and Shino saw us. In an instant, her expression shifted to something that looked much more like shame, a look I'd never seen on her face before. She sprinted away from us, unlocking the back gate to the compound and running out into the night.

Mieko stared after her, an equally uncommon look of surprise on her face. Then she looked in the direction of the Retreat, at the opposite corner of the Full Moon, and back down at me. "Follow her, Risuko. I don't know what's happened, but Shino may be a danger to others tonight—or she may be in danger herself. Just keep an eye on her!" She ran toward the Retreat. "I must go check on Mai."

"Yes, Mieko-*san!*" I called to her, and sprinted out the gate and into the night.

———

had no sooner stepped out into the space between the back wall of the Full Moon and the cliff than I regretted not taking back the *wakizashi*. The half-moon was well above the trees to the east, but its light somehow made the night feel even darker. An owl called out—a greeting or a warning, I couldn't say.

I looked around for Shino but saw no sign. I didn't think she'd have been able to reach the woods to either side of the ridge so quickly, and I didn't think there was anywhere she could hide at the base of the cliff, so I assumed she must have gone in the direction of the camps. Unable to think of any good reason for Shino to do that, I turned the corner and began to sprint toward the front of the compound.

Ahead of me, one of the guards at the gate shouted, *"Halt!"* I had to assume it was to Shino. I hoped she would stop.

When I reached the front gate, however, the two guards from early that morning were back at their stations, both on guard with drawn swords.

I approached them loudly, not wanting to surprise them. "Yukishiro-*san!* Aosagi-*san!* Did a tall girl with a flat face just run this way?"

Even though I was as unthreatening a creature as they were likely to encounter at the Full Moon, and even though I had done my best not to alarm them, both guards turned toward me in battle stances.

I stopped some ten paces from them, my hands at my shoulders. I was standing in the tall grass near where I'd jumped from the wall that morning.

Aosagi, the Matsudaira sentry, peered at me. "Who goes there?"

"It's the girl who climbed the arch!" barked Yukishiro, and they both lowered their weapons.

When I repeated my question, Aosagi grumbled and Yukishiro gave a sour snort. "She just ran by and wouldn't stop. I can tell you, we're a bit jumpy after last night. She's lucky we can't leave our post."

"I bet," I said. "Where did she go?"

They both pointed down the road between the two camps toward the valley.

I thanked them and took off down the path, trying not to startle any guards that might be stationed in either of the camps. I had passed through the two tent compounds without incident when I finally caught sight of a figure that could only be Shino, kneeling by the two pyres.

As I began to step toward her, consumed with curiosity, I felt a hand close on my shoulder.

I had asked Mieko how I could possibly anticipate surprise. The answer, it turned out, was training and allowing my body to think for itself.

My elbow found a soft midsection—I was fortunate that whoever it was wasn't wearing armor. I felt an *oof!* on the back of my neck. Before my mind had even begun to react to the threat, my leg had stepped around and behind the attacker's and my arm swept them back over my shin, sending them off-balance onto their back, driving what little breath was left to them out of their lungs. I stepped around with the other foot, just as I had practiced against Aimaru that morning—and many other mornings—and raised my fist, ready to drive my knuckles into the attacker's unprotected throat.

Do no harm.

In my hesitation, I blinked.

The dark face goggling up at me, expression shocked as Torimasa's had been, was Jolalo-*san's*. He gasped, much like the salmon Usako and I used to toss out of the creek beneath the bridge by our village.

We had laughed at their gasping then. I didn't feel like laughing at all now.

"You can't just grab someone like that!" I said between clenched teeth. I forced my fist down to my side.

He croaked. "No. It. Is."

I wanted to go after Shino—she was still by the pyres, I could see—but I didn't feel I could leave Jolalo-*san* there. I knelt beside him.

After a few wet gasps, Jolalo was able to pant and then to breathe deeply. Eventually he sat up, holding his middle, and said, "Never . . . sneak up . . . on Risuko-*san*. Never, it is."

I couldn't help giving a surprised laugh. "That's probably a good idea. I'd appreciate that."

"*Hai.*" He tried to push himself up but fell onto his backside. "Oof."

"Are you all right?"

"Only . . . pride hurt . . . it is," he grunted, and shot me an embarrassed grin.

"You're lucky, then, Jolalo-*san*." I didn't say, *If it had been one of the older women instead of me, you would probably be dead.* "Why did you do that? You frightened me."

"Am sorry, it is." He tried once more to stand and this time managed to get upright. "Wanted just to talk to Risuko-*san*, it is."

"Why would you want to talk to me?" I couldn't imagine why anyone would want to do that.

"Where did you learn to use a sword, to—" He mimed the elbow strike that I had used on him just then. "From you father, it is?"

"Oh." I couldn't tell him the purpose of the Full Moon, obviously. And I didn't feel like discussing the fact that *Otō-san* was dead. "Some from my father, yes. And . . . from a lot of teachers."

He nodded, still rubbing his middle.

"You could have spoken to me at mealtime, Jolalo-*san*."

"Risuko-*san* was not—" He gasped again, bending over. "Was not at meal, it is."

"Oh. I am sorry, Jolalo-*san*. I had to play at the wake."

"I know, it is."

I was about to tell him that he didn't need to end every sentence with it is—that it didn't sound more polite, and that in fact it was a bit confusing—when Shino marched by, still disheveled, muttering, "'Watch the night.' Right. 'Saying prayers for the souls of the dead.' Sure. *Baka*." She gave a derisive snort and disappeared back into the camps in the direction the Full Moon.

At once I was worried for the monk—had she attacked him? "Pardon me, Jolalo-*san*," I said as calmly as I could. "I must go and . . . bring some ceremonial materials to the monk."

He nodded and looked as if he were going to ask if he could join me.

I strode away. "Good night, Jolalo-*san!*"

He waved a hand. "Good night, Risuko-*san*."

When I reached the pyres, the monk's white form was flat on the trampled grass, and I was terrified that Shino had in fact hurt him—but when I stepped closer, I could hear him snore. Looking him over quickly, I could see no sign of injury.

Relieved, I returned to the back gate of the Full Moon.

Inside, Mieko stood, once more calm.

I told her what I had seen—though I left out the incident with Jolalo.

She nodded, saying that she had gone to see Mai, who had been quite drunk, and who told Mieko that she and Shino had had some sort of *encounter*—I nodded, realizing that, of course, they must have gotten into a fight. That Mieko had made sure that Mai drank some water and went to sleep, and that as she had left the Retreat, she had seen Shino come in the rear gate and go back to our dormitories. So all was apparently well.

She walked me back to the initiates' dormitory.

Relieved that a day that had started with tragedy had ended with nothing worse than a comedy of errors, I wished Mieko a good night.

It had been a long, difficult day.

The next day would be even longer—but I fell asleep happily ignorant of that fact.

21—The Bear

When I went to the Retreat the next morning to bring Mai her breakfast of bean curd and rice—she was on the same *yin* diet as Toumi—she was still fast asleep, curled up in her bedroll like a piglet that's just been separated from its mother. Mai's thumb was in her mouth, and her expression was soft and at peace in a way I had never seen it.

Scattered next to her lay three empty wine bottles—clearly she had broken into the stores to get more after she'd finished the one I'd brought her. No wonder Mieko had said she was drunk. No wonder she was sleeping so soundly.

I knew Kee Sun would be furious, but I couldn't say that I blamed her.

I found myself thinking of Torai, the short Takeda cook, barking at the monk about not having any spare *sake*. Strange. We had barrels of it.

I left the bland food where Mai would find it when she woke, cleared away the empty bottles, and returned to the kitchen. There I found Lady Chiyome and Mieko standing with Emi. Mieko was holding a quiver of four long arrows—white shafts, white feathers for the fletching.

"Ah, my squirrel," said our mistress, "there you are. Captain Hara asked for these to be ritually purified for the funeral today. I would like you two to take these back up to the hot springs." She leaned forward. "And keep an eye out for that Matsudaira deserter, Kobayashi, yes?"

"Yes, Chiyome-*sama*," we said. Emi took the quiver, and we walked back along the path up the hill we had taken the day before.

When I asked what they needed the arrows for, Emi shrugged. "I suppose they're going to use them to light the pyres."

"Oh."

———

We were walking up the spoiled-egg stream toward the hot springs. The smell made me think of our conversation the day before—about our fathers. I thought Emi might be lost in the same memories since she looked thoughtful and perhaps a little sadder than usual (though it was, as always, hard to tell).

She glanced over, saw me looking at her, and gave a half-hearted shrug.

"What are you thinking about?" I asked.

"*Otō-san,*" she sighed. "Mine. Toumi's. Yours."

"Me too."

We walked on in silence for a bit before she added, "About funerals. Did . . . Did you even have a funeral for your father?"

"No."

"Oh. That must have been hard."

Now it was my turn to shrug. "I guess. We've never really been sure he's dead, though he must be. We just know he went into the castle . . . and never came back."

Now Emi's expression was truly sad. She put her arm across my shoulder. "That must be hard. Not knowing."

"It's been terrible for my mother. She still expects *Otō-san* to walk in the door, I think." I have so many memories of Mother weeping, staring out at the cherry tree in our courtyard. "Usako and I were sad, I guess. But we didn't understand."

Emi nodded. "I think the funeral helped that—helped me and my mother accept that he was gone. But it was scary too. The flames. The smell . . . " She shuddered. "I was so young, I didn't really understand everything that had happened either, any more than you and your sister. But I knew he was gone."

My arm found its way around her shoulder, and we walked in silence the rest of the walk up to the pool.

The monkeys watched glumly as Emi and I approached the waterfall. I once again removed my shoes and jacket and stepped into the warm pool. Once I had ritually cleansed myself, I turned to Emi and asked for the first arrow.

All white, as I had noticed, it was also unusual in that the steel head was hollow, almost like a tiny cage. When I raised an eyebrow, Emi called over the roar of the cataract, "To hold the flame."

"Oh." I began the purification blessing, dipping the tip of the arrow into the falling water to cleanse it.

"Is that a thanksgiving prayer?" Emi asked.

I handed the arrow back to her and nodded. "My father used to do this with his swords every New Year."

She pouted and dried the missile with a cloth that she'd brought, so at least my jacket would be dry this time. "I . . . " She handed me the next arrow. "I envy you those memories."

I nodded. There didn't seem to be anything else for me to say— I couldn't blame her for envying me. Continuing the prayer, I washed that arrow and then the third.

When she handed me the last, I found myself saying, "I know Toumi doesn't have any clear memory of her father other than his death. Do you?"

Tears jeweled Emi's eyelashes—or perhaps it was just the mist from the waterfall since her expression was no more downcast than usual. "Not really. My mother talked about him all of the time, and so I remember her stories, of course. And I can remember his face. He was always smiling." She gave me a sad almost-grin.

I returned it. "I bet." Still looking at her, thinking how hard it was for one person to have suffered so much loss, I began muttering the prayer again and pushed the arrow into the flood.

I anticipated the downward pressure of the water but was completely unprepared for something to yank the arrow *into* the waterfall.

"Wha—" I gasped. Then I realized that one of the monkeys behind the falls must have grabbed the arrow, and I saw red. Without thinking, I dove through the torrent into the space behind, growling as I came—though of course the sound of the falling water completely drowned me out.

There, its teeth bared in a threatening grin, one of the little monkeys— probably the same one I'd chased the day before—shook the stolen arrow at me.

A group of three or four others gazed from the churning pool, farther along on the other side.

"Little *baka!*" I yelled, and waded toward the creature.

As it had the last time we'd faced off, it clambered up toward the seam at the top of the sloped rock, clicking its teeth at me.

Think I can't climb, do you? I scrabbled my way up the wet stone. I used both hands to pull myself toward the armed monkey, which continued to grasp the arrow and growled at me.

I looked over my shoulder to make sure the others weren't going to attack from behind. They weren't; they were grooming each other.

I saw Emi push through the waterfall behind me and begin to make her way carefully up the rock slope.

The monkey with the arrow watched us warily as we crept up towards its refuge, clearly becoming nervous—I knew enough about wild animals to know that they're most dangerous when they're frightened, so I tried smiling and holding out my hand.

It didn't work. The little thing just howled at me, showing off teeth as sharp as a cat's.

My attempt at a peace offering having failed, I barked at it like old Naru's big black dog that used to make Usako cry all of the time.

Astonished, the monkey backed up, eyes wide, turned, threw the arrow into a crease of shadow where the ceiling met the stone wall, and fled down to the water and back to its friends.

I cursed, climbing the rest of the way up the wall, and felt in the crease.

It was wider than it looked, hidden in the shadows at the top of the wall. I couldn't feel the arrow—in fact, I couldn't feel anything back there but smooth stone. The space sloped downward as far as I could reach my hand.

Pushing myself up, I realized that the opening was in fact more than big enough for me to fit through. I peeked over the edge, seeing nothing but shadow.

I did feel, however, a faint, dry breeze.

Emi pushed up next to me and called, *"Can you see the arrow?"*

I shook my head. *"I'll have to go down!"*

"Do you think the oni *is down there?"*

I had forgotten what Lady Chiyome said about the entrance to the ogre's lair being behind the waterfall. I gazed down into the darkness. *"Only one way to find out!"*

Cursing the little monkey—and then apologizing to the *kami* of the spring—I slid my upper body through the opening.

I still couldn't feel the arrow, which struck me as odd, until I realized that the cave beyond sloped downward. Not steeply, but with enough of an incline that when the monkey tossed the arrow in, it must have slid past my reach.

I almost gave it up for lost at that point.

Still, I knew that the archers would expect four arrows, not three, and I thought the lost one couldn't be too far down. The dry air flowing past me carried a scent of . . . something. Birds. Something. It was strangely familiar, and I found that I had to investigate.

I shimmied through the crack. The edge was smooth, as if worn by years of passage. The recesses were dim, and so I reached down, my fingers searching for the thin shaft of the arrow. I couldn't feel anything, so I reached farther—

And slid on my belly down into the dark.

I tried to stop myself with my hands and feet, but that just pushed me from one side of the chute to the other. I was screaming—until I slid, face-first, into a sandy floor.

The arrow rested right in front of my nose.

There was light—a vertical slash of light cut off by a large, lumpen shape.

Spitting sand out of my mouth, I grabbed the arrow and stood, blinking.

To my shock, I realized that I was in the cave on the cliffside above the Full Moon.

The ogre crouched between me and the cave's front entrance.

Only, I realized, I could see *through* the monster, could see ribs of light among the ribs of shadow.

Ribs.

My throat thick with fear, I shuffled closer to the looming shape.

Like a mountain valley revealed by a rising mist, the shape became clear to me: a skeleton. A huge skeleton with an enormous, sharp-toothed skull. And through its jaws what I had taken to be tusks were what looked to be long, thick thigh bones.

It still looked terrifying. But it was definitely, unquestionably not alive.

I stood, breathing, staring at the bones. I pushed the arrow through the ribs, disturbing a fluttering hide made of spiderweb.

I began to laugh.

"I think it's a bear."

With a yelp, I spun, holding the arrow out in front of me like a dagger. Mieko's voice in my head said, *That's more weapon than you need to defend yourself.*

The man was leaning against the wall of the cave. Lit from the side by the slit opening on to the cliff, his features were deeply shadowed, but I recognized the sunken-cheeked, sad-eyed face from the woods—from the wake the previous night. "Kobayashi-*san?*"

He blinked, his brows twisting. "How—"

There was a grunt behind me, and Emi slid into the back of the cave. At least she had managed not to fall face-first, so her mouth wasn't full of sand.

The Matsudaira deserter gave the two of us a puzzled look. "Did they really send two girls to bring me back?"

"No," said Emi, dusting herself off. "We were here preparing the arrows for the funeral tonight."

I raised the missile in my hand. "One of the monkeys grabbed this one and tossed it down the chute there."

He gave a dejected smirk. "Yeah. Funny little idiots, aren't they."

"Funny," I grumbled, and Emi gave a controlled chuckle.

"So," he said, standing up straighter, "no one knows I'm here."

My sense of alarm increased, and I could see Emi tensing. He wasn't wearing a sword, but I could see a knife tucked into his belt.

"They know you're not down in the valley," said Emi, voice even.

I tried to match her calm, though my pulse was racing. "And we saw you yesterday, in the woods above the waterfall. We told our mistress, and she's told the lords."

"Ah." He deflated again, like a pufferfish that's gotten over its fright. His eyes drooped as he gazed at us. "You're the two girls I saw go behind the falls yesterday." When we nodded, he looked toward the bright opening. "For a bit, I thought I might hide out here. Stay here. Wait till my comrades and the Takeda left. Disappear into the countryside . . . " He shrugged.

"I'm sorry," I said, surprised that I meant it.

"Oh, I knew it wouldn't actually work," he sighed, and slid down the wall until he was squatting, staring at the sandy floor. "I just sort of hoped . . . "

"Do you have any family, Kobayashi-*san?*" I asked.

"No." He shook his head. "The Matsudaira army has always been my family. Been in service to the clan since I was younger than you. Lucky me." He shot us a dispirited smile. "Luckier than Fatso, at least."

"Than Kumo-*san?*"

He nodded. "The cook. Uh-huh. Had a wife. A whole bunch of kids—all daughters, I think, near the border, in Picnic Valley." He shook his head. "Two years ago, while we were fighting the Imagawa on the other side of the province, a group of raiders came into the village. They took what they could carry and burnt what they couldn't. Most of the men were helping clear the road that day—that's probably why the raiders attacked. And the women and the girls . . . " He closed his eyes. "Fatso's family. All gone."

"Oh, no," Emi said.

Kobayashi nodded glumly.

"I guess that's why he's always so protective of us," I said to Emi.

"Well, he would be," agreed the soldier.

We all considered that for a painful moment.

"Kobayashi-*san,*" I asked, not wanting to be thinking about dead parents or dead children, "what happened the other night?"

His eyes, which had looked almost sleepy, flew open.

"Don't you want someone to know?" Emi prodded.

"I'm going to die," he whispered, "because of what happened that night. Sa— The Takeda guard's already dead. And I'll be dead soon."

I knelt in the sand before him. "What happened, Kobayashi-*san*?"

He moaned. "Nothing. We just . . . " He took a breath and squared his shoulders. "We took over at the Hour of the Rooster, and it was real quiet. Then, just before midnight, this Takeda officer comes up—he's a bit tipsy—and asks if we want to join him for a little, you know . . . " He mimed quickly drinking a cup of wine. When we nodded, he deflated again. "So . . . the next thing I remember is Aosagi shaking me, telling me he was there to relieve me. The moon was high. Me and the other guard had . . . fallen asleep." His face—brows, mouth, nostrils—all seemed to collapse, a mask of shame and sorrow. He began to weep.

Feeling terrible for him, knowing that there was almost certainly nothing that we could do to help in any way, I looked to Emi, who just shrugged. I bent forward and looked into his face. "Kobayashi-*san*, you were drugged. There was poppy juice in the wine. You didn't just fall asleep."

"Oh." He considered this and then shook his head. "It doesn't matter. I still shouldn't have taken the *sake*. I neglected my duty and dishonored the *mon*. And . . . " He shook his head slowly. "And now I've abandoned my post. I deserted. I'll be executed. Or I'll be hunted down and slain like an animal. Or I'll starve to death here in the hills."

I glanced at Emi, who was looking at me. I wondered if she was considering, as I was, the impossible choice our fathers had had to make.

She nodded as if she knew what I was thinking. "Kobayashi-*san*," she said, "you can at least still do your duty." When the former sentry scowled at her, she leaned forward. "The man who drugged you and Sato-*san* was himself murdered."

"Yes," he sighed, and nodded at me. "You played at the wake."

I nodded back, thinking, *Ah, so it* was *you I saw.* "Kobayashi-*san*, do you know what that officer was doing? He climbed into the Full Moon—that's why he drugged you, and that's where he died."

"He did?" Kobayashi screwed up his face. "Why would he do that?"

When I didn't have any answer, Emi said, "Well, that's what we're all trying to figure out."

"Strange." His monkey-like face bowed down in an exaggerated pout almost worthy of Emi, the guard grunted. "Mind, I did hear him fighting with someone just inside the gate the night before. I was on the evening shift, so it was just before the gates closed."

Emi and I both perked up. She asked, "Was it Lieutenant Sakai?"

His pout now turned to a frown. "Why would they talk?"

Because of Mai, I thought, and I could tell Emi thought so too.

"Was it him?" I asked.

Kobayashi clicked his teeth, then shook his head. "No. I know Sakai-*san's* voice. I couldn't recognize this one. It was kinda . . . flat. And nasal. I was on the wrong side of the gate to see whoever it was, but he and the Takeda officer were talking about money." He held up his hands apologetically.

Money! "Who was the other guard with you that evening?" I probed. "Was it the same sentry you had duty with the night before last?"

Again the former guard shook his head. "No. It was . . . What was the name? Tadashi? He wasn't very talkative, and there were a lot of folks coming in and out that evening, so we were at attention. Not like . . . " He shuddered.

Emi and I nodded in understanding—he and Sato had had the opportunity actually to talk. To let their guard down.

"Kobayashi-*san*," Emi said, "you should come back with us. You have important evidence that may help catch the killer."

When he scowled at her, I pressed the point. "Surely Matsudaira-*sama* will be merciful if you come back willingly and help solve the crime."

He chewed on one cheek, then the other. Then, once again, he shook his head. "Let me think about it." Now he grimaced. "If I let you go, you'll just tell."

"We promise not to tell either of the lords or any of their men, Kobayashi-*san*." I looked at Emi, who nodded, and so I continued, "We swear it on the souls of our dead fathers."

"Oh, well, then." He gave his first sad smile in some time. "Go. I will consider what you have said." He bowed his head.

We bowed back and stood. I considered scrambling down the cliff, but I knew that Emi would never make it down the long, steep climb, and so I made my way with her to the back of the cave. Before we left, I glanced first at Kobayashi, who hadn't moved, then at the skeleton in the middle of the cave. I nodded at it. "When I first saw this, I thought it was an *oni*."

Kobayashi gave a low chuckle. "Fair enough. But no. See the teeth? Big and sharp in the front, flat and wide in the back. That's a bear. Huge, mind, and I don't think it could have got here under its own power—too big to make it through that chute behind the falls, no way it could have climbed up the cliff. Wonder who brought it all the way up here?"

I had no idea, nor did Emi, and so we said goodbye and made our way back up to the pool.

As we were walking back down along the stream, Emi mused, "You swore that we wouldn't tell Matsudaira-*sama*, Takeda-*sama*, or any of the soldiers."

"Yes."

"But you didn't say anything about not telling Lady Chiyome or the *kunoichi*."

A little embarrassed but also a bit pleased with myself, I shrugged and smiled. "No. No, I didn't."

22—Samurai Orphans

We reported to Chiyome-*sama* in her quarters once again.

Once again, she seemed pleased that we had found Kobayashi and that we'd uncovered another potential witness but hardly happy with what we'd achieved. "And you couldn't have talked one cowardly deserter into returning to his general?"

I couldn't think of anything to say to that.

Emi answered, "He wasn't going to come. And he wasn't sure he could let us go. Murasaki-*san* convinced him we weren't going to turn him in, but the only other choice we had would have been to attack him. We probably could have won, but we might have been injured, and he'd almost certainly have been killed, and then we wouldn't be any further ahead than we are now."

"Perhaps," granted our lady, her face twisted as if the admission were painful. "And perhaps he will come and turn himself in. The funeral is at noon, just after the midday meal. If he's not here by sunset, take the Little Brothers and drag the ruffian back out of his lair."

I bowed in acknowledgment but had to point out that the Little Brothers would hardly fit through the chute—they were far broader shouldered than the deserter.

"Fine," grumbled Lady Chiyome. "Then bring Mieko, Hoshi, and, oh, Rin. They'll be able to haul the little weasel back. And he might even be alive if they feel like being careful."

"Yes, Chiyome-*sama*," Emi and I said.

She nodded at the quiver in Emi's lap. "Go, bring those arrows to Captain Hara. He's out at the meeting grounds. And then get back to the kitchen. I'm sure you're needed there—though I doubt anyone will be any hungrier at midday than they were at breakfast."

"Yes, Chiyome-*sama*," we repeated, and then we were gone.

———

We let the cooks know where we were going, but the preparations for the next meal seemed to be proceeding smoothly, and so Kee Sun waved us away and told us to get back as soon as possible to help serve.

Toumi glared at us, but it mostly seemed to be out of habit.

Aimaru and Kumo-*san*—Fatso—both smiled, while Torai-*san*—Shorty—glowered, though whether it was at us or that was simply his resting expression, I couldn't have told you.

We were making our way back out the gate when Emi said, "Murasaki?"

"Hmm?"

"Do you think Matsudaira-*sama* would really have Kobayashi-*san* executed?"

I considered this, glancing at the sentries currently standing at attention outside of the Full Moon. Could one of them be—I shook my head. "I don't know. I mean, he'd certainly be punished, don't you think?"

Emi nodded. "Yes. Discipline is important. And honoring the emblem of the clan. I guess I just wonder—is fear of punishment the best way to maintain discipline?"

"I don't know," I admitted. "I mean, without it, why would soldiers run toward battle instead of away from it?"

"Respect for their lord?" she suggested. "Honor? Our fathers made that choice."

"Our fathers refused an order. And they suffered the consequences."

"Yet they acted with honor."

"Your father and Toumi's," I sighed. "Not mine."

"His act honored you. And your sister. And your mother." I glanced over, but her face was empty of expression. "I wish mine had made that choice."

I tried to shake the image of Emi and Toumi watching their fathers' suicides out of my head. "I wish they'd never had to make any choice at all."

After a few steps in silence, she nodded grimly.

The meeting area was out on the ridge top, opposite where the pyres were still standing ready. The monk appeared to be talking to the corpses once again—praying for them, most likely. His two helpers were sitting on the ground, apparently playing *go*.

The lords and their captains had been meeting in an enclosed area circled by a heavy curtain—a *jinmaku*. At the side farthest from the Full Moon, facing south, two sentries guarded the entrance.

"Begging your pardons, sirs," I said as we approached. "We need to speak to Captain Hara."

"Why do you need to speak to Hara-*san*?" asked the Takeda guard. It was the young one I had met outside of Takeda-*sama*'s tent the morning that we'd found Torimasa's body.

Emi lifted the quiver with its white arrows. "We prepared these for the funeral. Our lady told us to return them to Hara-*san*."

The sentry's lip curled in annoyance, but he nodded. "Fine. Stay here. I'll see if he'll come." He nodded to the Matsudaira guard and stepped inside.

"He doesn't seem very happy," said Emi.

To our surprise, the Matsudaira soldier laughed. "Tadashi-*san* doesn't trust you Full Moon girls." When we blinked at him, he gave an apologetic shrug. "He's convinced you had something to do with that death the other day. Not sure how such a lovely group of ladies could have had anything to do with such an ugly mess!"

Emi and I both agreed that would be unimaginable, and he laughed again.

"Sir," I asked, "the soldier who deserted, the one who was outside our gate?"

The guard's face was suddenly somber. "Kobayashi."

"Yes. What do you think Lord Matsudaira will do when they catch him?"

He winced. "You ladies probably don't want to think about such things."

Emi bowed her head. "We are fortunate to live in such a peaceful, protected place, it is true, but there is trouble everywhere these days. Even apprentice *miko* such as we have experienced . . . much."

He winced again but returned her nod. "Yes. Of course. Why do you wish to know?"

I was going to tell the truth (or part of it at least)—that we were interested in learning more about our lord's new ally. Whether he was stern or merciful.

Emi, though, shared a slightly different truth. "We are orphans—orphans of samurai. We care about questions of duty and honor."

The sentry, a common soldier, bowed to us. "Matsudaira-*sama* is a strict commander but just. If Kobayashi turns himself in—well, he's been fighting for our lord since the siege of Temple Castle, which would have been before you girls were born. They've been through a lot together. I'd imagine, if Kobayashi-*san* comes in on his own, Matsudaira-*sama* will be as merciful as he can be."

That didn't do much to reassure me, but it was the best we could hope for. I bowed, and Emi followed me. "Thank you, sir."

He bowed back. "So . . . Samurai orphans?"

The flap to the *jinmaku* opened, revealing Captain Hara. "Yes," he murmured. "Samurai orphans."

Emi and I bowed, and she held out the quiver. "Hara-*san*, we prepared these arrows for the ceremony. Lady Chiyome told us to return them to you."

"Hmm." He took the quiver. He seemed about to turn back into the meeting when his eyes narrowed, and I felt as if I were being skinned by one of Kee Sun's thinnest blades. "Hanichi-*san*. Kano-*san*—"

Whatever he was about to say, or ask—and I wasn't sure I wanted to know what that might be—he was interrupted by a noise from behind him. A low, gruff voice—Captain Baba's, I think—growled, *"But if we move all of our troops west to support the attack, we'll leave our northern border undefended! The Hōjō will sweep right through Worth and Swift River, straight into your territory!"*

A higher voice—Captain Tokimatsu—growled back, *"But without the support—"*

Hara-*san* sighed and gave a grim chuckle. "Fighting in the war room again. I'd better get back before it comes to blows." He bowed his head. "Ladies."

We bowed back, and he was gone.

On the way back into the Full Moon, a question that had been troubling me for months bubbled up: "If Takeda-*sama* wanted Lieutenant Masugu to carry the battle plan to warn Oda-*sama* that the Matsudaira are planning to betray him, why did he have Masugu come here and wait the whole winter? Why didn't he send him on the Great Eastern Sea Road? That wouldn't have been blocked by snow."

Emi stopped, considering that for a moment. Looking back at the *jinmaku* that surrounded the meeting area, she murmured. "Well, they're only actually planning the attack now."

"So?"

"That plan in the letter wouldn't be accurate. And by the time Masugu reaches the capital, the Takeda and Matsudaira will be close behind." She bit her lip. "This way, Takeda-*sama* can look as if he's actually loyal, while the warning he's sending is for the wrong attack."

"Huh." I frowned. "That's. . . not very nice."

"*Daimyo* have different rules than you and me," she said with a shrug. "If they were nice, they wouldn't need *kunoichi*."

I thought of Chiyome-*sama*'s map, the huge, multicolored game of *go*, and shrugged back. "Come on. Let's get back and help in the kitchen."

As Lady Chiyome had guessed, appetites were as scarce at the midday meal as they had been that morning. I imagine the prospect of the coming funeral was weighing on everyone's mind—it was certainly weighing on mine—but I could tell that the meetings had been less than harmonious. The blue-white frost between the Takeda and Matsudaira sides of the Great Hall made me and Shino scurry even faster to serve everyone.

No one was eating, however.

Well, Jolalo was eating, sitting at the bottom of the Matsudaira table. He gazed around the room in open curiosity, as if waiting for the excitement to start.

The commemorative bowl of rice at Torimasa-*san's* place seemed to suck all life and conversation out of the hall. The chopsticks, stabbed into them upright, felt like a warning.

When Toumi and I started bringing full bowls back into the kitchen, the cooks all looked at us glumly, but they didn't grumble—even they knew that the soldiers were thinking about anything but food.

As Kee Sun began to prepare a meal for me to bring to Mai, Kumo sighed. "But why do they have to attend the funeral? Surely these poor young ladies can be spared from such a distasteful duty."

"Flower-girlie wants Bright Eyes there to play again. And all of the girlies need to be there. I'll tell yeh, I think Chiyome wants to have a nice, pretty wall between the two armies."

Kumo sighed again, but nodded. "I wish that they could be spared such . . . unpleasantness."

Torai grunted and shrugged. "Well, that leaves the three of us to pluck and butcher all those chickens." He turned to Kee Sun. "Are they out in the storeroom?"

Kee Sun shook his head. "Nah. In the pantry. Bright Eyes, take this to Foxy-girlie." He held up a covered bowl of the rice, vegetables, and fish the rest of the guests had been served but had barely touched.

"No *sake?*" I asked.

He smirked. "Nah. I think she's had more than her share o' that."

Though I agreed with the cook, I had a feeling Mai herself wouldn't—and I was right.

"*Baka yarō!*" she growled when I told her what Kee Sun had said. I wasn't sure whether she meant me or the cook, but I honestly wasn't about to ask, and she didn't give me the chance. I had seen Kee Sun after a night of drinking, looking like a bear that's been rolling in pine sap. Mai looked more like a tiger with a headache. "What does he expect me to do, sit out here and pick my nose! *Che!*"

"Um . . . You could . . . Do you need some more paper to draw on?"

"Draw?" Her furious expression twisted. She gave an angry laugh. "Why would I want to do that, you stupid mouse? Stupid drawings . . . " She looked away from me.

"Well . . . Your drawings of Shino-*senpai* were so—"

"Get out." She grabbed the bowl from me. When I tried to say something—anything to calm her down—she screamed, *"Get out!"*

She slammed herself down on the *tatami,* turning away from me to grab her chopsticks. But I was sure that I could see tears silvering her eyes.

I got out.

Back in the kitchen, Sachi was waiting for me. It was time for the funeral.

23—Smoke and Flame

As we set up once again to play at the head of the two pyres, I couldn't help but think through all of the strange events of the previous night. Would the funeral be as eventful as the wake? Would Lieutenant Sakai come again—and if he did, would there be a fight between the two armies?

The monk slowly circled the shrouded bodies on their beds of stacked wood. He was chanting under his breath—as he passed near us, I could once again hear vague phrases about "the Pure Land" and "the Western Paradise."

A sharp scent told me someone had soaked the pyres with oil. They were ready for the flames. The paper offerings from the night before fluttered in a gentle breeze from the west.

It seemed unreal.

I had finished tuning. Sachi-*san* was playing a section of "The Empty Sky" over and over—trying to get the mournful tone just right, I supposed.

How did you disappear into the blank, blue sky?

Shino plucked at her *koto*, one string and then another, apparently at random. She was looking toward the Full Moon.

"Shino-*senpai?*" I found myself asking.

Her gaze shifted back to me. It was dead. Or not dead—deeply buried, like a fire that's been banked for the next day.

"Did . . . " I wanted to know what had happened between her and Mai the night before. Had they fought? What about? Did I really want to know? "Did Mai-*senpai* show you the drawings she did?"

The masked heat flared. "Shut up, Mouse-*chan.*"

"Yes, Shino-*senpai.* Sorry, Shino-*senpai.*"

She went back to plucking haphazardly at the *koto*. She looked away from me, now glaring at the pieces of paper swaying on the branch that connected the two pyres.

Was that . . . Atop all of the zigzag *shi-de* streamers lay what looked much like the sheet of Mai's drawings that I'd seen the night before—even the grease stains that showed the text on the back were the same. *Why would Shino want to burn something so lovely?*

Shino was clearly in no mood to talk about it. Before I could ask or investigate, both armies began to stream out of their camps, and Lady Chiyome led the inhabitants of the Full Moon through the gate. Again, the women were in *miko* red and white, while Aimaru, Toumi, and the Little Brothers were in blue.

Lord Takeda and most of his followers were in white mourning robes. Many of the Matsudaira were dressed that way as well.

We played again while everyone settled back into the same configuration as the night before—first "The Empty Sky" and then "The Deer's Call."

We do these things, I found myself thinking as I played, for the souls of the dead. But truly—truly—the rituals are for the living. To help us to let go. The dead souls will depart whether we mourn them or not—so long as we allow them to.

Where do they go? Even the delicate white snow falls where I can touch it.

Shaking my head slightly, I tried to concentrate on my fingering.

The monk, swaying in his own rumpled wide-sleeved white robes, continued chanting some prayer—I couldn't make out what he was saying over my own playing. At some point he fell silent, and I saw him staring at the paper offerings. A smile flowered on his round face, and he stepped forward, grabbed Shino's drawing, and began to pray more energetically.

Four Takeda archers didn't sit. They broke off, each carrying a lit torch, a long bow, and one of the white arrows that Emi and I had blessed at the waterfall. The open cage of each arrowhead was stuffed with an oil-soaked rag. They took up position behind us. I could smell the smoke from their torches.

Once everyone was in place, Sachi brought us through the final refrain to silence.

The monk gave a sermon almost identical to the one he'd delivered the night before: this life, this world, is impermanent; only the soul is eternal, and our choices will affect the soul as it migrates from one life to the next, one body to the next. Whereas the night before his flat Estuary accent had seemed almost bored, as he delivered the funeral sermon, he seemed strangely excited.

All of us listened seriously. The only sound aside from his voice was the wind in the green grass and the occasional crackle of the torches behind us.

Finally, he brought his oration to a close and turned away from the bodies. He nodded at the archers.

Oil-soaked rags sizzled, catching fire behind us.

Sachi raised her flute to her lips, a signal that we should prepare to begin playing again.

I raised my *samisen*, but my attention was not on her or on the next piece—were we playing "Cherry Blossoms"? "Empty Sky" again?

Instead, all I could seem to notice was the piece of paper in the monk's hand. Shino's drawings were still visible—perhaps that's why he saved it from the coming flames?

Through one of the grease stains, however, I could read in reverse two *kanji* characters—武 and 田. *War* and *rice paddy*.

Takeda.

Before I could say something—what? to whom?—there was a whistle overhead as four flaming arrows shot into the two pyres and then a low *whoosh* as they burst into flame.

Smoke poured out of the oil-soaked wood, and the breeze blew it straight toward us. I coughed, blinded, and even Sachi stopped playing.

It *was* "Cherry Blossoms." I'd missed the beginning.

Quickly the fires caught, and the two bonfires roared into full flame. The heat forced the smoke up, and my eyes cleared.

The monk stuffed the scroll into a voluminous sleeve.

Sachi, Shino, and I managed to begin playing, though the crackle and howl of the fire probably muffled our music for anyone other than us.

Us and the monk, of course. Who had rescued the scroll that Torimasa-san had hidden in the storeroom. The scroll we had all been searching for since the day before. But . . . why? And how?

Shino had gotten it from Mai. Where had Mai gotten it from?

From the stores. When she'd gone to fetch her bedding, right after Aimaru had found it there.

Baka. Baka yarō! I was a complete idiot. Of course Mai had found it! Did she have any idea what it was? Probably not, or she wouldn't have been doodling on the other side.

But why had the monk grabbed it? What would a holy man possibly need . . .

Well, the thought came to me, what would a shrine maiden need with troop locations or movements? She wouldn't. Not if she were just a *miko*. Not if she weren't a *kunoichi*.

The twin bonfires blazed in our faces. We played on, though it almost certainly wasn't the best that any of us had played, even Sachi-*sensei*.

Emi had talked about her father's funeral being scary. About the smell. I hadn't been sure what she was talking about, though I'd attended a few funerals back in the village.

Sitting a stone's throw from the two burning pyres, I knew what she meant. There was the scent of burning wood, of burning flesh—both smells I was familiar with. But this was different, somehow. Unsettling.

These two men had been walking and talking and laughing two days before. Now their bodies were being reduced to ash and their souls released to the next life.

Somehow, I couldn't believe that either of them had attained release from this round of sorrow. Would they come back as men? As ants?

I thought of the straw amulet we'd tucked back into Sato-*san*'s sleeve. I hope that it protects you, I thought, wherever you go.

As all of these sad thoughts passed through my mind, I kept an eye on the monk, who was chanting again, barely audible even a few steps away over the roar of the fires.

He was a spy, of that I was certain. Aimaru said that he'd never seen the man or his helpers in the valley before. And Sachi said that he spoke with an Estuary accent. He wasn't local.

Who was he spying for? Lord Oda? For the Uesugi?

He had said that Estuary was in Armory Province—that was to the north.

I remembered Baba-*san* yelling that if the Takeda moved all of their troops away from the northern border, it would leave all of the Takeda territories open—

To the Hōjō.

Lady Chiyome's many-colored map flashed before my mind's eye even as I continued playing my *samisen*, as I tried to match Shino's rhythm.

The main island, Honshū, like the fat body of a trout. In the east, at the belly of the fish, masses of Takeda red and Matsudaira blue. Ringing them to the west, Lord Oda's white and the yellow of the Uesugi. And north, the orange of the Hōjō.

Yes. Of course Lord Hōjō would want to know exactly how many troops the Takeda could field.

I wanted to talk to Emi and Toumi about this. They seemed to understand these things better than I did.

But I was certain that the monk was supposed to be the one who took the list of the Takeda armies away. Was he who Torimasa had meant to give the scroll to?

Perhaps not—since the monk hadn't arrived until after the lieutenant was dead.

Which meant there was someone else. Probably someone with a name beginning with a T, the initial written on all of the IOUs in Torimasa's tent.

What was the monk's name, anyway?

Could he have killed Torimasa? Could his helpers?

If he was a spy as well as a monk, perhaps he was an assassin as well. If so, he wasn't as skilled as Mieko-*san*. Then again, as I understood it, few were.

As the fire burned on, the shapes of the two dead men no longer recognizable in the flames, soldiers began to stand and to leave.

How many of these have they seen? I wondered. With so many dead on all sides, probably a lot. Would that make it any easier?

From the tears in the eyes of a number of the Takeda, I gathered that, sometimes, it didn't help at all.

The Matsudaira didn't seem to be crying, but they seemed just as sober, just as thoughtful. Perhaps the simple thought *Someday that will be me* affected even those who hadn't known the two Takeda soldiers.

I couldn't find Lieutenant Sakai's face in the throng. All of the other Matsudaira officers were there, including Lord Matsudaira and his nephew. The lieutenant with the scar on his cheek, however—the one Mai had been flirting with the first night, the one who'd fought with the dead man over her—he was nowhere to be seen. Perhaps he stayed away as the Takeda lieutenant, Itagaki, had told him the night before. Perhaps he didn't want to make a scene.

Sakai didn't begin with *T* either.

If the monk wasn't the murderer, then who was?

Who was the person who'd gotten Torimasa-*san* to betray his duty? It seemed likely that it was the person the lieutenant had owed all of that money to. *T.*

Lord Matsudaira had left, along with all of his followers and many of the Takeda. Lord Takeda himself and his officers still sat, however, watching the cremation of their comrades.

Sachi signaled us at last, and we put our instruments down.

"Well done, as always, ladies," said the monk with a chuckle.

"Thanks," said Sachi, licking her lips, which were dry from the smoke and the long stint of playing the flute.

"Please," I asked, "may this humble servant know Your Reverence's name?"

He shot me a bemused grin. "My ordained name is Junkeishō. Why do you ask, child?"

"Oh, just curiosity, Junkeishō-*san*." As he began to turn, I asked, "And why did you hide that scroll in your sleeve?"

His head whipped around, but rather than attack me, as I had been worried that he might, he began to sprint in the opposite direction.

Straight at the four archers, who were still standing at attention behind us.

Sachi shouted, *"Stop him!"*

The archers—one of whom was Itagaki-*san*—responded immediately. One used his bow to trip the running monk. The other three used their feet to incapacitate him, two pressing down on his arms and Lieutenant Itagaki standing on the back of his neck.

"Don't kill the man, Itagaki," said Lord Takeda, who was suddenly standing at Shino's side. Surprised, she pulled back. "Well, Sachi, what did the man do, pinch you?"

The other Takeda crowded around us. I could see Lady Chiyome and the *kunoichi*, slim red and white birches, through the thicket of warrior cedars.

"No, my lord," Sachi said, "or he'd be without a hand. No. He took something from the pyres before they were set alight. A piece of paper." She looked at me and raised her eyebrow.

Dry mouthed, I looked down at the monk, who'd stopped struggling beneath the soldiers' weight. I hoped he could still breathe. "I think he has the . . . the list in his left sleeve. The list that the dead man sneaked in to leave in our storeroom."

Itagaki reached down, keeping his foot on the back of the spy's neck, and snatched the scroll out of the grass-stained sleeve. He held it out to his general, who looked it over gravely, then nodded at the bonfire. "How did this get here?"

Shino gave a choking gasp, and for a moment I thought someone had stepped on her throat. No—she was gawking at the drawings of her in Takeda-*sama*'s hand.

Mieko said, "I believe that our other senior initiate, Mai, drew those figures on the back, not knowing the significance of the paper itself."

Lord Takeda turned the list over, looking at the drawings of Shino dancing the Sixty-four Changes. His captains' eyebrows rose, but Takeda-*sama*'s face remained stony. "Very pretty," he said.

Shino was now staring down at the ground, face red as the setting sun.

Mieko put her hand on Shino's shoulder. "Shino here went to visit Mai last night. To ease her isolation. When Mai showed Shino what she had drawn,

Shino was, she told me last night, embarrassed. The two of them got somewhat . . . carried away. Is that not so, Shino-*chan*?"

"Yes," Shino groaned.

Carried away. That was one way to say they fought like she-dogs over a leftover bone.

"Risuko-*chan* here and I saw Shino leave the compound with the scroll in her hand, isn't that so, Risuko?"

"Yes, Mieko-*sensei.*" When the weight of all of those gazes didn't lessen, I gulped. "Um. Mieko-*sensei* sent me to make sure that Shino-*senpai* was all right, while she checked on Mai. I followed her out here. By the time I reached the pyres, she was already leaving. I saw the monk there on the ground, just like he is now—only asleep."

"Praying for the souls of the dead," grumbled Shino.

"So he didn't see her put the scroll there."

Lord Takeda grunted, then looked around. "So how did this Mai get the list in the first place?"

My mouth opened before I had time to think better of it. "I think she found it in the storeroom while she was getting bedding, after Lady Chiyome sent her to the Retreat."

Lady Chiyome gave a sour laugh. "Did she now? I don't know which is more of a curse—clever girls or stupid ones. Risuko, go fetch Mai from the Retreat. We have some questions for her. Again."

"My lady!" gasped Shino, suddenly coming to Mai's defense, just as she had the day before. Truly—I never understood those two.

Lady Chiyome raised her hand. "I doubt she's in any trouble. But we need to talk to her. As we need to talk to this ruffian in monk's robes. Risuko, go. Now."

"Yes, my lady!"

———

I sprinted up the path between the two camps. Both armies were busy after the ceremony. At the gate, I greeted the guards. "Hi, Yukishiro-*san*, Aosagi-*san!*"

"Hey, Risuko-*chan!*" they called as I ran by.

I ran past the stables and the men's dormitory, past the storeroom—the door was open, so someone must be in there—and under the boughs of the huge hemlock toward the Retreat.

The door was open there too. "Mai-*senpai?*"

No answer.

I peered into the small building. It was still stale with the reek of her *sake*-guzzling, and there were scraps of paper and such around the interior, but no Mai. Strange.

Well, she'd sneaked out before to get wine. Perhaps she'd done it again.

I jogged along the back of the Great Hall toward the well. She'd probably been caught in the kitchen pantry trying to sneak more *sake*, I figured. Well, Kee Sun could yell at her after Lord Takeda had asked his questions.

I stepped back into sunlight as I rounded the corner of the Great Hall into the kitchen courtyard.

There was Mai.

Strung up by her ankles from the same hook where the pig had been hung to bleed out.

Mai's sharp face was just as wide with shock as Torimasa's had been, but her mouth was set in her fierce snarl of a grin.

And like the pig's, her throat had been slit into a second smile.

24—Desecration

We say that the sunset is red, but it isn't. It is a mix of orange and gold and a million wonderful hues—but it isn't truly red. Nor are cherry blossoms—though the fruit certainly is.

Blood, however, is true red—redder than any cherry.

A fan of red spread out in front of our dormitory. Mai's blood, spraying out when her throat had been cut. While she was alive, or it wouldn't have sprayed out with such force.

A large wedge with no blood sliced into one side of the scarlet fan, however. So she'd been attacked from the front. And her attacker would be covered in blood.

Ignoring my knees, which wanted to give way, I stumbled over to the gong by the kitchen door and started banging on it, shouting, *"Help!"* Then I stopped, realizing that I might be calling the murderer as much as aid.

The door behind me slid open, and I jumped to protect myself, raising the twisted old spoon that we used to ring the gong.

Kee Sun and Aimaru both gawked at me. They were covered in feathers—their hair, their coats—and their faces looked anything but concerned.

That is, until I pointed across the courtyard to where Mai's body was strung up.

Kee Sun swore furiously in Korean.

Aimaru just gasped, "Oh, no!"

Aosagi, the Matsudaira guard from the front gate, ran into the courtyard. "What's— Oh!"

Kee Sun turned to the soldier and barked orders as if he were a commander or as if the man were a scullery minion. "Get. We need Lady Chiyome here now and Lord Takeda. We need troops. Now. *Get!*"

Aosagi took off toward the front gate at a full sprint.

"Fatso! Shorty!" shouted Kee Sun. *"Get yehr lard guts here now! We got trouble!"*

The two cooks appeared after a few heartbeats. "What's the matter?" asked Kumo, trying to pull his jacket closed over the large belly that tumbled out over his trousers.

Torai honked a nasal "What?" He was fully dressed, but his sleeves were stained with blood.

Kee Sun just pointed, as I had done, across the courtyard to Mai's body.

Torai stared at her, his mouth and eyes wide.

Kumo turned and tried to cover my eyes.

I pushed his hand away, immediately feeling badly for doing so. *Did he see his wife and daughters like this?* "I've already seen it, Kumo-*san*. I was the one who found her."

Kee Sun swore again, jumping past Aimaru back into the kitchen. I looked at my friend and to the cooks to see if they knew what he was doing. They clearly didn't.

I pointed at Torai. "You! You killed her!"

"What?" He blinked at me. "What are you talking about?"

Lord Takeda and his officers entered, along with Lady Chiyome, the Little Brothers, Emi, Toumi, Shino, and the *kunoichi*. They all stopped, staring at Mai's corpse.

Shino began to wail. Again, Kumo tried to shield the ladies' eyes from the body, but Toumi was even less patient than I had been. Holding the older girl, who was weeping, Toumi snarled, "Back off, Fatso."

Kumo looked as if she'd bitten him.

"What," said Lady Chiyome, her voice cold as hail and her face as white, "is going on here?"

"He murdered her!" I howled, pointing at Torai, who gawked at me. Then I pointed at the interrupted fan of blood in the gravel. "Whoever killed Mai was standing in front of her. See! And he's the only one covered in blood!"

When everyone turned on him, Torai held up his red-splattered hands. "Of course I'm covered in blood! We've been butchering chickens for hours! Some of us have clean clothes back in the men's' dorms"—he gestured at Kumo—"but me, I've been working dawn to midnight every day, no one to clean my clothes! I was looking for a clean jacket in the stores." He snorted. "'Course, only ones I could find were too big"—he flicked his chin first at the Little Brothers, then at me—"or too small. It's chicken blood!" He held his arms wide, then lowered them, turned to Lord Takeda, and gave a quick bow. "Takeda-*sama*, come on! You know me! Why would I do something like that?" He nodded toward Mai's body.

"That's an excellent question, Torai," the Mountain rumbled. "Is there anything you'd like to tell me?"

The cook turned as white as the chicken down on Aimaru's head.

Our cook stalked out of the kitchen, carrying several long butchering knives and Masugu's sword. "Masugu's blade ain't been touched this time, but one of the cleavers is missin'," he announced.

Kumo held his hands out, palms up, his head bowed down. "I was going to clean the blade properly after I changed. I must have left it back at the Bull Pen, I'm afraid." Where everyone else seemed incapable of looking away from Mai, he couldn't seem to bear to look at the horrible sight of her body. Not that I could blame him.

At that moment, Lord Matsudaira strode into the courtyard, followed by his officers, including Lieutenant Sakai. Their expressions shifted swiftly from concern to shock. As with the rest of us (aside from the Matsudaira cook), their attention was arrested by the spectacle of Mai's corpse displayed on the Full Moon's wall.

Lady Chiyome bowed stiffly to the two *daimyo*. "My lords, I demand justice for my girl—for this desecration of my home and of my follower. This evil cannot have been committed by any of my servants—we were all at the funeral, and no woman could have lifted her body so. I extended the hospitality of the Full Moon to my lords and their companies, yet one of your followers has defiled and dishonored that hospitality. Someone—someone in your employ—has committed two murders here, and one of them of an innocent girl who was due to take *miko* robes next week at the full moon." She gestured to her red- and white-clad women. Perhaps none exactly innocent but none of them deserving to be slaughtered like a fat sow.

Shino sobbed again in Toumi's arms.

The two lords stared at Lady Chiyome and then at each other. I am sure that neither of them was used to being spoken to in such a manner, yet they clearly understood that her anger was justified, as was her demand for justice.

"As this tragedy has taken place in my domain," said Takeda-*sama*, his eyes drawn back to Mai, "I shall call a tribunal to investigate this terrible crime." He looked around at all of us assembled there. "Since, as Chiyome says, both my soldiers and those of my lord governor of the Three Rivers must fall under suspicion, and since, as she put it, this defilement touches her honor as well, I propose that we three serve together as magistrates, investigating the matter of these two murders."

"My lord governor of Worth proposes wisely," said Lord Matsudaira. "I agree."

Chiyome-*sama* bowed again, lower and more gracefully. "My lords honor this humble widow." When they acknowledged her with nods, she stood straight again. "I trust my lords will consent to hold the tribunal in my hall. I do not think any of us wishes to remain here. And someone," she continued, still looking at the lords and their retinues, "see to the poor girl. Dignity was never her greatest strength, I'm afraid, but she deserves to rest in a less obscene manner, don't you think?"

All of the men winced and looked away at last. Captain Tokimatsu and Lieutenant Itagaki volunteered to see to it.

Lieutenant Sakai began to offer to help as well, but his general stopped him. "No, Sakai. I imagine that your evidence will be required."

"I . . . Yes, my lord."

Matsudaira-*sama* nodded again, grimly, then looked to Takeda-*sama*. "Perhaps our physicians should examine the poor young lady." Now he glanced to Lady Chiyome. "If our hostess consents."

"Oh, I consent, my lord," the old woman said. "I don't think there's any question about how she died, but I am sure that the doctors will at least confirm what seems obvious."

"Even so," Lord Takeda said, and ordered Aosagi, the Matsudaira sentry, to fetch the two physicians and to inform both camps of what had happened.

Lord Matsudaira added, "And let them know that we are conducting an investigation. They should see to their duties but be prepared to give evidence."

Captain Baba stroked his beard and said to the older Matsudaira captain, Ietada-*san*, "We should arrange for new sentries on the front gate. Our lords will need our man Yukishiro and your Aosagi here to testify about who came and went."

The soldiers fell into a discussion of duty rotations and personnel schedules. Captain Hara told Aosagi, who was looking overwhelmed, that he should also send word to fetch formal robes for both generals.

Lady Chiyome clapped her hands, and silence fell once again. "Very well, it is agreed, then. My lords, come and join me in the Great Hall. It has been some time since it has served as a courtroom, but my women can make it ready, I am sure. Mieko, please assist these gentlemen." She nodded to Tokimatsu and Itagaki. "See to it that they treat our poor lost child with proper respect, as I am sure they would in any case." As everyone began to shuffle off to their duties, she turned to Kee Sun. "While I'm sure it's the last thing on anyone's mind, we still need to see my household and two armies fed. Do you think you'll be able to manage it?"

Our cook tore his eyes from Mai's dangling corpse. "Ay, Chiyome. It may be a wee bit later than the troops would like, but we've still got plenty from the last meal, and we'll be able to grill the chicken if we get a move on. Come on, girlies, Moon-cake."

Kumo and Torai too began to follow him back into the kitchen. When I began to trail along, however, Lady Chiyome halted me with a dry hand on my shoulder. "Alas, my squirrel, I rather think you'll be needed as a witness. No cooking for you."

"Again," muttered Toumi, but for once she looked pleased to be allowed back into the kitchen.

Lady Chiyome arched an eyebrow and shook her head. "Come, Risuko. If my guests are going to get gussied up to play judge, I'll need you to help make me more presentable as well. Mieko is busy. Come."

"Yes, my lady."

———

Lady Chiyome did not in fact require much help at all. I held a brass mirror while she freshened her white makeup and applied rouge. Then I helped her into a stiff, heavy silk kimono—black, with a pattern of crossed willow branches stitched in gold thread and the white disk of the Full Moon over her heart.

Once she had dressed, she turned to me. "Tell me, Risuko. What exactly happened?"

I sighed and described what I had seen from the moment that I left the funeral until the moment that I had rung the gong. There wasn't much to tell.

She pinched the bridge of her nose. "And that doesn't answer any of the questions we had about the monk."

"Oh." The monk. I had completely forgotten about him. "I think he is a spy. For the Hōjō, I think."

"Is that so?" She gave a chuckle—one that sounded forced. "What makes you say that?"

"Well," I murmured, trying to remember the line of reasoning that had seemed so clear while I had played the *samisen,* "he's got to be a spy. Why else would he take the list of Takeda troops?"

"He liked the drawings of pretty girls?" Again she chuckled. "No. I think you are right about that. And why for Lord Hōjō?"

"Well," I said, gazing down at her map, searching out the Full Moon, and then looking north, "Sachi-*sensei* said that he has an Estuary accent." I pointed at the dot that marked the town amidst a swarm of orange stones.

"Did she indeed?"

I nodded. "Is she really from Armory Province herself, Chiyome-*sama?*"

"Oh, yes. I found her there on one of my first trips hunting for recruits. Her in Seashore"—she pointed to a small dot on a peninsula near Estuary—"and Hoshi in the other half of Dark Letter, in Uesugi territory." She pointed to where the Uesugi armies were represented in bright yellow to our west. "Well, if anyone could spot another Armory native, it's Sachi. Mind, she herself is proof that just because you're a spy and from Armory Province, you aren't necessarily working for Hōjō Ujimasa."

"No, my lady."

"Still, your deduction seems sound."

I looked at the provinces around Dark Letter Province, where the Full Moon was located. "Are the Uesugi and the Hōjō allies, my lady?"

"You'd think so, wouldn't you? But no: the Hōjō used to be our allies, along with the Imagawa. Since the Imagawa began to topple, however, the Hōjō have been fighting with both us and the Uesugi over the provinces of central Honshū. Dark Letter, of course, and Wild Heights." She circled the provinces with her finger. "It's like a group of starving dogs fighting over who's going to eat a poor squirrel." She winked at me. "Of course, Lord Takeda isn't a dog—he's a tiger."

I looked down at the stones, laid out like a many-hued game of *go* on the map. It made my head spin.

"Now, Risuko, before we go down to start the tribunal, tell me: who do you think killed that poor girl?"

Mai, I thought, but of course did not say. "I don't know, my lady," I answered, but my earlier suspicion wouldn't let me leave it at that. "Torai, our lord's cook—he was covered in blood, my lady."

"Yes," she sighed. "I heard you accuse him as we arrived. Of course, as he said, he'd been butchering chickens. But why would he do such a thing? Did you ever see them together?"

I thought about it. Kee Sun forbade Mai and Shino from entering the kitchen, and Mai had been banished to the Retreat since Torimasa's murder—most of the time that the Takeda had been at the Full Moon. I'd rarely seen Torai outside of the kitchen. "No. No, my lady." The only time I had seen the Takeda cook in the Great Hall, he had been talking to . . . "I did see him talking with the monk, my lady."

"Hmm. Yes. Interesting." She gave a curt nod. "Come, Risuko. It is time to get some answers."

25—White Sand, White Snow

We descended back into the Great Hall, which Mieko and the other women had transformed. The side tables had been moved back to the walls, the head table was covered in cloth to serve as a platform, and all of the decorations—bowls of flowers, scrolls on the walls, and such—were gone.

And in front of the head table, they had spread a circle of white sand.

"Ah, well done," Lady Chiyome said to Mieko. "It's been a while since we had to use this hall as a courtroom."

Mieko bowed. "Thank you, my lady. Yes. Seven years."

"Yes," sighed Chiyome-*sama*. "After the last time, I hoped we wouldn't have to hold another trial here."

I was about to ask what had happened seven years before, but at that moment the doors to the hall opened, and the two lords entered, followed by their soldiers—not just the officers but many of the samurai and common soldiers from both camps—and the *kunoichi* as well. The Portuguese priest and Jolalo slid to the back wall by the now-closed doors to the kitchen.

Lord Takeda and Lord Matsudaira strode to the head table, where Lady Chiyome joined them. They all bowed to each other.

I turned back to the door to see the last entrants—the Little Brothers, who were holding the monk Junkeishō between them, limp as a dead chicken.

He looked almost unrecognizable. His white robes were stained with grass, mud, and what looked to be blood. I had to assume it was his own. His eyes flitted around the hall, the only sign of life in his face, which was also covered in dirt and grass and looked to be bruised and battered.

A hand took my elbow, pulling me to the center of the hall, and I nearly responded (as I had the night before) with violence, but Sachi-*san's* voice, unusually solemn, whispered in my ear, "Come on, Risuko. You need to be ready to testify."

Oh. I was going to testify. It was bad enough to have to tell the lords about what I had seen, about what happened. But to do it in front of everyone . . .

I shivered.

Sachi squeezed my elbow and then let go. "You'll be fine."

"*Hai*," I tried to say, but I think it came out as more of a whimper. I took a breath. "Sachi-*sensei?*"

"Hmm?" Her eyes followed Lady Chiyome, who was talking with Lord Takeda.

"What happened seven years ago?"

"Seven years?" Her attention was still on our lady and the two lords, who were seating themselves—although their descent was so dignified, it felt more as if the platform were rising to meet them.

"Chiyome-*sama* and Mieko-*san*—they were saying something about the last time the Great Hall was used as a courtroom?"

"Oh!" She covered her familiar smile, which seemed out of place in this room of solemn-faced men and women. "Yes. Lady Chiyome's steward, Oshitori, was murdered. It was awful." She leaned down and began to whisper into my ear. "Of course, he was pretty awful, as it turned out, but—"

But before she could tell me the story, Baba-*san*, the Takeda captain, barked out, "Sit!"

We all sat.

Lady Chiyome looked first to Lord Takeda and then to Lord Matsudaira. When they both nodded, she peered out at the packed hall, freshly made-up face grim. "One of my girls has been murdered." A murmur rumbled through the hall, but she continued, silencing it. "Someone killed her—quite brutally, quite nastily. And this is the second murder here in my home in the past few days. My lords and I have convened this court to discover who has committed these outrages and to see that the ruffian who did this suffers for his crimes. Do you all understand?" The last question came in a low, wolfish growl.

All of the soldiers, Matsudaira and Takeda, muttered that yes, they understood.

Shino gave a sniff.

"Good." She didn't look happy—but then Lady Chiyome rarely looked happy, and I didn't blame her for being less than pleased at that moment. She indicated the floor in front of her. "Now the sand here—it's white to represent purity. And truth." She leaned forward. "It is also, of course, the color of death. If we call you to kneel here, please stick to the truth, or death will come."

Huffed gasps, grunts, grim chuckles, and hisses of surprise filled the hall, but again, we all murmured that we understood.

Knowing that I would be one of the ones to kneel on the sand, I fought to calm the breath that wanted to flee my chest like a startled quail.

Sachi gave my elbow another squeeze, no doubt to reassure me. It didn't, but I appreciated the attempt.

Once the hall had again fallen silent, Lady Chiyome continued, "We will begin with this morning's murder, since that one is so fresh and raises so many unanswered questions." She bowed to the man on either side of her. "My lords, since I know . . . knew the victim, may I call the first witnesses?"

"Of course, Chiyome," said Takeda-*sama* with a nod.

Matsudaira-*sama* too nodded and added, "And we shall ask questions as well, naturally."

Our mistress bowed again, even lower. "Naturally." She surveyed the hall, her eyes falling on me (and startling the quail back into flight) before passing on. "Shino. You knew the victim best. Come and kneel."

Shino stood there for a moment, still unsteady. Hoshi encouraged her forward and helped her kneel in the sand before stepping back to Sachi's side. Shino gave herself a small wet-dog shake, took a breath, then touched her forehead to the sand. "My lady. My lords."

His voice low and seemingly gentle, Lord Matsudaira said, "Tell the court your name and how you knew the victim."

"My name is Shino, my lord." She was staring down at the sand, hands folded in her lap, and her voice, though low, held steady. "M— The victim and I came to the Full Moon at the same time, three summers ago. Lady Chiyome found us on a trip south. I am from a village in Fountain Province, and she was from the city in River Bend. We have been training here since and became senior initiates last winter."

At Fuyudori's sudden fall.

The lord asked, still gently, "So you were friends?"

I could see her shoulders tighten, then relax. "We shared a sleeping pallet, my lord."

She didn't say that they did so because neither one of them could allow the other any privilege or advantage.

Lord Takeda's voice was pitched much more threateningly. "You were the one who told us the victim couldn't have killed my lieutenant."

"Yes, my lord."

"Do you maintain that claim?"

"Yes, my lord." For the first time, Shino looked up, and I could see from the straight line of her spine that she had found her ornery self. "She and I shared a bed for six months. She could not have left it without waking me."

Takeda-*sama*'s eyes narrowed. "Unless you left it together."

"We did not, my lord."

"Perhaps you killed my lieutenant and then killed your accomplice to cover the crime."

"I—" Shino's shoulders bunched, as if she were about to reach for one of the knives she usually wore.

Lady Chiyome held up a hand. Her voice came once again as a growl. "Remember where you are, Shino. Remember *to whom you speak*." The old woman's eyes flicked not toward the lord who had been accusing Shino but toward the one who, I remembered, could not know that we girls of the Full Moon were trained in far more than rituals to serve the old gods.

There is telling the truth, apparently, and then there is telling all of the truth.

"Apologies," mumbled Shino. I watched her shoulders descend—through an act of sheer will, apparently—so that her posture once again resembled that of a maid serving tea. "My lord. My lords. Me and . . . Neither of us could have done any such thing. Not that way, for sure."

I heard her unspoken implication that yes, they were perfectly capable of killing Torimasa, but if they'd done it, they wouldn't have done it in such a ridiculous manner, setting it up to look like suicide.

Lady Chiyome and Lord Takeda both nodded, understanding her as I did.

Knowing Shino and Mai, I assumed that they would have killed him in some different ridiculous manner—brutal and thorough—and then disposed of the body where it would make trouble for someone else.

Mai's death was brutal, but would Shino have hung her rival like a pig or a goat to bleed out just outside her own dormitory? Also, her current almost convincing attempt at appearing to be polite was about as far as Shino's acting ability extended. Barking, snarling, and grumbling Shino could do. But to pretend to cry the way she had when she'd seen Mai's body?

No. Shino couldn't have done that. I granted what she'd said with a nod and saw that Takeda-*sama* and Chiyome-*sama* were mirroring me.

Lord Matsudaira too nodded, but since he couldn't know what Shino or Mai were or weren't capable of, he seemed to be trying to reassure the remaining *senpai*. "We must ask these questions to get to the bottom of this tragedy."

Shino bowed. "Of course, my lords. My lady."

Lord Matsudaira continued, "And did you share a bed with her last night?"

"No." A note of misery crept into her voice. "After the lieutenant's death yesterday morning, Lady Chiyome sent her to the Retreat."

"The Retreat?" asked Lord Takeda.

Lady Chiyome explained, "A cabin on the far side of the compound where our women spend their moon time."

"Oh." Both lords looked as if they were trying to hold in expressions of distaste. Not the sort of thing they had to deal with, living with armies of men. "Of course."

Lady Chiyome gave her sour smile. "It also serves as a place to isolate troublemakers. Now Shino, you did see the victim last night, didn't you?"

"Yes, my lady."

"And why was that?"

"Well . . . " Shino's shoulders bunched again, but this time it looked as if she were trying to defend herself rather than preparing to attack. "After the wake for the lieutenant, I brought her some . . . something to drink. I know it's hard being stuck in the Retreat all day, and even worse, all on your own."

Lady Chiyome chuckled. "So you brought her rice wine."

"Um. Yes, my lady. But . . . Um. She'd already got some. I think Kee Sun sent her some with her meals."

Not that *many bottles!* I fumed silently.

Lady Chiyome smirked. "I see. And did she talk to you?" When Shino didn't answer, our mistress gave another chuckle. "Have a fight, did you?"

"No!" she groaned. "We just got . . . carried away. A bit. We . . . I kind of ran out of the Retreat. That was the last time I saw her." Tears thickened her voice. The clenched shoulders were now quivering and the straight back bending like a pulled bow.

"Indeed." Chiyome-*sama* held up the paper Mai had drawn on. "And did she show you this scroll?"

Shino was plainly crying now. "Yes, my lady."

"This is you, isn't it? These drawings on the back?"

"Yes," sobbed Shino.

"And is that what got you . . . *carried away?"*

"Yes."

Lord Takeda broke in. "And did she show you the other side?"

Startled, Shino gave a hiccup but then answered simply, "No. No, my lord. Why would she?"

He grimaced. "And when you ran out, you brought this scroll to the funeral pyres to be burned."

"Yes, my lord."

"Why?"

"Because . . . Because it was embarrassing, my lord. That she'd . . . And I was upset, like I said, so I thought I'd make it part of the sacrifice."

"And you had no idea what this paper was?"

"No, my lord."

"Can anyone confirm that she was alive when you left?"

Again, Shino hiccuped. "When I ran out of the Retreat, I saw Mieko-*sensei* and Risuko-*chan*. Risuko ran after me, but I think Mieko-*sensei* went to talk to . . . to her."

Lady Chiyome nodded. "I'd like to call Mieko to confirm that. Shino, you're—"

"Pardon me, Lady Chiyome," Matsudaira-*sama* broke in. "May I ask one more question?" When she nodded, he turned back to Shino, who seemed once more to be holding in tears. "Girl, did the victim have any enemies?"

A knife-edged voice in my head said, *Only anyone who met her!* It sounded suspiciously like Toumi.

Shino, however, shook her head. "No. She got along with everyone. In fact, before the Takeda showed up . . . My lord, I think she was getting kind of friendly with your lieutenant, Sakai-*san*. But then she was kind of friendly with the dead lieutenant. I think Sakai-*san* was kind of angry about that." She ducked her head. "My lord."

"Indeed," sighed Lord Matsudaira. "Sakai, we will likely be speaking with you. But Lady Chiyome, you wished to call your girl Mieko?"

"Indeed, my lord. Shino, you're finished for now. But we may need to ask more questions." Hoshi stepped forward and helped the now-weeping Shino away from the sand.

Her place was taken by Mieko, who confirmed Shino's testimony: she and I had seen Shino run out of the compound. Mieko had gone and gotten Mai to go to sleep. "She was very upset."

She was very drunk, I thought, but I understood why Mieko didn't share that information.

Lord Takeda waved Mieko away, no doubt relieved not to have one of his premiere assassins kneeling on the white sands of truth testifying before Lord Matsudaira. He stared at me. "Kano-*san*, come forward."

My knees slipped, as if suddenly filled with water. Sachi carefully led me to the brilliant white patch of sand. I nodded my thanks to the music teacher and knelt.

Lord Matsudaira asked, "Kano?"

"Yes, my lord. My name is Kano Murasaki. But everyone calls me Risuko."

His eyebrows were raised—he probably had some question about my father, but he nodded it away. "Ah. So you are the one who ran after Shino there."

"Yes, my lord."

Once I too had confirmed Shino's testimony, I told them that I'd last seen Mai alive when I brought her meals to the Retreat.

"And you saw this paper in the Retreat?" asked Lady Chiyome, holding up the scroll.

"Yes, my lady. When I brought her dinner last night."

"Yes," she sighed, "the grease stains bear that out. And did you see this paper again?"

"Yes, my lady. I saw the monk slip it into the sleeve of his robes at the funeral."

"Indeed." She shot a hawkish glare at the man between the Little Brothers. "And we'll be hearing from you too."

The jovial holy man whimpered.

Lady Chiyome turned back to me, her gaze just as intense. "And do you know what is on this paper?" When I frowned, she snorted. "No, child, not the drawings, lovely as they may be. The other side."

I gawked up at her and then at Lord Takeda. Did they really want me to reveal this secret document before Lord Matsudaira?

Takeda-*sama* nodded curtly.

"I believe it is an accounting of the current battle strength of the Takeda army." The hall, Matsudaira and Takeda, all gasped. Far behind me, I heard Jolalo speaking in his birdsong language to the priest. I continued, "I am fairly certain that the late lieutenant sneaked it into the Full Moon the night that he died in order to pay some debt. I think that he hid it in the storerooms before he died, and the victim found it there when she was getting bedding after you sent her to the Retreat, my lady."

Whispers filled the hall behind me. Captain Baba cut them off with a growled "Silence!"

Once quiet took hold again, Lady Chiyome raised an eyebrow at me. "Very interesting conjectures, Risuko, and we will explore them more fully. But now I would like you to tell us how you found the body."

I shuddered but told them about how I'd left the funeral to search for Mai, but after I saw the Retreat was empty, I had found her strung up behind the kitchen.

Both lords were staring down at me in their least pleasant, most predatory manner, but it was Lady Chiyome who leaned forward and snarled, "Did you kill her, Risuko?"

"What? No! I couldn't—whoever killed her would have been soaked in blood!" I held my shaking hands out, more or less clean, and then pointed at my blue jacket. "This is what I was wearing when I left you at the funeral, my lady, I swear. The killer was standing right in the— You saw how there was a gap in the blood. And as soon as I found her, I banged on the gong. And I couldn't have lifted her! And—"

Chiyome-*sama*'s scowl softened. "Again, all sensible points, my squirrel. But as Lord Matsudaira said, we must ask these questions. We will confirm what you have told us, but you are not a very likely suspect. Is she, my lords?" When they shook their heads, she called to the back of the hall, "You there! Foreign boy, by the door."

After a moment, Jolalo answered, "Me, it is, *senhora?*"

"Yes, boy, you. Go and tell the cooks that we need to have them come in and confirm Risuko's story, will you?"

"Yes, it is, *senhora.*" I heard the door from the hall to the kitchen give its familiar squeak as he slid through it.

"*Please!*" gasped the monk for some reason, but he only got half the word out before something covered his mouth. One of the Little Brothers' hands, probably.

"Now, Risuko, as we wait, you told me of some further conjectures concerning just whom our talkative monk friend was spying for."

The monk gave another muffled protest.

Matsudaira-*sama* grunted, "I hope, my lady, my lord governor of Worth, that you don't suspect the Matsudaira of being in any way involved in any of this."

Though Lord Takeda's face remained a mask, Lady Chiyome held up an open hand. "No, my lord. My young squirrel here, along with one of her teachers, discovered evidence of a different culprit. Risuko?"

I told them that Junkeishō had admitted to being a native of Armory Province, that he hadn't been seen in the district before the past few days, and so I thought it likely that he was acting as a spy for Lord Hōjō.

Behind me, I could feel the whole assembled crowd turn toward the monk, muttering what sounded like threats.

I remembered Sachi-*sensei* giggling once while showing us how to charm unsuspecting men out of information. *Soldiers don't like spies. Even cute ones!*

Before Junkeishō could be torn apart, the front door to the Great Hall opened, and two men entered, one a Matsudaira sentry and the other in rags. "General," said the one in armor, "Kobayashi has come to surrender himself."

26—Blank, Blue Sky

Behind Kobayashi and the guard, I could see a patch of sky that showed both bright blue and the white of gathering clouds. Perhaps it would rain. At least that might wash away poor Mai's blood. I shuddered.

Lady Chiyome whispered, "Risuko, you're done for now. Matsudaira-*sama* is going to need to speak to his deserter, and we may have some questions for him as well." When I sprang to my feet, glad to be able to retreat to the kitchen, she added with a snort, "And stay with Sachi. You're not off the hook yet."

Off the hook. Still shuddering, I made my way over to the music teacher as the sentry led Kobayashi to the white sand.

He nodded to me as he went to kneel before the three nobles. After he touched his head to the sand, Lord Matsudaira growled, "Where have you been, Kobayashi?"

The former guard's face was still sad and sunken, but there was a look of something like determination in his deep-set eyes. Head still bowed, he murmured, "I abandoned my post, my lord."

Another rumble like approaching thunder from the men behind me made it clear that soldiers didn't like deserters any more than they liked spies.

"Is that so, Kobayashi?" The Matsudaira general's face softened again so that it matched Kobayashi's sorrow. "You've never done anything like this, not in all of the years you've served under me, all of the battles we've fought in together. Why now?"

Outside the hall, actual thunder rumbled, followed by the wet sigh of falling rain.

Kobayashi's back rounded and then flattened, but his forehead remained pressed to the sand. "My lord . . . D'you remember the siege at Temple Castle, my lord?"

"Of course. It was my first real battle. I could never forget it." The lord nodded down at the prostrate man before him. "You were one of my guards that day."

"Yes, my lord. D'you remember, when the Oda showed up, a few of our troops panicked, ran off into the forest?"

"Yes, Kobayashi, of course, I remember that too."

"D'you remember what I told you when you wanted to ride after 'em and flog 'em?"

Matsudaira-*sama* gave a long sigh and glanced at the oldest of his captains, Hattori, who shrugged. "Yes. You said men can't always control where their feet are going to take them when faced with swords and pikes."

"Yes, my lord. And I may have said that heading off into the forest and flogging the men who'd run was only going to leave the men who'd stayed without a commander."

"It was good advice. What's your point?"

"Well, when I woke the other day, and realized . . . what I'd done, I was as surprised as anyone when my feet decided to run. And may I point out, my lord, that some of the men who ran into the forest at Temple Castle are behind me now, and they've been some of your finest soldiers."

"Again, Kobayashi, that is true. But they did not accept drugged wine while on duty, and while they abandoned their posts, it was during a pitched battle."

"Yes, my lord. I know, my lord."

"Then, Kobayashi, as a soldier who has always served me well—up until now—tell me, *why?*" The general's voice rattled with tamped-down anger, though his face remained sad. "And why, having run away, did you decide to return?"

"That girl behind me, my lord. Her and her friend." Both lords and their captains looked at me, eyebrows raised. When I just bowed, they turned back to Kobayashi. "They found me, where I was hiding up in the hills, and told me what happened to the officer that tricked me and, you know, the other sentry. That the lieutenant had been killed. And they told me you were investigating the murder and all. Said I had a duty . . . " His voice thickened. "Never turned my back on duty before, my lord. Never. I couldn't stay up in that cave knowing what I needed to do, even if it was the *last* thing I did. Which it probably is. So I came back, my lord. My lords. To help. And to face the consequences of what I've done."

"I see," sighed Lord Matsudaira.

Lady Chiyome cleared her throat. "Pardon me, my lord. Since this man may have important evidence regarding the two murders, may we question him?"

The general waved his hand.

"Two murders?" Kobayashi glanced up for the first time.

"Yes," said Chiyome-*sama*. "Two. The man who drugged you and one of *my girls.*"

Her tone made me jump—and I wasn't the only one. One of the soldiers behind me coughed to cover a gasp.

"Now, Kobayashi—that is your name, is it?"

"Yes, um, my lady."

"Good. What do you know about these murders?"

"Well, nothing about the second one, ma'am, I swear." Still bowed forward, he twisted his head toward me. "It wasn't your frown-faced friend, was it?"

I shook my head.

He nodded, closed his eyes, and then looked back up at Lady Chiyome. "Your girls asked if I'd heard the dead officer talking to anyone—"

To Sakai-*san*, Emi had asked.

"And I said, yeah, I'd heard him arguing with someone about money. Didn't recognize the voice. Flat, it was, like a goose honk." He pushed up and turned again, this time toward Junkeishō. "Sneaked down for the wake last night and heard His Reverence there, and when I woke up this morning, I thought the voice I'd heard sounded a lot like him."

"Like the monk?" asked Lord Takeda, his fierce gaze narrowing further.

The monk's eyes and mouth flew wide. Beneath the dirt and grass, his face was pale.

Kobayashi nodded. "Yeah. But then I realized not exactly. It was another voice, a lot like it, one I'd heard out in the courtyard while we were on watch."

At that moment the kitchen door slid open and Jolalo led the three cooks into the hall to back up my testimony.

Kobayashi gave a huff of surprise and pointed at the newcomers. "It was that one, there!"

Kee Sun looked up in shock. "*Me?*"

"No!" Kobayashi gave a humorless laugh. "Not him! The short one!"

Torai looked up, confusion and apprehension twisting his face.

"Brother!" called the monk. "*Run!*"

The cook started to sidle back through the kitchen door.

"Torai," snarled Takeda-*sama*, pinning him in place. "What have you done?"

———

The whole assembly stared at the Takeda cook, who stood staring back.

The only person not frozen was Shino, who pressed past the soldiers between them and howled at Torai, "*Shi-ne!*"

Torai unfroze in an instant and seized Shino, turning her. He lifted a thin boning knife to her throat. "Everyone stay away, or she'll—"

Whatever he planned to threaten, he'd picked the wrong girl. She may not have had poor Mai's skill with knives and garrotes, but as I said, Shino was a vicious close fighter. She grabbed the hand holding the knife and bit the wrist hard, then slammed her other elbow into the cook's gut even harder.

It wasn't one of the sequences we'd practiced in the hall against Aimaru, but it was clearly effective. Torai screamed, dropping the knife when Shino sank her teeth into his arm, and then crumpled once the elbow literally took his breath away.

"Nicely done," murmured Sachi.

The Takeda soldier next to her grunted in agreement.

Before Torai could hit the floor, Kee Sun's and Kumo's scarred hands grabbed their colleague and handed him to two officers—Takeda Lieutenant Itagaki and Matsudaira Lieutenant Sakai.

Takeda-*sama* growled, "Bring these two brothers up here." As the cook and the monk were dragged forward, he asked Matsudaira-*sama*, "May we conclude the matter of your deserter later?"

"Of course."

Lady Chiyome shot me a dry wink and added, "And perhaps we can hear again from my little squirrel. I believe that she will be able to shed some light on what these two ruffians have been up to."

As I walked somewhat unsteadily back to the front of the hall, Kobayashi left the sand and stood not far from me. His cheeks were still hollow and his eyes drooped, but he stood straight like a soldier for the first time that I'd seen.

I knelt back in the white circle—no longer even—and touched my head once more to the sand. "My lords. My lady."

When I looked back up, Lady Chiyome's expression was shrewd and cat-like. "Risuko, tell my lords what you found in the dead lieutenant's tent when you went to gather his funeral clothes."

"IOUs, my lady, for a lot of money."

"In fact," she said, holding up the scraps of ripped paper, "amounting to several gold *koshukin*."

"Yes, my lady."

"And to whom did the lieutenant owe these huge sums?"

"Most of them were made out to someone whose name began with a *T*."

"Like Torai, for instance?"

"Yes, my lady."

Lady Chiyome nodded to Lord Takeda, who ordered Captain Baba to have the cook's things searched. The captain gathered two soldiers and stepped out into a full spring downpour. The blank blue sky of the morning was gone, replaced by wet and grey.

Once they'd had gone off to the Bull Pen, Lady Chiyome asked me to repeat for the lords my reasons for suspecting the monk of espionage. I spoke once more about seeing the monk take the scroll and about his conversation with Sachi-*sensei* concerning his coming from Armory Province.

Lord Matsudaira said, "Yes, yes. We already know this."

"Of course, my lord," said Chiyome-*sama* with a bow. "Risuko, tell us: did you see the monk and the cook Torai together at all over the past few days?"

I had to think about that. "Yes, my lady. The holy man came into the hall and tried to go into the kitchen, and Torai led him back outside. And then yesterday afternoon, when we delivered the dead mens' clothes for the wake, they were having a disagreement. When Emi, Toumi, and I got close enough to hear, they told us they were arguing about rice wine. Torai-*san* said we couldn't spare any, but Junkeishō-*san* said it was very important for the funeral ceremony. But we have plenty of *sake*, and anyway, there wasn't any used in the ceremony!"

"No," said Lady Chiyome. "There wasn't. And now, Risuko, I'd like you to tell us: out in the courtyard, when you first discovered my girl's body, why did you accuse Torai of killing her?"

I thought carefully, picturing that awful scene. "Well, he was all bloody, of course."

"It was chicken blood!" Torai called out again from behind me.

"Silence!" growled Lord Takeda. "Was there anything else, girl?"

"Well . . . The past few days, he was acting very . . ." I closed my eyes, trying to focus, and a series of memories washed across my mind's eye. I gasped. "He kept trying to sneak out of the kitchen, my lords. To go to the stores." I turned toward him. As so often in the kitchen, his face was twisted with anger. "He was trying to find the paper that listed all the Takeda troops, my lords!" Now his face shrank with fear. "That's what he and the—and his brother, I guess—that's what they were arguing about, I bet: where the paper was. They were working together to get it back to Lord Hōjō."

Lord Takeda grunted. "Well reasoned, girl. Though with a fair amount of guesswork. My lady, my lord, let us question the traitors themselves."

Once more I returned to Sachi, who told me I had done well.

Soldiers dragged the monk and the cook forward and pushed them down onto the white sand of truth.

Junkeishō whimpered. Torai pleaded, "I didn't kill anyone, I swear! Please, my lord—"

Takeda-*sama* cut him off. "I've ordered you to be silent once already. If I have to ask you again, Hara here will cut off one of your ears. I'd have him cut out your tongue, but we want to hear you confess."

The cook trembled, joining Junkeishō in abasing himself, both lying flat on the sand—face and belly.

Lord Takeda continued, "Unfortunately for you, Torai, I no longer trust you. We have heard enough evidence of your conspiring with this— Are you two truly brothers?"

"Yes, my lord," both men said into the sand.

"And did you conspire to steal my military secrets for Lord Hōjō?"

There was a moment of silence. The soldiers behind me pressed forward to hear.

Voice quavering, the monk said, "Yes, my lord. Torai is our family name." And then he went on to explain how Lord Hōjō's spymaster had approached their father the previous spring at the inn their family had owned in Middlemanor for generations. The spymaster had complimented the inn and said what a shame it would be for such a lovely establishment to burn to the ground needlessly. That Lord Hōjō would be sure to protect the inn—and reward the family that ran it—if only they could provide him with some information that he needed. And so the father had sent his ordained son to contact the other—the one that had been a cook in Lord Takeda's army for years.

Lord Takeda tutted, "And so you betrayed me, Torai? After all this time?"

"My lord," the cook said, "please . . . I . . . I had no choice." At last he looked up but apparently didn't like the complete absence of compassion on his master's face, and so he collapsed once more into the sand.

His brother said, "They would have destroyed our family, my lord. What else could we have done?"

"You could have asked for my help. You could have fought," said Takeda-*sama*. "You could have died. As you certainly will."

Both men now began to cry, begging Lady Chiyome and Lord Matsudaira to intercede, pleading with all of them to show mercy.

The nobles' blank expressions offered none.

Captain Baba returned, waving a handful of strips of torn paper which turned out to match the IOUs. In his other hand, he carried a bloody cleaver. "This was under Torai's bed."

Lord Takeda pointed to the two cowering figures. His face as unforgiving as the cliff above the Full Moon, he ordered, "See them executed."

27—Ghost Blood

Captain Baba and his soldiers dragged the condemned men out to the angry calls of the soldiers, Takeda and Matsudaira alike. The execution party disappeared into the grey downpour, and the Little Brothers closed the door behind them, turning back toward the front of the hall. Their faces, which usually maintained a fairly tight balance between calm and good humor, were as angry as I'd seen them since the morning of the attack on the Mount Fuji Inn.

Lord Matsudaira gave a long sigh. "I believe that I must pass sentence as well. Kobayashi, kneel before us."

The deserter walked back to the sand, stiff legged as a stork, knelt, and bowed.

His commander stared down at him for a long moment and then said, "Kobayashi, you confessed here to having neglected your duty and to having abandoned your post. The punishment for these crimes, you must know, is death."

"Yes, my lord."

"You are a common soldier, and so I need not show you any mercy or consideration. Yet you have returned of your own volition and given testimony that helped my lady of the Full Moon and my lord governor of Worth root out treachery and murder, even though you did not have to. And you have served me long and well—well enough that I trusted you to serve as part of my personal guard. And so I will grant you this one favor, in return for the years of faithful service that you threw away: you may choose the manner of your own death."

After a moment, Kobayashi looked up. "What, my lord?"

"I condemn you to death." He said this almost kindly. "However, you may choose how you shall die. It is the best that I can do to repay you for having returned here so honorably."

"Th-thank you, my lord."

"Oh, Kobayashi, you are welcome. Now, before I must choose for you: what manner of death do you choose?"

Kobayashi looked around, eyes full, moonish circles, and, trying to imagine making such an impossible choice, I gave what I hoped was a thankful smile in return. He turned back toward the platform.

"Well?" asked Matsdudaira-*sama*.

Hanging can be slow and terribly painful, I'm told. Stoning? Poison? Beheading is supposed to be mercifully fast, but . . .

Kobayashi's voice came cracked but clear. "Old age."

Now it was Lord Matsudaira's turn to pause. He looked as if he'd put a persimmon in his mouth and tasted *kimchee* instead. "I beg your pardon?"

"I choose to die in your service, my lord. Of old age." Kobayashi bowed again. "If that's all right with you, my lord."

Around me, soldiers from both armies tried to stifle chuckles of surprise. Some succeeded better than others.

Lord Matsudaira closed his eyes and pinched the space between his brows. His ears turned pink. "I see." Regaining his composure, he glanced at Lord Takeda and Lady Chiyome, both of whom nodded back, more successful than the troops at holding in laughter but unable to hide it on their faces. "Get up, Kobayashi. I believe that you are late for duty."

The soldier leapt to his feet, kicking sand everywhere, and bowed deeply from the waist. "Yes, my lord! Thank you, my lord!" He turned, mouthing, *Thank you!* to me, and began to march out of the hall.

His commander stopped him, however. "Kobayashi. Consider yourself on report from now until that sentence is carried out. If you step out of line even slightly—if you break even the most minor rule or fail to follow any part of any order—I will reconsider this . . . punishment. Do you understand?"

Kobayashi bowed even more deeply and repeated, face set in a scowl so serious it looked a bit silly, "Yes, my lord. Thank you, my lord."

And then he walked out into the rain to take up his post.

I have promised to tell my story as it happened—not to get ahead of myself. But it pleases me to be able to break that promise so far as to say that Kobayashi did in fact serve long and honorably, first beneath Lord Matsudaira and then in the Tokugawa *bakufu*, the military government. He never rose in rank, remaining a sentry until he was grey haired and his hollow cheeks were lined with wrinkles. But having decided to return, he never abandoned his post again.

———

I returned to the kitchen with Kee Sun and Kumo and helped finish to prepare the evening meal—another of Torai's recipes, bland vegetables and grilled chicken, which Kee Sun decided to spice up. "Don't want to just serve what that *baesinja* planned, right?"

We all agreed—even Kumo-*san,* who seemed understandably thoughtful.

Toumi, Emi, and Aimaru had listened through the door. As we washed the chickens with the dark, peppery marinade, Toumi muttered, "Knew that short *baka* was up to no good."

I expected the cooks to admonish her, but Kee Sun looked as if he agreed with her, and Kumo was gazing up into the rafters, seeking some answer from the herbs.

We all concentrated on the work of preparing the meal, though I am sure the others were wondering whether the Torai brothers were already dead and how it had been done.

The kitchen filled with the sharp smell of the searing chicken and tang of onions and ginger in the wok.

That evening's meal was less quiet than the previous few—the officers from both sides of the hall were once again talking to each other, and Mieko and Sachi, along with the other *kunoichi,* were doing their best to keep the conversation light and far from murder and espionage.

Keeping the talk off dark topics didn't keep everyone's mind off them, however. The amount of *sake* that Shino and I poured was proof that the chatter and manic laughter was covering much gloomier thoughts.

Shino herself looked blank. Soulless.

"Are you all right?" I asked.

She didn't even snap at me, as I had expected, but simply shrugged.

As I refilled Mieko's *sake,* she whispered that she would meet me outside the kitchen at the Hour of the Pig, once the others were in bed.

Well seasoned as the food may have been, as we all ate in the kitchen that night, my thoughts were so far away that I don't think I tasted a thing.

Later, as we finished refilling the tubs, Emi voiced a thought that had been one of many swimming through my mind like a school of tadpoles in a muddy puddle. She asked whether we really thought that Torai—both Torais—had really been guilty of the murders.

"Who else?" grunted Toumi as she poured the last bucket into the hot tub.

Emi cocked her head in thought. "Well, I suppose I can see why they'd kill the lieutenant, since he could connect them to the espionage. But why her?"

Neither Toumi nor I had an answer for that question.

After Toumi and Emi were both snoring, I left the dormitory. Behind the closed door to the senior initiate's room, Shino was weeping, though she finally had sole claim to the privilege of the raised bed there.

I stepped out into the moonlit courtyard. The hook was empty and the gravel unstained. The rain had indeed washed poor Mai's blood away.

Poor Mai.

Even so, I could feel her spirit there in the dark night. It didn't feel like a happy spirit.

Not that Mai's spirit ever seemed very happy.

Mieko watched me cross the courtyard, her mouth set in a minute smile, though her spirit seemed no happier than that haunting the space outside the kitchen. "Come," she said, holding out Masugu's *wakizashi*. "Let's go outside."

As we walked into the moon-washed garden outside the wall, she unsheathed her own practice sword and asked, "Feeling ghost blood down the back of your neck?"

Startled, I just nodded, removing the short sword from its sheath.

Mieko looked up at the cliff—up toward the *oni*, or rather the bear skeleton that glared malignly out over the Full Moon. "Death always pains us. Even the death of someone we don't like very much. I do not know that I believe in ghosts, Risuko-*chan*, but I believe that death—especially violent death—stains our souls."

"Even violent deaths we commit ourselves?"

She was looking away from me still, but her shoulders tightened. "Oh, yes, Risuko. Always."

And then she whirled, aiming a devastating cut at my shoulder. I am sure, in retrospect, that if I had not stepped back and raised my own blade in a parry, she would have stopped her cut before it removed my arm. But at the time, I would not have said so. At the time, I only knew that I had to block her, and so I did.

We practiced as the moon continued its upward path, until I could see that Mieko's face was glowing not just with reflected light but with perspiration.

I, of course, was soaked.

When she bowed to me, marking the end of the lesson, a voice from the shadows by the wall called out, "Well done, ladies." Tokimatsu-*san*, the young Matsudaira captain, sauntered toward us, his hand resting on the grip of his own sword.

I found myself snapping into the Eight Phases, the most balanced guarding stance.

Mieko, however, remained at ease, her sword held one-handed by her side. "Tokugawa-*san*. You honor us. What brings you back here so late at night?"

He shrugged. "This is not the first time I have heard steel striking steel late at night toward the back of the Full Moon. Last night I was curious, but when I investigated, the sound was coming from inside the walls. Tonight . . . " He nodded toward us, a slight bow.

Mieko bowed back more fully and sheathed her sword. "I have been training young Kano-*san* here to defend herself."

His eyes flashed to me. "Of course."

"Risuko, sheathe your blade." Mieko's tone was light, but I could hear the sternness of the order beneath the tone.

I did so, though I kept the sheath in my off hand, ready to draw again.

Tokimatsu's gaze was still on me. "Kano. Are you by any chance . . . "

Forcing myself to look down and bow, I said, "Yes, sir. I am the daughter of Kano Kazuo." Then, because I couldn't stop the bitterness from seeping out, I added, "Late scribe of Serenity Province."

"Scribe." When I straightened, I was surprised to see his eyes wide and even more surprised to see the lord's nephew bow deeply to me, his hand leaving the handle of his blade for the first time. "Your father was much more than a scribe, Kano-*san*, as I am sure you know. Your father is the reason that I am alive." He straightened, his eyes flashing to Mieko. "And Masugu as well."

"Yes," she said.

"I remember you, Mieko-*san*. From Lord Imagawa's castle. From the night that Masugu and I carried my captain, Katsudama-*san*, back to his quarters." He narrowed his eyes, though his mouth remained in a wry smile. "Poisoned."

In all of the time I had known Mieko, she had rarely lost her composure. Now I heard her breath hitch. "I . . . I see."

"Yes," he answered, and nodded at our swords. "I too see. I see that the ladies of the Full Moon are, as we have been told, more than capable of defending themselves." When Mieko began to say something, he held up a hand. "I will not share this knowledge, Mieko-*san*, not even with my uncle. However, should I see you, or Kano-*san* here, or any other lovely ladies in *miko* or servant garb around the Matsudaira armies or in my uncle's court, I will consider their presence there to be, at best, suspicious. Do you understand?"

She bowed again. "Very well, Tokugawa-*san*."

He returned her bow. "Good. I wish you no ill, I promise. But my first loyalty is to my lord."

"Of course." Again, rare hesitation marked Mieko's speech. "Masugu has spoken of you. Often. He . . . was called to the capital. On duty."

"Ah. Well, perhaps I shall see him there. We will be leaving in the morning."

I blurted, "So soon?" It felt as if the two armies had been there for months, though it had only been a handful of days, and it had begun to feel as if the twin invasion would last forever.

The captain smiled. "Yes. So soon. Your lord and mine have both decided that, since the Hōjō are clearly looking for any opportunity to push into their territory from the north, planning an offensive toward the west at this moment would serve no one's best interests but the enemy's." He bowed again, the smile widening. "Ladies. It has truly been a pleasure. And please: if you see Masugu before I do, give him my best, will you?"

"Of course," we both answered.

28—The Ogre

The next morning, the Matsudaira camp was as busy as a wasp's nest that's been kicked. Tents coming down, horses being saddled, armor being put on.

In the kitchen, Kumo spoke little, and his gaze continued to be focussed somewhere else—somewhere outside.

For the first time, officers from the two armies broke ranks, with some Matsudaira sitting among the Takeda, and Itagaki sitting next to Sakai among the Matsudaira.

Jolalo-*san* kept looking at me, rather like a dog staring at a scrap of food on the table, willing it to fall.

It made me profoundly uncomfortable, even more than I could account for, to be honest. Even so, there was only me and Shino serving—and Shino was still moving far more slowly than usual—and so when their tea was empty, I had to be the one who refilled it.

Jolalo kept staring at me as I poured the genmaicha that we were serving that morning. (Apparently, Lord Matsudaira was particularly partial to the green tea flavored with toasted rice.)

When he started to say something, the priest beside him said a flurry of words in their twittering language, causing the bronze-skinned Portuguese boy to darken.

Then the priest said, his speech almost unaccented, "Thank you, my dear, for your service. João and I greatly appreciate the care shown by you and your mistress."

I blinked at him. "You speak Japanese!"

He smiled. "Naturally, it is."

"I had assumed that Jolalo-*san* was your translator!"

"I see," he said, his smile twisting slightly. "Understandable, perhaps, it is. I merely wished him to practice a language that for us very difficult, it is."

"I . . . Yes. It is. Understandable, that is."

Jolalo stammered, "R-risuko-*san*. An honor, it is. To know you, it is."

The priest chuckled and said something in Portuguese, once again making Jolalo blush.

———

When the meal had ended, I went back to the kitchen to help finish cleaning and also to say goodbye to Kumo-*san*, who had looked so hollow eyed ever since Mai's death.

The Matsudaira cook wasn't there, however.

"Gone to pack up," Kee Sun said with a shrug. "And I don't think yeh'll get much of a farewell outa Fatso. He's not been himself since yesterday."

I nodded. *Because of his daughters*, I thought. And I hadn't been myself either, truly—not for days. I thought of what Mieko had called *ghost blood*, the heavy spray of all the horror, dripping down my spine . . .

Cleansing.

I wanted to bathe myself, to wash away the bloodshed and violence. Not to forget what had happened to Torimasa, to Mai, to the Torai brothers, but to rid myself of the stain of their deaths, as my father had done every New Year at the small cascade above our village.

When all of the dishes were wiped clean and the little waste disposed of, I asked our cook if I could take Masugu's sword back to the springs. He waved me away in acceptance.

I took down the blade from the rack. When I asked Toumi and Emi to join me, they said they didn't want to miss Mieko's dance class.

That almost stopped me.

I wish it had. Almost.

I walked through the woods and up along the spoiled-egg stream. I passed the rocks where I had tripped Jolalo.

I tried to think about good things, positive things—but my mind filled instead with Mai's blood. With Torimasa's shocked expression. With the slouched figures of the cook and the monk, being led out into the downpour.

Lord Imagawa had placed the heads of traitors over the gate of his castle—gruesome. It had been an awful relief never to see *Otō-san*'s head there but terrible never to know what had happened to him.

The heads of the Torai brothers weren't hung over the gate of the Full Moon. They'd simply marched off into the rain, never to be seen again.

I reached the pool and the waterfall, watched once again by monkeys, who seemed more distrustful than curious now—though that may have been my imagination.

While the morning was cool, the mist from the waterfall was warm as always, and so I removed my jacket and my shoes with pleasure, laying them on the rocks along with the sheath.

Carefully, thoroughly, I went through the rituals—washing my hands and then the blade, though truly I was seeking to wash my spirit.

As on the previous visits, I could feel a presence watching me. It did not feel like the benign *kami* of the spring, however. It felt like the ogre down in the cave below. Kobayashi was almost certainly right—no doubt it was a bear skeleton, left to look over the Full Moon there since the time of legends, since before the Full Moon was built. But the spirit I felt was *oni*-like: angry, violent, malign.

Peace, I prayed, even so, offering thanks, attempting to embrace balance. *Rest easy.*

I do not know whether the spirit of the bear-ogre was placated at all, but my own spirit had settled somewhat when I heard a sound from behind me, over the roar of the torrent.

I broke off my prayer to the eight million spirits and turned, the cleansed sword in my hand rising to readiness.

On the bank, Jolalo was calling to me, hands cupped to his mouth, though he was only a few steps away.

Alarmed and curious as the squirrel that I will always be, I stepped toward him.

He bowed stiffly—a proper bow from the waist, not the odd, hand-waving, bent-kneed bow he'd offered a few days before. "Risuko-*san.*"

I let the sword tip drop, not aware of having raised it. "Jolalo-*san?*"

He was wearing the same strange black jacket, short pants, and tight leggings as usual, but now he had a flat cap on his head in the identical heavy material as the coat. His face was flushed, and he wore as hungry an expression as at breakfast. He closed his eyes for a moment, then said, "João."

"I beg your pardon?"

"João, my name, it is."

"Jo-lalo."

He spoke as if to an infant. "Jo."

Dutifully, if doubtfully, I repeated, "Jo."

"Ah."

"Ah." I felt silly, standing there, soaking wet in my undershirt, repeating nonsense syllables back to him.

"Oh."

"Oh."

He nodded and smiled. "João."

I frowned. "Jolalo."

He sighed and closed his eyes. "*Mãe de Deus.*" His eyes flashed back open, hungrier than ever. Then he grabbed me by the shoulders and, before I could pull myself free, rattled out, "*Amor é um fogo que arde sem se ver, é ferida que doi, e não se sente . . .*"

Stunned, I stood there, dripping.

And then he stepped closer to me, his cap hitting my forehead and falling to the ground, but before I could say anything about that, he pressed his lips to mine.

It felt strange. Funny.

I wanted to push him away, to stop him, but shock like cold honey slowed my muscles.

Finally, I raised my left hand—the one not carrying Masugu's sword—to his chest and, holding him firmly in place, stepped back, breaking the kiss.

His face was now dark and his eyes wide in a kind of terror. "*Opa,*" he groaned.

And then the eyes rolled back in his head and he slumped to the ground.

Behind him stood Kumo-*san*, his face no longer distant or kindly. He looked furious. In his left hand, he held the rock he'd used to cosh Jolalo. In his right, he raised a long, lethal knife to slash at Jolalo's exposed throat.

"*Kumo*-san!" I screamed—and when he didn't stop but began to swing the blade, I acted without thought and parried his cut.

It wasn't a pretty, precise parry such as Mieko-*sensei* had been drilling me to make, but it stopped Kumo's knife from slitting Jolalo's throat—

—just as Mai's had been slit.

"Kumo-*san?*"

His eyes flew up to mine, his face a mask of animal, bottomless rage.

"Why? Did you kill Mai?" The name slipped out in spite of my knowing better.

"*Monsters!*" he howled, raising his long blade again. When I shifted into the stance of the Two Fields, my sword tip inches from his belly, he stepped back in surprise, and I advanced, stepping over Jolalo's form, protecting him.

Kumo's glare flashed back up to me, and he growled, "Monsters. All of you, monsters!" His thick chest heaved. "I thought—you and Emi and even that Toumi, though she was a bit of a harridan—thought you were all *proper* girls, *nice* girls. But you're not, are you, with your fighting and swearing and drinking . . . " He sobbed but brought his knife to meet my sword. "That girl, that slut, drunk, saying, 'You're tall enough, Fatso, bet you broke his neck like one of your chickens!'" His face contorted, baring his teeth. "So I had to cut her throat, didn't I?"

Swallowing carefully, keeping my eyes focussed so that I could see both his twisted face and the knife, I said, "And you killed the lieutenant as well."

Another sob. "Thought he was sneaking in to abuse the girl. Couldn't have that!" Now anger throbbed through him once more. "Monsters. That Takeda officer. This one here!" He spat down at Jolalo, who groaned between my feet. "All of them! Not a one of them proper soldiers . . . or proper girls . . . "

"Like your daughters?"

"Don't you dare speak of them!" He brandished the knife, threatening me with it.

I did my best to stay still, waiting for an actual attack.

"Monsters like *him*"—he gestured at Jolalo with his chin—"destroyed my poor family. And monsters like that *girl*"—now he narrowed his eyes—"and you. All of you. Monsters. So yes, I killed her. Tossed my coat into the fires in the bathhouse, went to get a new one, put the blade under Shorty's bedroll . . . "

"And then you came back when I started ringing the gong, as if you didn't know a thing."

He gave a bear-like growl of a laugh. "Yes. And you accused Torai. Serves him right. Another monster!"

"But—but he didn't kill anyone!"

"He was a traitor. And a spy. He and that monk deserved what they got."

"Perhaps. And the lieutenant was certainly a traitor as well, though you couldn't have known that. But the girl you killed hadn't—"

"She was a monster, I told you!" he howled. He bared his teeth at me again, and there was nothing smile-like about it. I understood, suddenly, why the little monkeys had run away when I'd grinned at them. He raised his knife again. "Just like you."

I tightened my grip, preparing for an attack. One that I was fairly sure I could stop but only by killing the big cook. "Please, Kumo-*san*. I do not wish to harm you."

"Monster!" he screamed, and raised his knife for a horizontal cut—easy to block, but then—

His head jerked back, and a surprised cough exited his body along with a spurt of bright red blood.

Then he slumped to the ground, revealing the hilt of a knife protruding from the base of his skull.

And Emi, reaching for another blade in her belt, her eyes and mouth full moons of shock.

We looked at each other, then down at Kumo, who gave a long, relieved sigh, all anger flowing from his body with the breath and the blood.

True red.

"Saw him!" gulped Emi. "Toumi saw him follow you and Jolalo, and he seemed so strange, so she went off to get help, but thought I should . . . "

"Thank you, Emi," I said, stepping around the dead body to embrace her.

Before I could, however, she leaned forward and vomited all over my still-wet undershirt. Then she began to cry.

As I attempted to wipe myself clean and comfort her, Jolalo groaned again and tried to sit up before slumping back to the gravelly shore, holding his head. *"Ai, minha cabeca!"*

Epilogue—Heading Off

By the time Toumi arrived with Hoshi and Mieko, Jolalo was sitting up, still holding his head, and I had cleaned myself off again in the waterfall. I had even conducted the cleansing ritual once more—this time for Emi.

And also for Kumo-*san*, whose sad corpse lay on the rocks as baleful and yet as empty as the bear skeleton in the cave.

The *kunoichi* promised that they would take care of the dead cook. Emi and I led Jolalo, wobbling, back down the hill.

He didn't remember a thing about the encounter by the pool. When he tried to ask if he had said anything to me, whatever he saw in my eyes silenced him.

I didn't ask Emi if Kumo were the first person she had ever killed. I could see the answer in her trembling fingers and shallow breath.

"You did well, Emi. He would have tried to kill Jolalo. Me. He was dangerous."

She simply nodded.

Like her, however, I was troubled by the big cook's death.

Back at the Full Moon, I returned Jolalo to the priest's care, explaining that he had hit his head.

And with Lady Chiyome's help, I explained to Captain Tokimatsu that the Matsudaira cook was dead—and had been the murderer of both Torimasa and Mai.

He nodded in understanding, though his gaze searched for answers to unasked questions.

The Matsudaira left in as orderly a fashion as they had arrived—eighty-eight infantry and a dozen mounted troops in perfect rows.

A squadron of Takeda cavalry accompanied them.

No cook.

Only two faces turned back toward the Full Moon as they descended the road to the valley: Captain Tokimatsu's and Jolalo's.

Quickly, they too disappeared.

———

The Full Moon felt empty—though Lord Takeda and his forces stayed another day.

At dinner, the soldiers were buzzing like a bee's nest at apple-blossom time. Apparently, since the attack on the capital was off, Takeda-*sama* was planning to use the troops he had massed in Highfield to take Dark Letter Province away from the Uesugi once and for all. The general himself would be returning to Worth to plan a way to punish the Hōjō on his northern border.

After breakfast the next morning, Sachi came into the kitchen to inform me, Emi, and Toumi that the Mountain wished to speak with us.

Nervous—even Toumi—we made our way into the Great Hall and knelt before Takeda-*sama*. Behind him stood our mistress and Mieko-*sensei*.

After a moment of silence, Lord Takeda said, "Kano. Torugu. Hanichi."

"My lord," we answered in unison.

"I hear that we have the three of you to thank for solving much of the trouble of these past few days. I asked you, when you were first brought to my attention, whether you were truly your fathers' daughters. I see now that you are."

Shocked, I glanced up. Lord Takeda's tiger scowl made me lower my face back to the bamboo. "Thank you, my lord," I whispered.

Emi and Toumi echoed me.

"Yet it seems to me that, if you are truly worthy samurai daughters, then you deserve to have your honor fully restored."

Now all three of us looked up.

He dismissed our hope with a wave of his hand. "I was not the lord to remove your family honor. Only one *daimyo* can reinstate it. The one who wronged your fathers: Oda Nobunaga."

Emi and I did our best to remain silent, but Toumi couldn't. "What do you mean? Um, my lord."

He gave a mirthless laugh. "I mean, girl, that Chiyome is sending your teacher Mieko here on a mission to the capital and that I suggested to her that you three might accompany her. To . . . complete your training. You are not yet fully trained *kunoichi*, yet I have seen—and your mistress confirms—that you have the necessary skills. And that, once you arrive in the capital, having gained all of the many skills Mieko and the others practice so well, you would at last be able to avenge your fathers' disgrace."

Still bowing low, I looked to either side. I could see that Emi and Toumi were weighing Takeda-*sama*'s words and coming to the same conclusion that I was: we were being ordered to assassinate Lord Oda.

There being nothing else to say, we all answered, "Yes, my lord."

No harm.

He gave a satisfied grunt and stood. "I will leave the rest to you, ladies," he said, and strode out the door.

"My lord," we all answered—the three of us but also Lady Chiyome and Mieko.

When he was gone, Chiyome-*sama* gave her familiar sour smile. "Well, I did not think you would be heading off so soon. We shall miss you three troublemakers. Mieko, see that they're ready to leave. And . . . Oh, I can't spare the Little Brothers, but you can take Aimaru with you. Just in case."

"Yes, my lady," answered Mieko.

Lady Chiyome began to walk toward the stairs to her rooms but stopped. "Girls. I told you when I took each of you on that I had it in my power to give you something you did not even know you wanted. This was it. Do this well, and you will confer honor not only on your clans but upon the Full Moon itself. Fail . . . "

She did not complete that thought.

Once she had closed the door to her apartment, Mieko said softly, "Come, girls. We leave tomorrow at dawn."

THANK YOU FOR READING

BRIGHT EYES!

I hope that you enjoyed this tale of Risuko's continuing adventures. If you did, please tell your friends what you thought. Word of mouth is an author's best friend—and I'd like to think you'd be doing *your* friends a favor too! You can share an honest review on your blog or TikTok, post a pic on Instagram or Snapchat or a link on Facebook, or leave a review

on Amazon (risuko.net/amazon-bright-eyes),

on BookBub (risuko.net/bookbub-bright-eyes),

or Goodreads (risuko.net/goodreads-bright-eyes).

If you do write a review, please let me know where and when by sending the web address (URL) or a screenshot to

risuko@risuko.net—I'd love to know what you think!

Thanks again.

David Kudler

To be Continued in
KANO
Seasons of the Sword #3

Or read the prequel short stories

Find out more on
SeasonsoftheSword.com
Follow on:

Sneak Preview:

KANO

"My lady," sighed the Uesugi captain, "I can't let you and your party through without an escort—there's trouble on the other side of the province. And we've already had to send half of the garrison west, so I can't spare any men for an escort. I must insist you stay in Tiptown."

Mieko gave him her most disgusted Lady Chiyome glare. "Ruffian." She turned to me and Toumi, kneeling to her left in the captain's office. "What will Masugu-*sama* think if we don't arrive in the capital on time?"

I put my hand in her knee like the supportive lady's maid that I supposedly was. "I'm sure the *shōgun* will understand if his cousin, your intended, has to change the wedding date."

When Toumi gave a dismissive snort and muttered, "Sure he will," Mieko covered her face in her hands and began to wail.

I handed her a silk handkerchief.

The Uesugi commander ground his teeth, clearly unused to having to manage high-strung noble brides—or cunning *kunoichi*. "My lady. . ." He closed his eyes. "Can I get you something, my lady?"

This is the cue we had been waiting for. "Please," I simpered, "if this humble servant might fetch her ladyship some wine, that might help our mistress's nerves."

"Yes, yes," grumbled the captain. "The stores are immediately across the courtyard, to the right of the main gate."

As I bowed, Mieko sniffled, "Oh, you go with her, Toumi. She's always getting lost."

"Yes, my lady," said Toumi in a more than passably respectful manner. Really, if you didn't know her, you might almost have thought she was *sweet*.

Toumi and I scurried out into the courtyard of the Tiptown garrison. It was quiet. Eerily so, since we knew that they were about to be attacked. The soldiers there looked anything but alert.

Emi and Aimaru stepped past a ragged line of marching pikemen to get to us. Emi said, "Is, um, our *mistress* all right?"

I expected Toumi to make a joke, but she kept up her respectful maid facade, and so I answered, "Mieko-*sama* is very upset. The captain suggested that we fetch her some *sake*."

Aimaru nodded solemnly as he and Emi finally got close enough to whisper, "I'd like to see Mieko-*san* acting very upset."

"It's definitely weird," Toumi granted with a shrug.

Feeling that time was tight, I whispered, "Armory?"

Emi answered, "To the left of the gate."

Opposite the storeroom. One sentry at each door.

My heart began to thrash like a sparrow trying to escape a drying net.

Mieko had talked us through all of this as we rode from the Highfield garrison across enemy lines to Tiptown. I forced the sparrow down my throat and back into my chest. "So. We get the wine. Then I'll deal with the gunpowder. Toumi, you keep an eye on the door. Emi, you bring Mieko-*sen*. . . Mieko-*sama* the *sake*. And Aimaru—"

"Get the horses ready. Just in case."

They all nodded together.

Emi, Toumi, and Aimaru had all grown up on the streets of the capital. All three of them had done things like this in order to survive—risky, illegal things.

I had climbed up the outside of Lord Imagawa's castle near our village— but I had done it out of boredom. And while I would have been beaten (or worse) if I'd been caught, I had known I wouldn't be caught.

Who expected a little girl to climb up the stone walls of a castle?

But this? Walking into a room full of weapons in the middle of an armed fort that we knew was about to face an attack, even if the Uesugi didn't?

"Come on, Murasaki," said Emi, taking my hand and leading me across the courtyard. Aimaru split and sauntered out the gate toward where the horses we'd picked up in Highfield were tied.

When we got to the storeroom, there was a guard at the door, looking thoroughly bored. "This where the wine's kept?" asked Toumi.

When the guard just stared at her, I said, in my meekest servant-girl voice, "Pardon, sir, but the captain and our lady have commanded us humble servants to bring them *sake*. If the wine is stored here, may we enter?"

He rolled his eyes, but stepped aside.

The storeroom was huge — and a mess. Kee Sun would not have approved. Rats scurried as we walked past haphazardly stacked bales of rice and barley toward the back, where sealed jars of *sake* lay in a pile next to what looked like Uesugi battle flags mixed with summer jackets.

"How can they keep track of anything?" murmured Emi, her habitual frown deepening.

"Don't care," grunted Toumi, grabbing two jars of *sake*. "And they won't either after the Takeda kick them out." She handed one jar to Emi and the other to me. Then she grinned. "Think I'll take another of these, since it won't do them any good."

"Toumi!" Emi and I gasped.

She rolled her eyes at us. "Not for me, *baka*. You'll see."

Emi's frown now deepened to a scowl, and I'm sure my expressions wasn't much sunnier. However, we needed to keep moving—before our absence was noted. Or I lost my nerve.

As we came back out of the stores, Toumi nodded to the bored soldier and showed him the wine jar. "Thanks. Our bosses will be real happy." Then she flicked her head toward the guard in front of the armory, "Hey, what's the name of your friend over there?"

He stared at her again, then gave a grunt and said, "Joshi. Why?"

Toumi shot him a grin and sloshed her wine. "'Cause I'd like to be happy too, and I thought you and your buddy might want to join me."

He gave a gruff laugh. "Are you old enough to be drinking wine?"

"Old enough to want to!" answered Toumi with a grin that didn't look right on her face.

"Toumi!" Emi's voice was disapproving, and I think she was only partially acting.

"Oh, come on. You two get to go into where Lady Mieko and the captain are having their fun. I get to sit out here. Can't blame me for taking advantage of the opportunity. Come on." She winked at us and, as we walked away, said to the bored guard over her shoulder. "Be right back!"

"Are you sure this is a good idea?" I whispered.

"Hey, I'm not stupid," Toumi whispered back. "Not gonna actually swallow any of it. It's just like those endless drinking games Sachi-*sensei* made us play with water, right? And it's the best way of getting you into the armory, Mouse."

"All right," I conceded.

Emi added, "Be careful."

"Wow. I might almost think you care," she said with a grin that was more like her—knife-sharp and dangerous.

"We do," I answered.

Rather than answer me, Toumi called to the guard in front of the armory, "Hey, Joshi-*san!*" When the guard blinked at her, she gave her *sake* jar a wet shake. "Your pal at the storerooms was planning on showing me some drinking games, and said you might like to join us."

He tried to look stern, but licked his lips. "Zashiki said that?"

"Yup. Said you knew some fun ones."

"Oh, sure." He smiled, and I realized with a start that he didn't look any older than Aimaru. With a laugh, he abandoned his post and joined Toumi crossing the courtyard toward the much-less-bored-looking Zashiki.

I was about to point out that Toumi was actually frighteningly good at that when Emi whispered, "No one's looking. Go in."

And so before I could think about it, I moved my wine jar to my left hand, slid open the door to the armory, and stepped through.

Emi slid the door behind me, no doubt heading off to deliver the remain jar of wine to Mieko, and I was alone in a room full of the instruments of death and destruction.

The "armory" at the Full Moon was just a corner of the storeroom that held a dozen long-bladed glaives, a half-dozen swords, a handful of bows, stacks of arrows, some helmets, and a few suits of armor. Plenty to defend Lady Chiyome's school for shrine maidens—and assassins.

The Tiptown garrison's armory was intended to supply a small army and defend the western half of Dark Letter Province from invasion by the Takeda.

Where the food and goods in the storeroom had been piled haphazardly, here the soldiers' equipment was arranged with the precision of a scribe's tools: neat stacks of long *katana*, short *wakazashi*, and even shorter daggers, sheathed, but still deadly. Pikes and glaives, long and short bows, bushels of arrows, mounds of neatly piled armor parts—helmets, gauntlets, chest plates, bracers for the arms, pauldrons for the shoulders, sabatons for the feet, greaves for the legs, and more.

And in the very back corner, on wooden pegs all of the way to the high ceiling, perhaps forty muskets, and below them the things that made those strange looking contraptions of metal and wood lethal: boxes that I knew must contain bullets and thirty or so sealed ceramic canisters marked 火薬. *Gunpowder.*

Captain Yamagata, the Takeda commander of the garrison at Highfield, had simply told us to *neutralize* the Uesugi guns. He hadn't cared how.

Earlier that day, crossing a ford over a small, quick river, Mieko had asked us how we would do such a thing.

Toumi had answered very simply, "Use a flint. Boom."

Mieko had actually laughed at that. "True. That would be extremely effective. It would also probably kill whichever of us managed to do it, and would put the Uesugi on high alert, which Yamagata-*san* and his men would rather we not do, since they are marching only a few hours behind us. Any other ideas?"

Aimaru had suggested stealing them, but had granted with a smile that there was probably too much to take, and someone would certainly notice.

Emi had suggested smashing the jars, but Toumi had pointed out the sound would again certainly attract notice, and I added that they still might be able to use some of the powder.

Mieko had smiled in approval, and then said, "Risuko-*chan*, you grew up near a castle. Did you ever watch the musketeers training?"

I'd nodded. I'd loved to spy on them from the pine trees near our village, watching them fire at targets set against the base of the cliff below the castle.

"Did you ever watch them when it was raining?"

I'd frowned as I rocked unsteadily on the back of the Takeda charger. "Yes, once." I had visualized the chaotic scene. "They were practicing, when we were hit by a sudden shower. They went scurrying, covering everything with tarps and umbrellas!"

"Yes. I will tell you all a secret about gunpowder: once it gets wet, it can't ever be used. Even a tea-cup's worth of liquid poured into a canister of gunpowder will turn it into so much dirt."

"Oh!" I could see what she was suggesting. "So we get their powder wet, and make it so they can't use their guns, like Yamagata-*san* asked, and it doesn't make any noise!"

Emi had jumped in, saying, "And they won't even know what's happened until it's too late."

I opened my *sake* jar, and then took the lid off of the first canister of gunpowder. The smell was an odd combination—a bit of the familiar scent of charcoal and a touch of the rotten-egg scent from the hot springs above the Full Moon. I poured what seemed like a tea cup of wine in, put the lid back on the canister, shook it, and moved to the next canister.

Do no harm, my father had begged me as he walked away that last time, toward Lord Imagawa and his doom.

Well, I wasn't hurting anyone, was I? In fact, I was making it so the musketeers couldn't hurt anyone.

I was also making it so they couldn't defend themselves. I wasn't sure whether my father would have approved or not.

I was very conscious of how long it was taking me to sabotage each container of black powder. I tried to be as quick as I could while still being careful, not letting any of the powder spill.

I was putting the lid back on the last canister when I heard the door to the armory slide open.

"You really don't need to show me! I believe you!" Toumi's voice, which she was trying to keep as light and jocular as before, had an edge of panic that set off my own fear like a spark to unspoiled gunpowder.

"No, no, no," said Zashiki, the storeroom guard, sounding as if he'd had more than a tea-cup's worth of *sake* himself. "You must see, we have over forty muskets, the Takeda wouldn't dare attack us here."

"Tha's right," slurred the young guard, Joshi, "they'd be idiots t'even try!"

Hearing their footsteps, I realized that I had little time to hide, and so, without thinking, I did what I do best: I climbed.

To be Continued in

KANO

Seasons of the Sword #3

Coming Soon!
Find out more on
SeasonsoftheSword.com

Follow on:
twitter.com/RisukoKunoichi • risuko-chan.tumblr.com
facebook.com/risuko.books • instagram.com/RisukoKunoichi
risuko.livejournal.com • tiktok.com/@kanomurasaki

Glossary

*The straight line over some vowels (for example, ō or ā) is called a **macron**. It indicates that the vowel should be given a longer sound.*

-chan—child

-ko—ending meaning that the word is a girl's name or nickname

-sama—my lady or lord (honorific)

-san—sir or ma'am (honorific)

-senpai—senior student (honorific)

Ai, minha cabeca! (Portuguese)—Oh, my head!

Amor é um fogo que arde sem se ver, é ferida que doi, e não se sente. (Portuguese)—"Love is a fire that burns unseen, a wound that aches yet isn't felt."—Luis de Camões

baesinja (Korean)—traitor

baka, baka yarō—idiot, complete idiot (offensive)

baka ama—stupid woman (offensive)

bakufu—the military government headed by the *shōgun*

Benten—Buddhist deity of beauty and art (also known as Benzaiten)

Bishamon—Buddhist deity of strength and war

busu—ugly person, usually used for women (offensive)

byeong-shin (Korean)—idiot (offensive)

che—interjection (not particularly offensive)

daikon—a large, white, mild radish

daimyo—lord (roughly equivalent to an English duke or earl)

dōmo arigatō—thank you very much

genmaicha—green tea flavored with toasted rice

go—a Chinese game of strategy

gō—actions (in Buddhism, *karma:* the spiritual weight of your actions or *karma* determines your next life)

hai—yes

hanyak (Korean)—herbal medicine

hiragana—phonetic script used for Japanese words for which there are no *kanji*

ichi—the number one

jinmaku—circular, curtained enclosure used in military camps

Jizō-bosatsu—the Buddhist saint (*boddhisatva*) of lost children; he is often portrayed with a blank face and large sleeves in which he protects the children

kami—spirit or god; Shintō tradition says there are eight million, but that figure is meant simply to suggest "beyond number"

kanji—Chinese ideograms; over three thousand of these non-phonetic characters are widely used in Japanese writing

karma—In Buddhism and Hinduism, the sum or weight of one's actions, which determines one's next life

katakana—rounded phonetic script used for most foreign words and for emphasis (similar to italics in English)

katana—a samurai's long, curved sword

kimchee (Korean)—pickled cabbage, often spicy

kudzu—Arrowroot, a fast-growing vine

kitsune—a mischievous nine-tailed fox spirit

koshukin—gold coin, worth fifty silver *monme* or about 1000lbs
(450 kg) of rice, enough to feed four people for a year

koto—a long, plucked, stringed musical instrument, like a zither

ku or *kyu*—the number nine

kumiho (Korean)—mischievous fox spirit (similar to a *kitsune*)

kunoichi—"nine in one"; a special kind of woman trained as an assassin,
bodyguard, or spy

Kwan-um (Korean)—the Buddhist saint (*boddhisatva*) of mercy and
beauty; called Kwan-yin in China and Kannon in Japan

Mãe de Deus (Portuguese)—interjection meaning "Mother of God"

miko—shrine maidens; young women who assist at Shintō festivals and
ceremonies

mizutaki—a hot-pot dish made with fish, chicken, or some other meat

Mochizuki—"Full Moon"; the clan of Lady Chiyome's late husband

mogusa—mugwort; formed into pellets and burned (with the lit end
away from the flesh) as a stimulant and as a way to celebrate
children's aging during the New Year festival

mon—the emblem of a noble house (like the European coat of arms)

monme—silver coin worth approximately twenty pounds (9 kg) of rice

Mukashi, mukashi—"Long, long ago" (traditional beginning to Japanese
folktales, similar to "Once upon a time")

nattō—fermented beans

no—preposition meaning of, in, or from

oni—ogre, monster

Okā-san—Mother

opa (Portuguese)—oops

Otō-san—Father

Risuko—Squirrel (a girl's name or nickname)

samisen—a long-necked, five-stringed instrument, similar to a guitar or banjo

senhora (Portuguese)—my lady, ma'am

sensei or *-sensei*—teacher (honorific)

seppuku—ritual suicide (also called *hara-kiri*)

shi-de—Paper streamers, usually cut in a zigzag shape, for use in Shintō rituals

Shi-ne—Die! Drop dead!

Shintō—the native religion of Japan; Shintō believes that there are many gods or spirits (*kami*) inhabiting different parts of the natural world and is frequently practiced side by side with Buddhism

shakuhachi—a long flute carved from bamboo

shōgun—the emperor's warlord

shoyu—soy sauce

soondae (Korean)—blood sausages

tatami—a straw mat that is traditionally used to cover floors in Japan

torī—a large arch or gateway usually found at Shintō shrines or temples

wakizashi—a samurai's short sword; traditionally used for defense and for committing ritual suicide (*hara-kiri* or *seppuku*)

Wihayeo (Korean)—Cheers!

yang (Chinese)—the male force

yin (Chinese)—the female force

Place Names

I have translated most of the place names in the book; after all, the names aren't exotic to a speaker of Japanese! The translations are my own, and sometimes aim more at a poetic than a literal translation of the name.

There is in fact a village called Mochizuki in Nagano (what used to be Shinano or Dark Letter Province). It is not very far from Midriver Island (Kawanakajima), the site of several of the greatest battles of Japan's Civil War era. I couldn't help but set the estate of the Mochizuki family there. The estate itself, however, is entirely of my own imagining.

Armory Province—Musashi

      Estuary—Edō (later known as Tōkyō)

      Middlemanor—Fuchū

      Seaside—Yokohama

Dark Letter Province—Shinano

      Full Moon—Mochizuki, Shinano Province

      Highfield—Ueda, Shinano Province (Takeda controlled)

      Midriver Island—Kawanakajima, Shinano Province

      Tiptown—Sakaki, Shinano Province (Uesugi controlled)

Fountain Province—Izumi

Great Eastern Sea Road—Tōkaidō

Pure Beauty Province—Mino

Rising Tail Province—Owari

River Bend Province—Kawachi

Serenity Province—Tōtōmi

      Pineshore—Hamamatsu-shi, Tōtōmi Province

Three Rivers Province—Mikawa

      Picnic Valley—Shitara-chō, Mikawa Province

      Temple Castle—Terabe, Mikawa Province

Quick River Province—Suruga

White Mountain Province—Yamashiro

      Capital—Kyōto, Yamashiro Province

Winged Flight Province—Hida

Wild Heights Province—Kōzuke

Worth Province—Kai

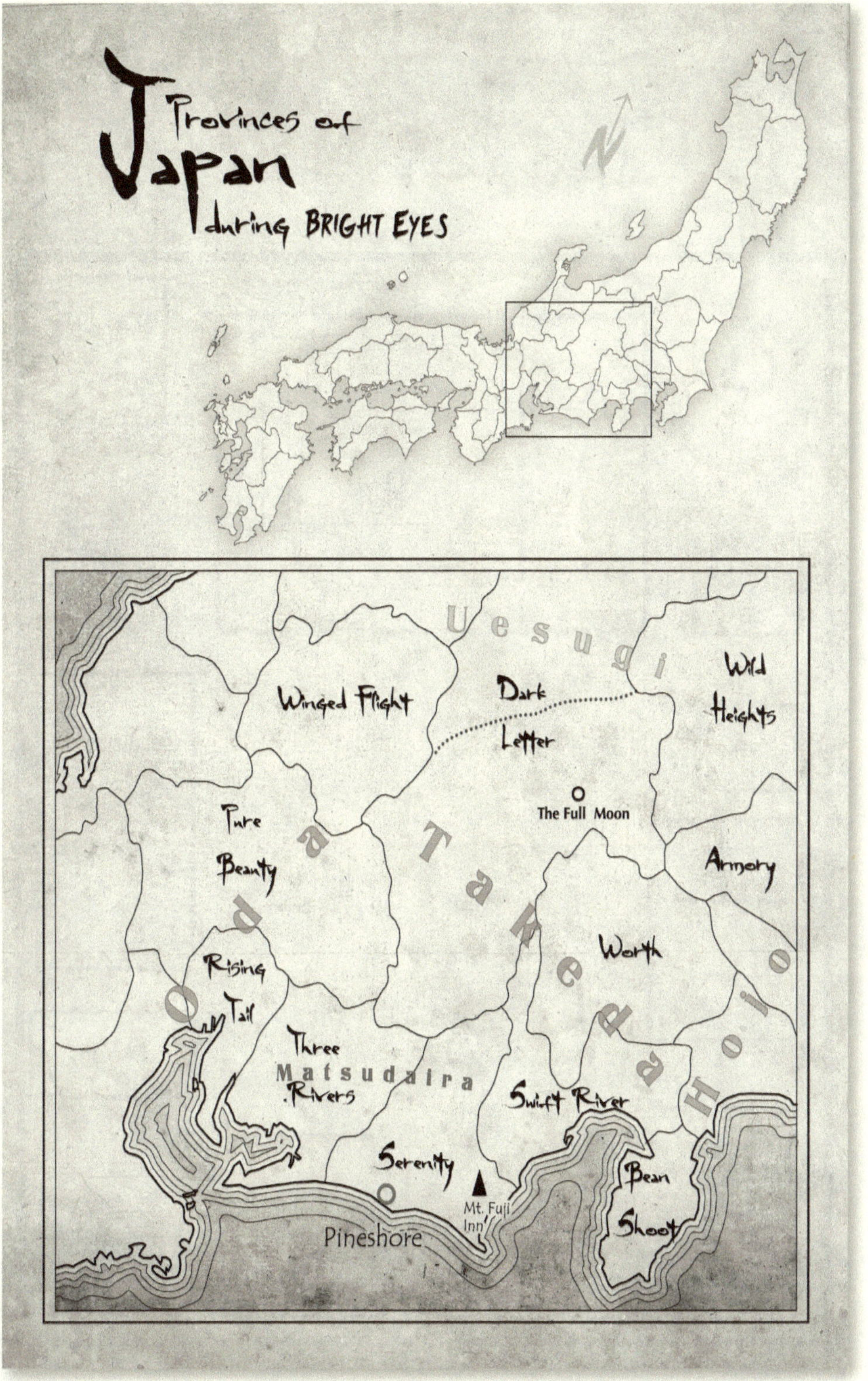

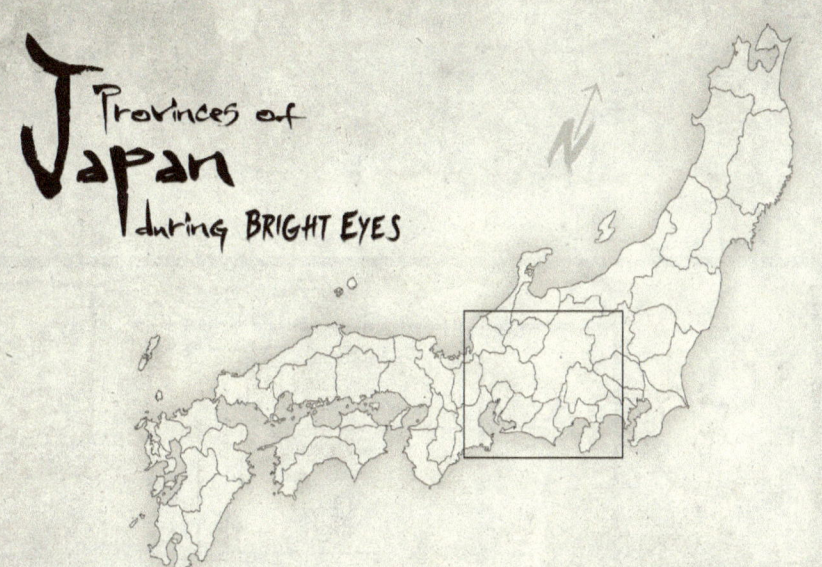

Provinces of Japan during BRIGHT EYES

Uesugi

Winged Flight

Dark Letter

Wild Heights

The Full Moon

Pure Beauty

Oda

Takeda

Armory

Rising Tail

Worth

Hojo

Three Matsudaira Rivers

Swift River

Serenity

Mt. Fuji Inn

Bean Shoot

Pineshore

The Full Moon

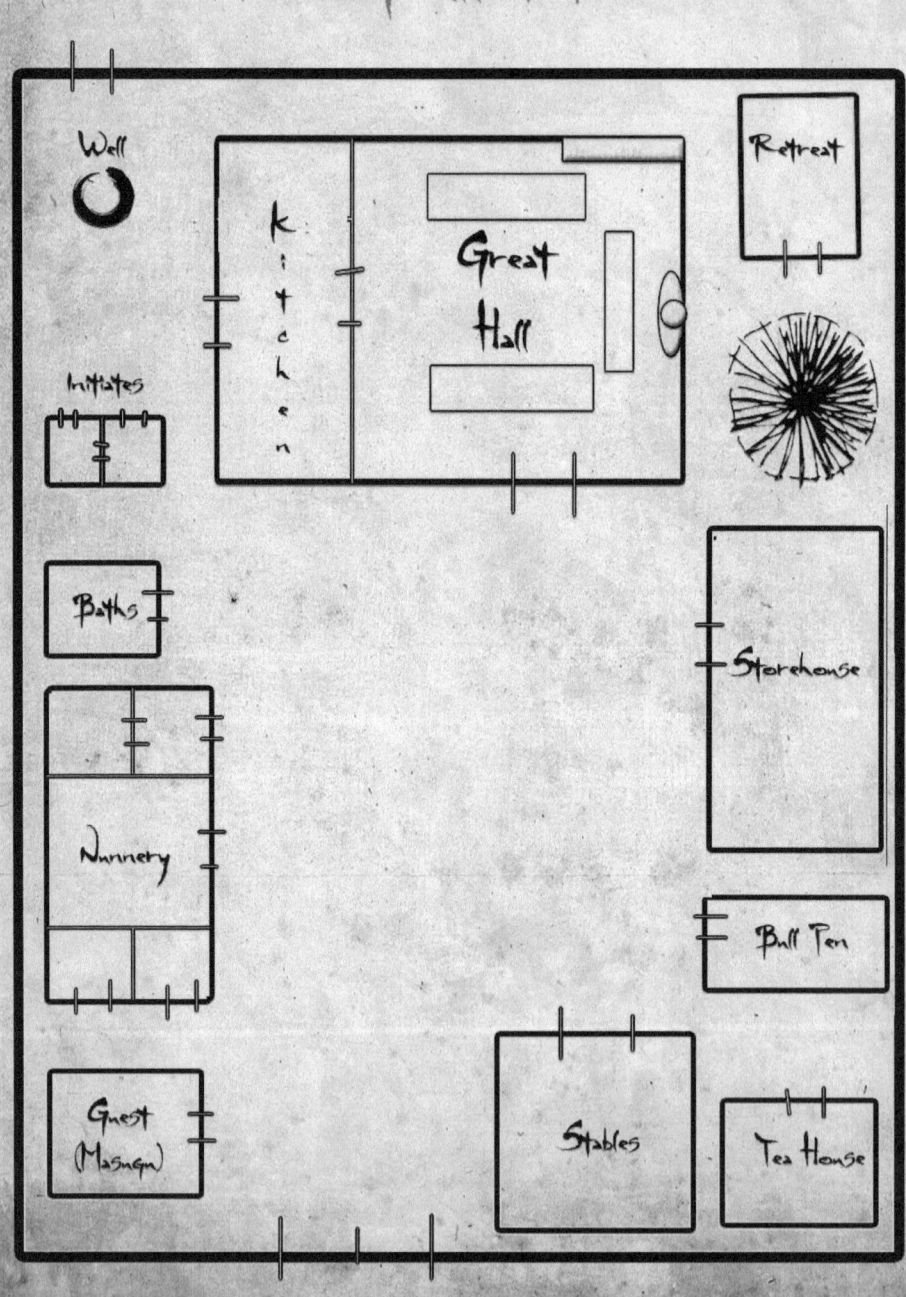

Author Note and Acknowledgements

One of the challenges of writing historical fiction is balancing the two halves of that genre name: *historical* and *fiction*.

To keep my writing historical, I do a lot of research and try to keep the setting, events and characters as close to what really happened as I can. (Even four and a half centuries later, it's easy enough to find out about battles, famous births and deaths, alliances, betrayals, plagues, and so on—the big, society-changing events. What people ate for breakfast? Not so easy.)

Of course, writing an exciting story doesn't always allow me to keep all of the facts strictly accurate.

For example, there's no record that I am aware of showing Lords Takeda and Matsudaira planning to turn on Lord Oda and invade the capital in the spring of 1571. Then again, the times being what they were, I'd be shocked if they didn't at least consider it.

Also, at this point in history, Lord Matsudaira was no longer going by the name Matsudaira Motoyasu. Instead, starting in 1567, as part of his break with the Imagawa, he had taken the name by which he would become famous: Tokugawa Ieyasu.

To give you an example of the sorts of decisions that I've made to tweak history, I chose not to have the lord governor of the Three Rivers go by his later name for a couple of reasons: first, knowing that not all of my readers would be comfortable with Japanese, I didn't want his name to be too easy to confuse with *Takeda*, since they would appear side by side so often; also, I didn't want yet another *T* suspect for Risuko & Co. to chase; and finally, I assumed that some of my readers would be familiar enough with Japanese history to know how his story turned out. Don't want to give away the ending, you know?

I did give his (fictional) nephew the more famous family name, which comes from a river where the clan originated—in Wild Heights (Kōzuke) Province.

If you were wondering what Jolalo and Father Francisco were doing at the Full Moon, Portuguese missionaries and merchants did visit Japan during this period. In fact, they were the ones who had introduced the muskets that had revolutionized Japanese warfare in the decade before this book takes place. (Later, there would be Spanish, Dutch, and English visitors to Japan—before the *shōgun* closed the borders of the empire to all foreigners in 1639.) The Jesuit missions in Japan at the time of *Bright Eyes* served a religious purpose, obviously—but they were also gathering information and seeking alliances for both the Portuguese crown and the Vatican. So Lady Chiyome and Lord Hōjō weren't the only one to think of using religion as a guise for espionage!

The poem about the sky and the snow that Lady Chiyome writes on the dusty storeroom floor for Aimaru was (as my little literary critic says) written by Lady Izumi Shikibu, a contemporary of Lady Murasaki, Risuko's name-sake. They both lived at court and wrote in the first decades of the eleventh century. Lady Izumi is mostly known for her occasionally racy diaries—but this short, sad poem was (as Risuko was about to tell Lady Chiyome) written in response to the death of her daughter. My translation is adapted a bit to serve its purpose in the book, but I think remains true to the meaning and spirit of the original.

By the way, I'm not entirely sure how the bear skeleton made its way into the cave above the Full Moon. I have thought a lot about who brought it there and when—members of a prehistoric tribe living in the hills above what would become the Full Moon about ten thousand years or so back, before the Jōmon people brought agriculture to Japan. I could tell you all about them. . . But that's a whole other book!

In any case, I hope that you found this book both accurate and exciting, as true historical fiction should be.

When *Risuko* first came out, I joked that if it takes a village to raise a child, it takes an army to publish a novel. That army has continued to grow, and it is a pleasure to be able to thank them once again.

First, I'd like to thank Brenda and Donal Brown, who read the manuscript for *Risuko* long before it was finished and provided both their wisdom and their apparently bottomless enthusiasm, which sustained me through many of the darkest passages in my journey to bring Risuko's to print. They also introduced my book to Danielle Svetcov (see below), for which alone they deserve literary Elysium—if they hadn't already earned it in a thousand other ways. The dedication for this volume is the least that they deserve.

I've never thanked anyone for helping with a sneak peek, but I can't *not* acknowledge Robin LeFevers, whose wonderful His Fair Assassin and Courting Darkness series inspired Risuko's sabotage of the Uesugi arsenal in the preview chapter of *Kano* above. When I reached out to her, she pointed me to her source, a fun book called *Gunpowder: Alchemy, Bombards, and Pyrotechnics—The History of the Explosive That Changed the World* by Jack Kelly. By the way, if you like my Seasons of the Sword novels, I highly recommend hers, which like mine feature a group of young medieval women being trained to serve the gods—and to become assassins. (Her books take place in fifteenth-century Brittany and France, and feature a great deal more fantasy and romance than mine, but I think you'll enjoy them as much as I did!)

Danielle Svetcov of Levine|Greenberg|Rostan Literary Agency continues to represent these books as they seek out new audiences. Kendra Arimoto, Alexis Boozer Sterling, and Maury Sterling are currently working to bring Risuko's world to one of those audiences, the world of video, which excites me enormously, and I hope excites you.

Robin Larin provided a sensitive, thoughtful, thorough copyedit that improved this book in many ways. She provided a wonderful answer to the question, *Quis editorem edit?* ("Who edits the editor?")

The Risuko Beta Team provided incredible feedback as I was completing the book. A heartfelt *dōmo arigatō* to One Anjana, Stephanie Curtner, Azalea Dabill, Stephen Gerringer, Suzanne Hartog, Rob Henn, R. Mar, Ania Mieszkowska, Michael Lambert, Shannon, Carson Smith, Cherrie Walker, and a small army of anonymice for helping me see where I'd gone wrong (and right).

Without the Kickstarter backers who backed the campaigns that supported the launches of *Risuko* and *Bright Eyes*, this book literally would not have been published. Margot Avery, Kendra Arimoto, Roger Beckett, Isaac "Will It Work" Dansicker, Sylvia-Michelle Hostetter, Alithea Howes, John Idlor, Ania Mieszkowska, Empress Diana and Imperial Princess Amara of the Most Illustrious Lee Dynasty, Lenhoff Family, magycmyste@gmail.com, mywayhoff11@aol.com, Ripley Patton, Roman Pauer, Cara Melia Pico, Jason Png, Ritske Rensma, Jeremy Reppy, Kalilah Robinson, Roy Romasanta, Rachel S.,

Riccardo Sartori, Ken Schneyer, Robert Walter, Susan R. Woodward, Eron Wyngarde, Heesung Yang, and yet more anonymice—you are angels in every sense of the word.

I must once again thank my middle-school English teacher, who (as you may remember from *Risuko*) happens also to be my mother, Jackie Kudler. She served as one of my first readers for this book. Her fine eye for detail and narrative through-line was as helpful now as it was when I was thirteen—and much more welcome.

My wife Maura Vaughn has probably read *Bright Eyes* more than anyone other than me. Having been fortunate enough to be her husband for over three decades, I consider her Chiyome-level insight, Masugu-level support, and Mieko-level patience almost more than I deserve. Almost.

Last and greatest as always is my debt to my own two daughters, Sasha and Julia. When I began writing *Risuko*, they were young—in Julia's case, too young to read the book on her own. (If you listen to the audiobook, the accent she takes on as Kee Sun was inspired by mine as I read her the early manuscript.) As I publish *Bright Eyes*, they are now both women, wonders in their own rights, with much to offer the world. I continue to hope that I have captured half of their spirit in Murasaki and her friends.

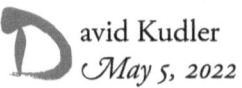avid Kudler
May 5, 2022

SEASONS OF THE SWORD
BOOK THREE

COMING
SOON

KANO

D A V I D
K U D L E R
AUTHOR OF *RISUKO*

 **DAVID KUDLER** is not afraid of heights. He just has a healthy respect for depths. "I'm as surprised as anyone," he says, "that I've written a series of books featuring a girl who loves to be as high up in the air as possible."

An editor and author, he lives just north of the Golden Gate Bridge with his wife, actor/teacher/author Maura Vaughn, their author-to-be daughters, and their (apparently) non-literary cats.

He is the founder, publisher, and editor-in-chief of Stillpoint Digital Press. Since 1999, he has overseen the publications program of the Joseph Campbell Foundation, for which he has edited three posthumous volumes of Campbell's previously unpublished work (*Pathways to Bliss*, *Myths of Light* and *Sake & Satori*) and managed the publication of over ninety print, ebook, print, audio, and video titles, including the third edition of the seminal *Hero with a Thousand Faces*.

Risuko and *Bright Eyes* are the first novels in his four-book Seasons of the Sword. He is also writing a series of prequel stories called Kunoichi Companion Tales for his newsletter subscribers.

His children's picture books *The Seven Gods of Luck*, *Shlomo Travels to Warsaw*, and *How Raven Brought Back the Light* (the last two co-written with his wife Maura Vaughn) are available as The Winter Tales.

He is currently hard at work on *Kano*, the third book in the Seasons of the Sword series.

For more information about David Kudler and his writing, visit

SeasonsoftheSword.com

You can also follow him on social media:
twitter.com/dkudler • davidkudler.tumblr.com
facebook.com/davidkudlerauthor • davidkudler.pinterest.com